THE HARTFIELD INHERITANCE

'I bequeath my entire estate to my cousin Rowland Sandiford of Merryn Park in the county of Wiltshire, on condition that within six months of my death he marries my granddaughter Merab Eliza Hartfield...' Such was old Julian Hartfield's outrageous will. What could Merab do? She might be almost penniless, but she was not going to submit to her grandfather's bullying tactics—and she was certainly not going to marry the rude and overbearing Rowland Sandiford! Nor did Rowland have any intention of marrying a plain, twenty-six-year old spinster—especially while pretty, flirtatious Kitty Parminster was free. But could it be that Grandfather knows best after all?

THE HARTFIELD INHERITANCE

Elizabeth Hawksley

Chivers Press • Thorndike Press
Bath, Avon, England   Thorndike, Maine USA

This Large Print edition is published by Chivers Press, England, and by Thorndike Press, USA.

Published in 1997 in the U.K. by arrangement with Robert Hale Ltd.

Published in 1997 in the U.S. by arrangement with John Johnson Ltd.

U.K. Hardcover   ISBN 0–7451–6917–1 (Chivers Large Print)
U.K. Softcover   ISBN 0–7451–6918–X (Camden Large Print)
U.S. Softcover   ISBN 0–7862–0853–8 (General Series Edition)

The text of this Large Print edition is unabridged.
Other aspects of the book may vary from the original edition.

Set in 16 pt. New Times Roman.

Printed in Great Britain on acid-free paper.

British Library Cataloguing in Publication Data available

Library of Congress Catalog Card Number: 96–90524

To my daughter, Tamsin,
with love.

CHAPTER ONE

The stagecoach rattled and lurched over the cobblestones of the main street causing at least two of the occupants inside to clutch at each other to avoid being thrown against the window. It swayed round into the inn yard and finally came to a halt.

'Fifteen minutes, ladies and gentlemen,' shouted the guard. 'We leave again in fifteen minutes.'

An ostler and a stable-boy had come out of the stables and were busy unpoling the sweating horses. Someone let down the coach steps and opened the door for the passengers to descend.

'King's Head, Cirencester, ladies and gentlemen. Coffee? Tea? Refreshments indoors.' He glanced at two ladies, both in black, with an experienced eye. The older one was pale and looked ill, the younger one, who was looking around her with wide-eyed interest, was probably her daughter. Little money, he guessed. He doubted whether they would have more than a cup of coffee apiece and he couldn't expect much of a tip. Losing interest, he turned away.

The ladies got out, the younger one first. 'Well, here we are, Mama.' She turned to the inn-servant and said firmly, 'Could you please

1

arrange to have our trunks taken down? Those boxes there.' She pointed to two shabby leather trunks on the roof.

The man turned and spat on to the cobblestones, and hailed one of the inn-servants who was hovering in the doorway. ''Ere, Joe. Take the ladies' trunks.'

'Come along, Mama,' said the girl cheerfully and followed Joe into the inn. Joe had summed up the finances of the ladies about as accurately as his superior, but he was a kindly young man and he felt sorry for the older lady, looking so pale and worn. He elbowed open the door of a small parlour with a fire burning brightly in the grate. 'No one will disturb you here, ladies. Shall I bring you some coffee?'

The elder lady began to shake her head, but her daughter intervened. 'Yes please,' she said, decidedly. 'Come and sit down, Mama. You look exhausted.'

The mother sank down, coughed painfully into her handkerchief and said in a thread of a voice, 'My name is Mrs Hartfield. We are being called for.'

'I will enquire, madam.' Joe left the room.

There was silence. The elder lady removed her bonnet and held her thin hands to the fire. It was nearly September and not particularly cold, but she seemed to feel chilly. Mrs Jonathan Hartfield, a widow of about forty-five, was small and finely made; it was easy to see that she had once been very pretty. Her

2

eyes, now sunken, were large, well shaped and of a warm brown. Lines of pain were etched into her forehead, but her mouth was still a lovely curve and her hands and feet were beautifully moulded.

Her daughter, Merab, was eighteen, taller than her mother and still rather skinny, for she had grown too fast over the last few years and had not yet filled out. Her hair was a thick, dark curly mass which she somewhat inexpertly tried to confine in suitable braids and she had inherited her mother's lustrous dark eyes, which were her best feature. Her black dress, unskilfully lengthened, did not suit her. She was normally a lively girl, but just now she was anxious, for it was she who was responsible for their journey.

But she had had no choice. Her mother's health had always been delicate, but after her father's death a couple of months previously, it had deteriorated with frightening rapidity. Jonathan Hartfield had only been able to leave them £1,000, which brought in £50 a year, and how could they live on that with the doctor's bills becoming an ever-increasing item? Perhaps they could have managed if Mrs Hartfield's health had been good, for she had been a singing teacher before her marriage and she might have been able to find some pupils. Merab herself had not long left school, but the Misses Goodison's seminary had been a cheerful place in which to gather a few ladylike

3

accomplishments. Merab was all too aware that the education it offered hardly fitted her for being a governess, which was the only career open to her. Even if she had found a post—she might, she thought dubiously, have been capable of teaching younger children—what would have become of her mother?

After her husband's death, Mrs Hartfield had written to her unknown father-in-law, as was proper. There had been a cold acknowledgement. Not that she expected more. As she said to Merab, 'Mr Hartfield swore he would cut your papa off without a penny when he married me. And he did. He did not even let your papa know when his brother Edmund was killed on the hunting field. Not that dear Jonathan cared for his brother, who indeed sounded a most unpleasant man, but to learn of it through the newspapers! It was a severe shock, as you may imagine.'

Fortunately, Jonathan's godfather had left him £1,000 which he had settled on his wife, and there had been a few hundreds from the sale of some family bits and pieces that were his, and this had given Merab an education. Jonathan had never regretted the step which had led him to leave a cold, autocratic father and bullying older brother for marriage with the lovely Abigail Cooper, whom he had first met when she had a singing engagement at an evening party.

Sadly, it was now plain that Mrs Hartfield

was not going to get well. Her lungs had always been delicate: 'Too much standing about in draughty halls,' she had said vaguely. 'And when I was younger, I was heedless. A singer should take care of her throat, you know, but I was careless and often forgot my wrap.'

Finally, the doctor had taken Merab aside and said bluntly, 'I'm sorry, Miss Hartfield. Her right lung is badly infected. A very settled way of life is necessary.'

Merab swallowed and said after a moment's silence, 'I understand.' But her heart sank. Her mother would need the best care. And how could they afford doctor's bills on a pound a week?

That evening Merab wrote to her unknown grandfather. It was not an easy letter to write. If he had not become reconciled to her father, his only surviving son after her uncle Edmund's death, nor offered her mother anything at her husband's death, what chance was there for her to persuade him to help her mother now? Probably very little, but she must try.

To her surprise, a fortnight after she had written, she received an answer. The welcome was grudging at best, and Mr Hartfield sent no money, but nevertheless he told them to come to Hartfield Hall and, in return for the £50 a year towards their keep and Merab's help with the housekeeping, he would support them. He gave them the stagecoach directions and said that he would see to it that a conveyance awaited their arrival at the King's Head, Cirencester, on the afternoon of September 3rd, 1809.

The door opened and Joe appeared with the coffee tray. He placed it, together with a small plate of biscuits, on a table next to Mrs Hartfield. 'There is a message, madam,' he said. 'Farmer Willett will drop you at Hartfield Hall on his way back from market. He'll be here in about an hour. Earlier, if he sells the pigs.'

Merab began to giggle. The idea of travelling in a cart with pigs had a certain appeal, but she was not so young that she did not see her grandfather's callousness in allowing a very sick woman to be conveyed in this fashion.

However, when Mr Willett arrived they found the arrangements less Spartan than they had feared. The driver's seat was properly padded, the pigs had mercifully been sold, and Mrs Hartfield and Merab were able to sit next to Mr Willett in comparative comfort and even to keep warm with a rug thoughtfully provided by Mrs Willett. Farmer Willett himself was a kindly man of about fifty with a cheerful, rubicund face and Merab's natural optimism began to return.

Perhaps things would not be so bad as they had feared.

*   *   *

6

Merab could not have known it, but the arrival of her letter had been fortuitous, for, by the same post, Mr Hartfield had received a black-edged notification of the death of his cousin, Mark Sandiford, who he had decided should be heir to the Hartfield estate. Mr Sandiford was sixty-nine and had been ill for some years, but Mr Hartfield, a sprightly seventy-seven himself, had not taken his cousin's illness very seriously. His death, therefore, came as a profound shock.

Mr Sandiford, a second cousin, was the only one of his relatives for whom Julian Hartfield had felt even a mild affection. Once, long ago, a ten-year-old Julian had saved the two-year-old Mark from drowning and had felt a mildly proprietorial affection ever since. The adult Mark had kept this good opinion by never showing the smallest tendency to hanker after the Hartfield estate. In fact, he had assumed that the disinheriting of Jonathan Hartfield was mere bluff and that in the end his cousin Julian would do the decent thing and leave Hartfield to his surviving son.

But Mark had died, and therein lay the rub. For Mark's son, Rowland, now aged twenty and up at Oxford, was pursuing a course of which Julian Hartfield violently disapproved. It was not gambling or women, (Mr Hartfield would have regarded these as a normal, if regrettable, part of a young man's education) it was politics. Rowland was imbued with ideas

7

most unsuitable to his rank, and had become infected with all the Godwinian nonsense of universal male suffrage and other ridiculous notions. On the last occasion he had been to stay, a conceited young puppy of about eighteen, he had dared to suggest that his cousin Julian should start a school in the village! As well encourage a hotbed of revolution! 'First a school and then it'll be sedition and Radical pamphlets: I'm not having any of that at Hartfield. Reading and writing for the lower classes only encourages discontent.'

Now Mark was dead and Rowland was the next heir to Hartfield—unless Julian Hartfield changed his mind. So when he opened Merab's letter he did not, as he might have done, fling it straight into the waste-paper basket. He still intended Rowland to be his heir (Julian prided himself on never changing his mind), but it would do the boy no harm to learn that there were others, more nearly connected, to whom he could leave the estate if he so chose.

In the meantime Mrs Hartfield—for so he supposed she must be called—and her daughter might come. The girl could make herself useful. The housekeeper, Mrs Barden, was getting old and had already spoken of going to live with her daughter. He would let her and this Merab creature—ridiculous name!—could earn her keep and take over the housekeeper's post.

It didn't sound as if Mrs Hartfield would last long, but long enough, he hoped, to convince Rowland that she and her daughter represented a serious threat.

He reached out and tugged at the bell pull.

*　　*　　*

Mrs Barden could scarcely wait to get back to the kitchen. Indeed, for one who was amply built and usually on her dignity, she fairly ran. 'Just think! Master Jonathan's wife and child are coming!' she cried. 'Oh, he was such a lovely boy. Always had a kind word.' She patted a stray wisp of grey hair back into place and placed one hand over her still palpitating bosom.

Tilling, the gardener, who had just brought in the day's vegetables, looked at her. 'Now why would he do that?' he asked, scratching his head. 'When he wouldn't forgive Mr Jonathan even after Mr Edmund was killed. It don't make sense.'

'He isn't exactly making them welcome neither,' retorted Mrs Barden. 'He's told me to prepare the East Room and that little cubbyhole next to it.'

*　　*　　*

Farmer Willett's cart turned off the main road and through an ornamental gateway. 'This is

9

it, ladies. Hartfield Hall.'

'It looks a bit neglected,' observed Merab, peering round. The gateway was twined over with ivy and what had once been a gatekeeper's cottage was deserted. The cottage garden was overgrown and several of the windows had been boarded up.

'Mr Hartfield's a bit near with his money, if you know what I mean, miss. The land's in good heart, he don't stint on that, and essential work is always carried out. But he don't do more than that.' He remembered suddenly that he was talking to Mr Hartfield's granddaughter and fell silent.

The house, when they rounded the bend, was an unpretentious grey stone building built in the previous century. Its shape was strictly symmetrical with a portico over the front and three windows on either side. A small flight of stone steps with a curving balustrade went up to the front door. The lawn in front was, Merab noticed, neatly trimmed; there was no obvious neglect and yet the house seemed uncared for. Perhaps it was just that there were no plants to soften the grey stone, no roses or honeysuckle to climb those austere walls.

The cart stopped. Mr Willett clambered down and went to knock at the door and then turned back to help the ladies descend and to take the trunks out of the back of the cart.

The front door opened and Mrs Barden came down the steps. Merab and Mrs Hartfield looked at each other. Who was this? And why was Mr Hartfield not there to welcome them?

'I am Mrs Hartfield,' said Mrs Hartfield with gentle dignity, 'and this is my daughter. I believe we are expected.'

Mrs Barden dropped a curtsey. 'I am Mrs Barden, madam, the housekeeper here. Master is out and won't be back till late. But please come in.'

She turned to Merab who was looking around her with interest. Here was a chip off the old block and no mistake. 'Come in, miss,' she said. 'We was all very fond of Mr Jonathan and you have a look of him.' Mr Jonathan had just such an ungainly quality as a young lad, she thought.

Merab gave a smile, which lit up her whole face. 'My father was very good-looking,' she said laughing. 'I doubt whether I shall ever be his equal.'

'When he was about your age he was all legs and angles, just like a young colt,' said Mrs Barden, allowing herself a smile.

'Then there's hope for me yet,' said Merab. 'Poor Mama has given up on me. She was expecting a daughter slim and petite like herself and she has this giraffe instead.'

'Nonsense, Merab,' Mrs Hartfield smiled in her turn. 'I'm very well pleased with my tall daughter. And thank you for your welcome, Mrs Barden. I'm sure you will not take it amiss if I say that we did not know what to expect.'

11

Having escorted them upstairs and shown them to their rooms, Mrs Barden left them. She promised Mrs Hartfield that one of the maids would bring her some supper on a tray and a warming pan for the bed: 'For I can see that you're tired, ma'am, and you'll be glad to get to bed, I'll be thinking.' She then turned to Merab and said, a little grimly, 'Mr Hartfield has asked you to dine with him this evening, Miss Merab. He dines at half past six, so I shall come and take you down to meet him in the library shortly before the gong goes.'

'Th ... thank you, Mrs Barden,' stammered Merab.

'Poor pet,' said Mrs Barden to Mr Tilling when she got back downstairs to the kitchen. Mr Tilling had been summoned to help take the ladies' trunks upstairs. 'Looked as white as a sheet, she did. And I couldn't blame her.'

Meanwhile, Merab saw her mother settled, gave her her drops and went to her own room. There was a branch of candles on her dressing-table and Merab, after a swift glance around the room, went to look at herself in the glass. What she saw did not reassure her. She was looking pale and there were dark rings underneath her eyes and, oh horror, a spot on her chin. Her black dress looked travel-stained and her stockings were splashed with mud.

Some of these she could remedy. She rummaged in her trunk and found some clean stockings, her evening slippers, a clean collar and pair of cuffs. There was a wash-stand in one corner of the room and a maid had left her some water in a ewer. Merab washed her hands and face; the water was cold but it was soft and Merab felt mildly encouraged. She then brushed her unruly hair and did her best to smarten herself up. There was nothing to be done about the spot. What she did not see was that her thin face held a good deal of intelligence and those large dark eyes the promise of future beauty.

It wanted still ten minutes until dinner-time and Merab sat down on the edge of the bed and looked around. It was obvious that they were to be the poor relations, she thought. The tent bed looked all right—Merab gave a few discreet bounces—there were no lumps, but everything else looked as if it had been hastily brought down from some attic—as indeed it had. The dressing-table, for example, had plainly seen better days. There was a bow-fronted mahogany chest of drawers which had been recently polished, for Merab could smell the beeswax, but few of the knobs matched. The curtains had obviously been made for a different-sized window and the carpet on the floor was worn and had been inexpertly patched in one corner.

On the other hand, she told herself firmly, Mrs Barden was disposed to be pleasant, and so long as her mother was being looked after properly then Merab didn't see that she had any cause for complaint. There was no use looking back to what had been or what might have been. She had made the best choice she could and now she must make the best of it, for good or ill. What was it that Miss Goodison used to say at school? 'Rise above it, girls!' Well, she would try to rise above it.

A little before half past six Mrs Barden tapped on the door. 'I'll take you down, miss,' she said. She cast an approving eye over Merab. The child had tidied herself up, she noticed, and had done her best. God forbid Mr Hartfield was in one of his moods. 'Mr Hartfield is awaiting you in the library.'

What Merab saw as she entered the library was a tall old man, dressed in the knee breeches and powdered wig of the last century. His face was thin and lined, and under bushy white eyebrows glared a pair of cold grey eyes. The whole face was hard and rigid as if sunlight never shone on it.

As a child Merab had loved to hear her father talk of his youth and used to listen with pleasurable fear to stories of her grandfather's cold rages which made him sound far worse than the ogres in the fairytales because he could never be outwitted. Now she saw that her father had not exaggerated. Merab's heart sank and her hands became suddenly cold and clammy. She took a deep breath, stepped forward and curtseyed.

'Good evening, sir.'

14

The cold eyes raked over her. If any resemblance to his son softened him, he did not show it. 'Merab. Outlandish name.'

Merab drew herself up. 'It's in the Bible,' she said, nettled. 'She was a princess, daughter of King Saul. I was named after a sister of my mother's who died young.' She put up her chin. She had decided earlier that she would be courteous and pleasant, that her grandfather should find no want of manners in her to shame her upbringing. But that did not mean that she would submit to being bullied and brow-beaten.

Mr Hartfield glared at her, but said nothing more, only indicated that she should precede him into the dining-room.

Dinner was one of the most unnerving meals that Merab had ever eaten. Her grandfather sat in total silence and offered Merab no wine, though he drank steadily through a bottle himself. The dining-room was a large one and the table could probably seat two dozen people with ease. The cutlery was silver with the Hartfield crest on it and the china was obviously good, far above the earthenware plates that they always used at home. Most of the room was in shadow, for her grandfather obviously did not believe in wasting candles. There was a branch at Merab's end of the table and another in front of her grandfather and that was all.

At the end of the meal Mr Hartfield rang the

bell and Mrs Barden appeared.

'Mrs Barden, in future Miss Hartfield will take her meals upstairs with her mother. I find I can do without her company. They can have my wife's old sitting-room.' He turned to Merab and said, 'As for you, whey-face, you can keep out of my way.'

*   *   *

Heroines in novels have a habit in such circumstances of winning over any number of grumpy, elderly relations by their grace and charm; young men appear as if by magic in their vicinity and long-lost relatives turn up and leave them money. None of this happened to Merab. Her mother died peacefully the following year and in due course Merab took over Mrs Barden's post and, with the help of Mr Camberwell, the Hartfield lawyer, managed to negotiate a grudging twenty pounds a year out of her grandfather—about half what he used to pay Mrs Barden.

For the first eighteen years of her life Merab had been the cherished and petted child, now, suddenly, she was on her own. A lesser person might have quailed at the prospect of being incarcerated in a large country house with only a cantankerous old man for company. Merab decided—and in this she was her father's daughter—that she would create her own circumstances and have as satisfactory a life as she could manage, in spite of her grandfather.

She took the gardener into her confidence.

'Mr Tilling,' she said one day, shortly after Mrs Barden had retired and gone to live with her daughter, 'I want to keep some hens. I hope you can advise me.'

Tilling shook his head. 'Mr Hartfield wouldn't allow it.'

'I don't intend to ask him,' retorted Merab. 'You know as well as I do that he wouldn't like anything that might make me a bit of money.' She had decided that if she was to be the housekeeper then she would be firmly on the side of the servants—and that did not include a blind loyalty to her grandfather. Loyalty, in Merab's view, had to be earned.

Tilling looked at her with a grudging respect. 'Old Mrs Hartfield kept hens,' he offered. 'There was a place behind the kitchen garden.'

'Could you show me?'

On the way Merab outlined her plan. 'The village is in a disgraceful condition,' she said. 'There is only one well. Some of the cottages are damp and there is no school. Something ought to be done, but I am well aware that Grandfather will do nothing. But if I could earn a bit with the hens then I could at least do something, even if only buying up a stock of basic medicines.'

'You should go and talk to Farmer Willett,' said Tilling. 'He goes to market every week and doubtless could take in your eggs or even a

17

basket or two of vegetables.' He winked, for the vegetables would be Mr Hartfield's.

Merab smiled back. She had every intention of turning this into as large an enterprise as she dared and it was encouraging to know that she'd have Tilling's backing.

Two weeks later, the hen coop repaired, Merab got her hens and gradually she managed to make a modest profit. She did what she could for the village, but she discovered that this required some ingenuity, for her grandfather had a rooted objection to 'cossetting' and would have strictly forbidden Merab's gifts of nourishing broths and bottles of cough medicine if he had happened to hear of it. Fortunately, the villagers were quite as well aware as Merab of the clandestine nature of what she could do, and Mr Hartfield remained in ignorance of her activities.

Her grandfather lived another seven years and was cold and unyielding to the end. For the first five years, while he was still mobile, he would occasionally go up to London and Rowland Sandiford would be summoned from his Wiltshire acres to have lunch with his cousin at his club.

These meetings appeared to give Mr Hartfield little pleasure. True, Rowland's earlier Radicalism had toned down—or at least Rowland had had the tact to let it appear so—but he had had the temerity to start a village school and still wanted to go into

Parliament on a reforming ticket.

'Damned young fool!' Mr Hartfield had reported to Merab on his return. 'Fortunately, he won't get far. The Merryn estate ain't worth more than fifteen hundred a year for all his newfangled farming methods and it would cost him several thousands to get into Parliament.' After Mrs Hartfield's death Mr Hartfield had reluctantly allowed Merab to join the human race and occasionally summoned her down to dine with him. He never seemed to enjoy her company, she noted, but it did give him an audience for his views on Rowland's misdoings, and allowed him to tease her with mentions of the heir to Hartfield Hall.

'Perhaps he'll find a patron,' said Merab sensibly. She had been hearing about Rowland's iniquities on and off ever since she'd arrived and had some sympathy for her unknown cousin.

'He won't do it on my money,' snapped her grandfather. 'And don't think that that means I'll leave it to you either, whey-face. I'll leave it all to charity.'

Merab said nothing. She had heard it all before and besides, she did not entirely believe him. He might fulminate against Rowland, but she noticed that that did not stop her grandfather from summoning him again on his next trip to London. She once expressed a tentative interest in meeting her cousin, but, possibly to thwart her, the one thing Mr

19

Hartfield never did was invite Rowland up to Hartfield.

There was one bright spot for Merab: she had kept in touch with her old school friend, Amelia, now married to Sir Thomas Wincanton and living in Bath. Occasionally, Merab was able to pay them a visit. This would not have been possible if it had not been for Sir Thomas's kindness in sending a carriage for her and the first time Mr Hartfield had protested vigorously.

'You have a job to do, miss, and don't you forget it,' he had thundered. 'Visit Bath indeed! No, I won't hear of it!'

'Lady Wincanton has often urged me to go and live with her, sir,' said Merab. 'Now Mama has died, perhaps you would rather I did that?'

This was bluff on Merab's part. Dearly though she loved Amelia, Merab did not relish living on the charity of her friend and she knew that Sir Thomas would never agree to take her fifty pounds a year. But her grandfather had had second thoughts. Perhaps he, too, was thinking of that fifty pounds a year, which he had hung on to, or possibly he was thinking of the surprisingly efficient housekeeper he had gained for the paltry sum of twenty pounds a year. At any rate he grunted, 'Very well, you may go.'

On her return Merab found that he had docked her wages.

Her grandfather's enmity continued

unabated—possibly enhanced by the fact that, whenever he rode round his estate, he met her praises everywhere.

'And how is Miss Merab?' one of his tenants would ask.

Or some old woman from the village who was complaining about a leaking roof would say, 'I hope Miss Merab is well, sir. It's a ray of sunshine when she comes.'

Mr Hartfield would ignore them. Back home he said to Merab, 'I won't have you cossetting the villagers, miss. Don't believe in it. An idle useless lot they are. What were you doing at old Mrs Lane's, eh?'

'I read the Bible to her, sir,' said Merab. She also brought the old lady fruit from Mr Hartfield's orchard and an embrocation for her rheumatism, but this she did not say.

In one respect, however, country life suited her. When she'd arrived she was a somewhat gawky girl with a tendency to spots. But as the years passed her figure filled out, the long country walks gave her an elegance of deportment and the fresh air cleared her complexion.

'She could be such a pretty girl,' Mrs Barden said to Tilling. 'She has a lovely clear skin and beautiful eyes. But who ever sees her here?'

When Merab was twenty-six fate answered that question. A couple of years before, Mr Hartfield had had a minor stroke and Merab, under the guidance of the Hartfield lawyer, Mr

21

Camberwell, gradually took over the running of the estate. Her grandfather didn't seem to like her any better, but he unwillingly acknowledged her competence. It did at least mean that she was able to make a few small improvements in the village. Unfortunately, it also meant that she was no longer able to visit the Wincantons in Bath.

Finally, on December 6th, 1816, after a second heart attack and a week of sleepless nights for Merab, Julian Hartfield died, unlamented and unloved.

When it was over Merab stood by the bedside and looked down at the still body, whose face was as rigid in death as it had been in life and thought, I'm free. But the words meant nothing. All she felt was an immense weariness and a dry-eyed exhaustion.

Mr Camberwell came over that evening and arranged for a notice to be sent to the papers and wrote to Rowland Sandiford telling him of the funeral arrangements.

Merab awaited Rowland's arrival with interest. His youthful iconoclasm had always appealed to her and she assumed that a man who was concerned for the education of his tenants and the rights of the poor must himself be sympathetic. When she heard the carriage wheels she went out with some eagerness to greet him.

A tall well-made man of about twenty-nine stepped down from the carriage. Merab's heart gave an unexpected leap, for she saw to her amazement that he had the same unruly curly hair as herself. Then he turned to look at her and the words of welcome were frozen on her lips. For, in spite of the hair, he looked uncannily like her grandfather with the same aquiline nose and cold grey eyes. He looked her over indifferently and said, 'And who may you be?'

'M ... Merab Hartfield,' she stammered.

'I never knew old Julian had any by-blows.'

Merab flushed. 'I am Jonathan Hartfield's daughter, sir, and no by-blow. Surely you must have heard of me?'

Rowland's grey gaze raked over her. 'Never.' She could see his knuckles whiten. Without waiting for a response he turned and strode into the house. Merab, hurt and disappointed, slowly followed him.

It did not get any better. Rowland treated her with a chilling courtesy and ignored her attempts at explanation.

By the time the funeral came, Merab was exhausted. It was not the custom for ladies to attend funerals, so that afternoon she organized tea in the dining-room and waited for Mr Camberwell and her cousin to return from church for the reading of the will.

Merab had tried not to worry but, of course, she couldn't help wondering if her fifty pounds a year was safe. In her more optimistic moments Merab allowed herself to hope for a

23

small legacy. Cousin Rowland, naturally, would inherit the estate, but might she not hope for a small sum? A thousand or so would make all the difference between struggling to keep her head above water and a comfortable life. Her grandfather, in one of his rare softer moments, once said, 'I'll see you provided for', and smiled grimly. Merab had never dared ask him what he meant.

There was the distant noise of the returning carriage and Merab went to light the branches of candles, for the short December day was closing in. The maid went to open the door and in a moment Mr Camberwell, briefcase in hand, came into the room, followed by Rowland. The lawyer murmured a few words on the funeral but Rowland said nothing. Somewhat intimidated, Merab indicated that both gentlemen should sit down and rang the bell for tea.

'Tea, Mr Camberwell?' asked Merab, when the maid had entered with the tray. 'Mr Sandiford?' She did not dare call him 'Cousin Rowland.'

'Thank you, Miss Hartfield,' said Mr Camberwell, after waiting in vain for the younger man to speak. 'A cup of tea would be most welcome.'

When they had drunk the tea and eaten some of the fruitcake, Mr Camberwell said, 'With your permission, Miss Hartfield, I think I should go over the will now.'

'For God's sake let's get it over with,' Rowland spoke harshly.

Merab looked at him in surprise. Surely he knew he was to inherit?

Mr Camberwell waited until the maid had cleared the table, then took out some papers, put on his glasses, cleared his throat and said, 'I must assure you both that Mr Hartfield made this will against my advice. However, it is all perfectly legally drawn up and valid.'

The room suddenly became very cold. Oh my God, thought Merab, it all goes to charity. The will was dated the previous year, shortly after Mr Hartfield's first heart attack and the first page or so was the usual provision for the servants, pensions for Mr Tilling and Mrs Barden and a year's wages for the maids, Mary and Jenny, and the cook. There was a small legacy to the parish church and ten guineas each to the vicar and his wife. Merab's thousand pounds was restored to her full use. Merab closed her eyes thankfully.

Then Mr Camberwell cleared his throat and read, 'I bequeath my entire estate and all monies accruing to my cousin Rowland Sandiford of Merryn Park in the county of Wiltshire on condition that within six months of my death he marries my granddaughter Miss Merab Eliza Hartfield of Hartfield Hall, Gloucestershire. If either party declines then the whole estate is to be divided equally between The Society for the Succour of

Widows and Orphans and the Queen Charlotte Fund for distressed Mariners.'

Merab felt all the blood drain from her face. 'Was my grandfather mad?' she enquired faintly. 'This ... this is outrageous!'

Rowland stood up. 'Very pretty,' he sneered. 'This is your doing, I see. Not only did you have an eye on the estate, you wanted to snare a husband as well!' His eyes swept over her contemptuously, her darned black gown, her unfashionable hair-style, her pallor.

'How dare you!'

'Mr Sandiford...' began Mr Camberwell, in consternation. 'I really cannot allow you to ...'

Rowland interrupted him. 'Oh, I dare speak the truth when I see it.' He turned to Merab. 'Look at you, dowdy, knocking thirty, how else could you get a husband! You schemed your way into this.'

Merab was so angry that she found her voice shaking. 'A moment's consideration—not that you seem capable of anything that could be considered thought—' she said icily, 'would have allowed you to see that my grandfather never in his life did anything other than what he wanted to do. Not only is this the first that I have ever heard of this preposterous idea, I will tell you here and now that I will have nothing whatsoever to do with so disgraceful a scheme!' She turned to Mr Camberwell. 'So I suggest, sir, that you inform the two charities of the windfall in store for them.'

She rose as she spoke, turned on her heel and left the room.

CHAPTER TWO

Miss Kitty Parminster, only daughter of Sir John and Lady Parminster of Parminster Hall in the County of Wiltshire, whose blue eyes and dancing nut-brown curls were the despair of all the young men within a twenty-five mile radius, sipped at her coffee in the breakfast parlour and said, 'Papa, you've hardly said a word to me this morning! What is it that so engrosses you in that horrid newspaper?'

Her father lowered the paper, folded it up and handed it across to her. 'There, Miss Curiosity, Old Julian Hartfield is dead.'

Miss Parminster's blue eyes widened. 'Rowland's old cousin? The one who is to leave him the estate?'

'The same.' Sir John eyed his daughter shrewdly. 'Now listen, Kitty, I know you fancy the fellow and young Sandiford has made it pretty plain what *he* wants, but until we know what the will says I'm not allowing the affair to go any further.' The Parminster estate marched with Merryn Park and Sir John had known Rowland since he was a boy and liked him, but the Sandifords were not rich for Rowland's grandfather had left the estate

27

burdened by debt.

Kitty pouted. 'But Papa, I have money of my own, you know.'

'I've nothing against Rowland, mind, though he does have some damn fool Radical ideas, but your dowry of ten thousand pounds means that you can look a lot higher than Sandiford, whose estate is worth barely fifteen hundred a year.'

'But I love him!' The ready tears sprang into Kitty's eyes and hung trembling on the ends of her lashes.

'That's as maybe. You're an extravagant little puss, Kitty, you wouldn't be able to carry on as you are used to if you were to be Mrs Rowland Sandiford, you know.' Kitty's chin went up.

'Rowland would deny me nothing!'

'Unless he wanted to land in Queer Street, he would have to say "no",' said Sir John firmly. 'You could afford a month or so in Town for the season, maybe, but you couldn't expect all those pretty trinkets you conjure out of my pocket, puss.'

Kitty smiled. She could twist men round her little finger, she knew. She had always done so with her doting papa and saw no reason why her husband should not do the same.

'If old Hartfield's estate is valued at about twenty thousand and comes to Rowland, then that's different,' went on Sir John. 'He must settle half of it on you, of course, and the rest he can use improving his estate. He's always going on about the need to plough money into it. Personally, I think his rents are far too low; squeeze the lot of 'em is my view.'

'Rowland wants to bring it back to what it was before his grandfather took to gambling.'

'He also has the idea of going into politics—and that costs money,' continued Sir John. 'He'll have to give up that notion, of course. Well, we shall see. I shall do nothing precipitate.'

Kitty's pretty brow frowned down at her coffee. Papa could be so unreasonable sometimes. Of course she'd never love anybody else. Rowland was so handsome; she loved the way his hair curled wildly, the way his grey eyes shone so tenderly down at her, and she especially loved (though Papa did not know this) the one or two stolen kisses he had snatched. For a moment or two the tears threatened again, but then she cheered up. She was going over to tea with her friend, Lavinia Heslop, today, and Lavinia had a perfectly splendid brother who was just now on furlough from his regiment. Last time she had met him, Lieutenant Heslop had been very gratifyingly smitten, and Kitty couldn't help wondering if she would be offered a repeat performance.

She poured herself another cup of coffee and smiled reminiscently.

Over in the vicarage the Rev. George Heslop had also seen the notice of Mr Hartfield's death

29

and pointed it out to his wife. 'I daresay that means that Sandiford will soon be announcing his betrothal to Kitty,' he remarked.

His wife sniffed. 'I confess I cannot understand what he sees in her,' she said. 'I grant you Kitty is bewitchingly pretty, but I always took Mr Sandiford for a sensible man.'

'Sandiford won't be the first man to take himself a pretty but unsuitable wife. Look at Delilah.'

'Delilah!' echoed his wife, scornfully. 'We all know Rowland has political ambitions, and Kitty would be a disaster! I doubt whether she knows one political party from another. She is completely empty-headed and she'd ruin him within a couple of years.' Lavinia, she thought thankfully, was admittedly not as pretty as Kitty, but she had a much nicer nature.

'Perhaps marriage to Sandiford will steady her,' said the vicar mildly.

Mrs Heslop pointed out with asperity that whereas that might say much for his Christian charity it did not, in her view, say much for his common sense. Mr Heslop directed a quizzical glance at her from over his spectacles and picked up the paper again.

* * *

Rowland had spent an uncomfortable evening after the reading of the will in Mr Hartfield's library trying to convince himself that his dowdy cousin was 'on the catch'. But try as he might he could not conceal from himself that he had behaved with unpardonable rudeness and quite unlike any gentleman of breeding. Julian's presence seemed to linger in the library and more than once Rowland found himself looking round sharply whenever a coal fell or the wood creaked. The books stretched from floor to ceiling, musty old tomes with cracked bindings and above the mantelpiece was a portrait of his cousin, painted some twenty years ago and it seemed to Rowland that the face held a grim smile as if to say, 'You'll do as I say now'. Rowland's fist clenched in anger and frustration and he aimed a savage kick at the grate which sent a log crashing down and a shower of sparks fell on the worn Turkey rug. Cursing, Rowland stamped them out and poured himself another brandy. Damn him, he thought not for the first time. Damn him.

Rowland had been largely unaware of Merab's existence prior to his arrival at Hartfield Hall. True, his cousin had gone on about close relatives staying there when Rowland was younger, but he had always taken their existence with a pinch of salt, believing it to be merely an attempt to exert some pressure on his political views. In later years, whenever he had met Julian in Town, his cousin had not mentioned them and Rowland had assumed that either their 'existence' had been dropped or that, if real, they had gone back to wherever they had come from.

Merab's presence at Hartfield Hall was, therefore, a considerable shock and not a welcome one. A granddaughter, Jonathan's child, and living at Hartfield Hall for the last eight years! Rowland was not a mercenary man, but he had always been given to understand that Hartfield Hall would be his in the fullness of time, and here was this creature, of doubtful legitimacy, who had schemed her way into his cousin's affections.

What he saw was a tall thin woman in an outmoded gown of dusty black and with thick dark hair unbecomingly scraped back from her face. Her eyes, her best feature, were disconcertingly dark and lustrous and reminded him unpleasantly of an Italian contessa who had once ditched him for a richer lover.

Rowland could not get it out of his head that Merab was an impostor in some way. Why had his cousin never spoken of her? What hold had she had over him?

Underneath all this was anxiety over Kitty. If he did not inherit Hartfield Hall then he could say goodbye to all hopes of marrying Kitty. Even if her father allowed it, how could he let her marry somebody who could not afford to give her what she wanted? Part of him knew very well that Kitty would not make a suitable MP's wife, but he told himself that marriage would settle her. She loved him and of course what was important to him would be important to her too.

The morning after the disastrous will reading, however, Merab was not in the dining-room at breakfast.

Taken a pet, thought Rowland. His feeling of having behaved badly towards her was still uncomfortably with him. Perhaps it was true that the will had been as much of a surprise to her. She did not, after all, dressed as she was, look like the favourite granddaughter. And there was no doubt that she was right when she pointed out that Julian Hartfield had never been known to be influenced by anybody.

He did not like his new cousin, but, reluctantly, he recognized that he owed her an apology. At any rate it could do no harm and maybe they could do something about this appalling will. Might it be overturned? Could they argue Julian Hartfield's insanity, for example? He must speak to her. He rang the bell and Mary appeared.

'Send my compliments to Miss Hartfield,' he said, 'and ask her if she would be so good as to spare me a few moments of her time.'

'Miss Merab's gone, sir,' said Mary, not without satisfaction. Rumours had spread like wildfire downstairs and she and Jenny were agreed that Miss Merab had been treated something dreadful, poor lady.

'Gone? What do you mean, gone? Gone where?'

'I don't know, I'm sure, sir.' Mary stuck her nose in the air. 'Have you finished with your breakfast things, sir?'

'Never mind that. When she comes in, please give her my message.'

'She's gone, sir,' repeated Mary with relish. 'She packed her trunk last night and Farmer Willett collected her this morning about six.'

* * *

Sir Thomas and Amelia, Lady Wincanton lived in Pulteney Street, far enough away from the bustle of Bath to be quiet, but near enough to be within a ten-minute walk of the centre. It was Sir Thomas's great-grandfather who had made the family fortune during Bath's first building boom and until six years ago Sir Thomas had lived in Queen's Square, in the house his great-grandfather had acquired. But Queen's Square was no longer so fashionable as it once had been and Sir Thomas decided on his marriage that the newer Pulteney Street would offer a better address.

He had married late in life, being a good twenty years older than his wife. He was a kindly man, somewhat old-fashioned in his notions, who enjoyed having a young and pretty wife and liked to indulge her. But Lady Wincanton was well aware that his indulgence had its limits and that—though she would never dare to say so—he had inherited some of the narrow-minded provincial notions of his great-grandfather, who had been a grazier by trade.

It was tea-time in the Wincanton nursery on this chilly December afternoon, and Amelia Wincanton, a vivacious lady with light-brown hair which curled prettily on her forehead, was helping Nurse to persuade young Master Charles Wincanton to eat his bread and butter and keeping a careful eye on her elder son, Tommy, at the same time.

'Now come along, Charlie; look, bread and butter soldiers for you. Eat up now. There, in it goes.'

'I have a tooth loose, Mama,' said Tommy proudly. 'Look!'

'Not with a mouthful of cake, Master Tommy,' said Nurse firmly.

'Excuse me, my lady.' A maid poked her head into the nursery. 'Miss Hartfield has just arrived.'

Amelia straightened up slowly, one hand pressed to the small of her back. Merab here, she thought, whatever could have happened? 'Pray tell her I shall be down immediately.'

'Yes, my lady. Miss Hartfield is in the drawing-room with Sir Thomas.'

Oh dear, thought Amelia in dismay, Sir Thomas won't like this. She hoped he would not be in one of his moods of stiff propriety. Amelia went swiftly up to her room, took off her apron which had been protecting her gown from the nursery tea, smoothed her hair and picked up Merab's letter from the dressing-table. It had been written a week or so previously and had been little more than the bald announcement of her grandfather's death. Amelia had replied at once, begging her friend to come and stay. 'You have only to say when it is convenient,' she wrote. 'Sir Thomas will send the carriage for you. You know we shall love to have you.'

She had expected Merab to write in a week or so when she had had time to recover from the funeral. She and her husband had discussed it many times and neither could quite believe in the stories of Julian Hartfield's parsimony and meanness. 'She's his only grandchild, after all,' said Sir Thomas. 'I am sure he will leave her comfortably provided for.'

Amelia gave herself a last look in the glass, patted her stomach reflectively and went downstairs and into the drawing-room. A swift glance at her husband reassured her that he was in an indulgent mood.

'Merab!'

'Oh, Amelia!' Merab rose and embraced her friend. 'Forgive me. I had to come!'

Sir Thomas, a tactful man, rose to his feet. 'I feel sure you have a lot to say to each other, my dear. I shall see you at dinner.' Bowing to Merab, he left the room.

When Amelia had heard the story of the will, she was quite as shocked as Merab could have wished. 'So indelicate!' she cried. 'So distasteful a thing to do. If he did not wish you to have the estate he could at least have left you a reasonable competence. Did you not tell me that you were paying for your keep as well?'

'Yes, at least I thought I was. But Mr Camberwell told me last night that he had persuaded my grandfather to let that accumulate once I took over the housekeeping. It means that now I have something over fourteen hundred pounds. That's one comfort.'

'Pooh! What's that? Seventy pounds a year. Pin money! You cannot live on that.'

'Well, at least it's better than fifty pounds a year,' retorted Merab.

Amelia gave her friend a sidelong glance and then said, 'But tell me about Mr Sandiford.'

'He's rude, overbearing and odiously condescending,' said Merab roundly.

'Oh dear,' Amelia laughed. 'But good-looking?'

Merab considered. 'I suppose so,' she said grudgingly. 'Tall, brown hair, aquiline nose, which he looks down.' She paused, for some reason she could not mention her initial pleasure on finding that he had hair as curly and unruly as her own; it savoured too much of disappointment. 'No manners. He arrived two days before the funeral and barely spoke to me. We had our meals in almost total silence. He reminded me unnervingly of Grandfather.

After the will reading, of course, I was sure of it.' She winced inwardly, remembering the humiliation she had felt on being raked contemptuously by those cold, grey eyes. The last eight years had not increased Merab's store of self-confidence and she had felt as gauche and awkward as she had been when a gawky schoolgirl. The fact that Rowland's good looks had had their inevitable effect on the two Hartfield maids who remained, a giggling Mary and a blushing Jenny, who had vied to take up his shaving water in the morning had not helped. She sternly quashed her own confused feelings about her cousin's attractions, and said nothing to Amelia.

'Pity,' said Amelia. 'Of course, the blatancy of your grandfather's will is disgusting, no modest female could bear it. But there is no doubting that it would be a sensible solution.'

'Nothing, but nothing would induce me to marry Rowland Sandiford,' cried Merab. 'Would you want to marry somebody who told you that you were a dowd and accused you of setting out to entrap him?'

'I don't suppose I would,' admitted Amelia.

She said nothing more to her friend and the conversation turned to the little boys and the happy trivialities of Amelia's life. She smiled at Merab's enquiring glance at her gently rounded stomach and admitted that she was expecting a happy event in the summer. Later, however, in the privacy of the marital bedroom, Amelia was not so reticent.

'What do you know of Rowland Sandiford?' she asked her husband when she had related Merab's story.

'Pleasant chap. I've met him once or twice at my club when in Town. He had the reputation of being somewhat Radical in his ideas up at Oxford, but I imagine he has sobered up since. The only other thing I know about him is that he wants to get into Parliament on a Reform ticket and they say that he's head over ears in love with the Parminster chit.'

'Kitty Parminster!'

'Yes, that's her.'

Amelia thought for a moment. 'Haven't I met him then? Yes, I rather think I did a year or so ago. Doesn't his mother live in Bath?'

'I believe she does.'

Amelia sat down at her dressing-table and began to fiddle with her ivory-backed hairbrush. She remembered Mr Sandiford now, a pleasant, intelligent man. A little brusque, perhaps, but not uncivil. And whatever Merab might protest, he was certainly good-looking enough to satisfy the tastes of most females. So he was in love with pretty, silly little Kitty Parminster, was he? Why did men always fall for these insipid dolls? It was plain to anybody with an unprejudiced eye that Miss Parminster would be nothing but a liability. She would lead him a pretty dance, get him into debt and bore him within six months.

He had much better marry Merab.

Sir Thomas was watching her in the glass, a half-smile on his lips. 'I can read you like a book,' he said. 'Now, don't interfere, Amelia.'

'I, interfere?' exclaimed Amelia at her most limpid. She looked at him under her lashes.

'Baggage!' said Sir Thomas appreciatively. 'Come to bed.'

* * *

Rowland had plenty of time to regret his outburst. A meeting with the Hartfield lawyer had proved salutary. Mr Camberwell, a rather spare, dry man with receding grey hair and the faint trace of a Scottish accent from his youth in Edinburgh, had a considerable respect and a certain affection for Merab. He admired the way she had borne with her grandfather with courtesy and patience in spite of the provocations offered, and he had always done his best to do what he could to ameliorate her unenviable position. He found Rowland's outburst the previous evening both distasteful and grossly unfair and was not adverse to letting that gentleman see it. Mr Hartfield, the lawyer informed Rowland with a certain grim pleasure, might have been considered something of an oddity, perhaps, but he was in nowise mad.

'But why make such a will at all?' Rowland

expostulated. 'If he didn't trust me, why not leave the estate to Miss Hartfield, who was his granddaughter after all? That would have been understandable. But to propose a marriage between two people who are quite unknown to each other, why, it's outrageous.'

'Mr Hartfield expressed no affection for Miss Hartfield,' said Mr Camberwell carefully, 'but I think he had the greatest respect for her management. She bore an increasing burden of the running of the estate after his first stroke and, whilst he resented it, he also had a certain admiration for her.'

'Then why not leave Hartfield to her outright?'

'Possibly because he felt he had raised your expectations. Or it may be that he considered Miss Hartfield would be a steadying influence on your politics.' Mr Camberwell allowed himself a slight smile. He was sorry for the position Rowland was in, but he thought it would do the young man no harm to be taken down a peg or two.

Rowland picked up the paperweight on Mr Camberwell's desk and appeared to be studying it carefully. Eventually he said, 'I have been paying my addresses to a Miss Parminster, and I doubt whether her father is going to be happy about this. I cannot blame him. Miss Parminster is worthy of far more than I can now offer her.'

'I am sorry to hear this.' Mr Camberwell

looked at Rowland over the top of his glasses with rather more sympathy. 'You will feel it deeply. Nevertheless by the terms of the will we must wait until six months elapse from the date of Mr Hartfield's death before anything is done.'

'What will happen to the estate in the meantime?'

Mr Camberwell shrugged. 'I do not know. A temporary manager probably. I had hoped that Miss Hartfield would have stayed on. At least I could have ensured that she was paid properly.'

'Do you know where she is?'

'I do.'

'Supposing I decide that this marriage is possible after all?'

Mr Camberwell looked at him blandly. 'Then I should let Miss Hartfield know of your decision, naturally. But I should remind you that there are two parties in this, and from what Miss Hartfield reported to me I doubt whether you changing your mind would change hers.'

Rowland bit his lip.

He left Hartfield Hall that afternoon and returned to Wiltshire in a mood of towering resentment, a feeling augmented by the fact that Mr Camberwell had made his disapproval of Rowland's rudeness towards his cousin abundantly clear. He tried to dismiss the lawyer's only half-concealed scorn from his mind. Miss Hartfield refuse him? Unlikely! His estate at Merryn Park might be only moderate, but he had been courted by enough matchmaking mamas on the lookout for their debutante daughters to realize that he was a not undesirable *parti*. He had had sufficient more intimate relations with the fair sex for him to be confident of his personal attractions. Miss Hartfield, tall, skinny, and possessed of no personal attractions whatsoever, would be only too pleased if he should choose to drop the handkerchief in her direction.

Some few days later he was in Sir John Parminster's library. In fact, it was a library in name only, for there were very few books about. There were, however, plenty of hunting trophies; a couple of foxes' masks hung on the walls, together with a number of hunting prints and, in one corner, Sir John's discarded riding whip. Sir John had greeted Rowland civilly enough, offered him a drink, made a few jovial remarks about him having missed some good hunting; but about any proposed marriage he was adamant.

'I'm sorry, my boy, that it's turned out like this. Damn sorry for your disappointment in old Hartfield. It was not a gentlemanly thing to do in my opinion. He should have left it to you as he'd always meant to do and left your cousin an annuity secured against the estate. Or given her a few thousand. Granddaughter, too, eh? It looks bad.'

'I'm more disappointed about Kitty,' said Rowland, staring rather blindly down at his drink.

'Yes, yes,' said Sir John soothingly. 'But that's completely out of the question now. You must accept that.' He looked at Rowland's downcast face and added, 'You may not think so at the moment, but Kitty's not the wife for you. Bless me, she don't know one political party from another. And she's extravagant. Whoever marries Kitty will have to be prepared for a wife without the smallest notions of economy!' He laughed fondly.

Rowland forced a smile. 'Kitty deserves the best,' he said. 'I would not have willingly denied her anything. But I had hoped that as my wife she would have come to share my interests, and perhaps...'

'Moonshine!' interrupted Sir John with asperity. 'Kitty's a selfish little puss and would see no reason why she should not continue to have her new dresses and trinkets and a thousand other things. Men always think, God help them, that a young girl can be moulded. It's nonsense. Just as women think they can change the man they marry. They can't. You have to accept your partner for what they are. Compromise, that's what marriage is about. Adaptation and compromise.'

Rowland smiled ruefully. 'I've never been very good at accepting things as they are. I've always wanted to change the world.'

It was surprising what effect just being away from the pressures of Hartfield had on Merab's state of mind. For the first week or so at the Wincantons' she seemed to do nothing but sleep. The tent bed with its crisp chintz curtains with a swagged rose design and the comfortable mattress were unaccustomed luxuries and Merab woke each morning and looked about her with pleasure. She knew she mustn't stay for longer than a couple of months at most, and that a grim future as teacher or governess beckoned, but for the moment surely she might enjoy the comforts of the Wincantons' well-ordered house and relax? Several times Amelia found her asleep on one of the *chaise-longues* in the drawing-room, a book fallen down by her side.

'I don't know what's the matter with me!' Merab exclaimed, having woken up with a start as the butler came in with afternoon tea.

'You're run down and exhausted, that's all,' said Amelia. 'You've had years of waiting on that old curmudgeon, not to mention running the estate. And if he ever voluntarily considered that you might need a break, this is the first I've heard of it. You have a lot of catching up to do. Tea?'

Merab sat up and took the cup offered to her. 'It's strange. When Mama was still alive it was worrying and exhausting, of course, but I

45

had something coming back. We would talk about old times, she'd want to know how I was getting on with the flower bed Tom Tilling dug for me, that sort of thing. But with my grandfather I don't believe he ever spoke to me voluntarily in his life. He couldn't care less about what I was doing and thinking. It was his coldness and harshness that was so depressing. I used to think, what have I done to deserve this? I tried to please him, Amelia, truly I did. But it was no use. Even at the end . . .' She made a useless gesture with her hand and was silent.

After a moment Amelia said, 'I've heard one or two things about Mr Sandiford.'

'What sort of things?' asked Merab cautiously.

'He is desperately in love with a silly little chit called Kitty Parminster. Of course that'll be off now, I imagine. I cannot see her papa agreeing to the match in the present circumstances.'

'I hadn't realized.' Merab sipped at her tea. Perhaps that explained at least some of his fury. 'Dowdy', 'knocking thirty', 'scheming'; all those years of poverty and drudgery had left their mark, and Rowland's barbs had stung.

'What's she like?'

'Kitty Parminster? Nineteen, beautiful, selfish, lazy, spends money like water. And she was the toast of the season last year.'

'I can see then that I'd come a very poor second in the Kitty Parminster stakes,' said

46

Merab, trying to smile.

'Thank God!' retorted Amelia.

*   *   *

Rowland spent the next few days after seeing Sir John trying to blot out his depression by flinging himself into Merryn estate business. He had several meetings with his bailiff, visited a tenant farmer who had problems with a leaking roof and caught up with his correspondence. In the years following his father's death he had managed slowly but surely to pull the estate out of debt and next year would, if the harvest were reasonable, show a modest profit. Normally, this thought gave him a very real satisfaction, now, however, it all seemed pointless. Kitty would never be his wife and his plans for village improvements which he fondly imagined she shared felt like a wearisome burden rather than an absorbing interest.

Sir John had said that he thought it would only upset Kitty if Rowland attempted to see her privately and Rowland had no option but to acquiesce. Kitty felt otherwise. A little scented note was slipped into his hand after church by Kitty's giggling maid and here he was, waiting for her at their special place, a small copse which bordered the Parminster and Sandiford estates. In a few months' time it would be covered with a blue mist of bluebells, but now it was bare, save for where a few holly bushes lit up the cold winter's morning with their scarlet berries. It had been a frosty night and even now at eleven o'clock the hazel's bare twigs still glistened with rime. Rowland tethered his horse to a young sapling and dismounted. His feet began to get cold.

It was not until some twenty minutes later that Kitty galloped up. Rowland caught his breath. She was wearing a deep-blue riding habit which exactly matched the blue of her eyes. Her shining nut-brown hair was coiled up under her dashing riding hat with its curled ostrich plumes. Rowland immediately forgot his frozen fingers and went to help her down.

Kitty was in something of a pet.

'Well, sir. So you are jilting me, then?'

'Kitty darling! How could I argue with your father who wants only the best for you? I shall, in all probability, be no richer than I am now—at least for a number of years.'

'Do you think I care for that?' Kitty turned her lovely profile away. 'I have my own money after all.'

'Dearest, you know it's not possible. Don't make it harder for me.'

'Harder for you! What about me? Nobody cares about my feelings in all this, I notice! Have I been asked, or in any way consulted?' Kitty had attempted a small tantrum that morning at the breakfast-table but had been balked by her father's at once retreating to the

48

library and her mother saying firmly, 'Now, don't be silly, darling.' She had ridden to the spinney that morning in the pleasurable knowledge that she could vent her spleen on her beloved.

'Dearest Kitty, please don't cry.' Rowland looked helplessly round. 'You wouldn't like being the wife of a poor man, would you? How would you manage without all those new dresses every season?'

'Papa would pay for them!'

'No, he would not! I could not allow my wife to be supported by her father.'

'Why not? Papa isn't mean. And if you wouldn't sell one of your precious cows, or whatever, then of course, Papa would pay.'

For a moment Rowland felt a twinge of irritation, but stifled it. She was only nineteen and had been brought up by doting parents and never allowed to want for anything. Of course she could not help being a little spoilt.

'Kitty,' he began.

Kitty backed away. 'It won't make any difference, will it?' she said, pettishly. 'We can't marry, anyway, can we? And I consider it's all your fault! You should have buttered up this awful old cousin of yours and made sure you inherited. Well! I shall go now. What do you care if my heart is broken?'

'You don't mean that, Kitty!'

Kitty went back to her horse and gathered up the reins in one hand. 'Help me up, please,' she said coldly.

In silence Rowland did so. If part of him realized that her behaviour was that of a spoilt child, part of him could not help feeling devastated by the sight of that woebegone face—as doubtless Kitty meant him to be. As she turned to go, Kitty said, 'I would have married you whatever. Remember that!'

Rowland watched until she was out of sight, but Kitty did not look back.

That afternoon over tea and toast Kitty relayed the episode for her friend Lavinia Heslop's benefit. Her version of events, with Rowland's pusillanimity and her own noble fortitude, not to mention her parting remark which had somehow become embellished into a farewell speech indicative of martyred love, would have astonished Rowland considerably if he had heard it. Lavinia, a thin slip of a girl whose only pretensions to beauty were a pair of speaking grey eyes set in rather a thin face, listened with gratifying admiration. Kitty was so encouraged by Lavinia's reaction that she ate several slices of toast and jam and the girls ended with an animated discussion of the next ball and what they were going to wear.

Rowland, meanwhile, untied his horse and rode slowly back to Merryn Park. The house, when he entered it, looked lonely and unwelcoming. His feet echoed on the marble hall floor and the portrait of his grandfather seemed to stare mockingly down at him.

Rowland stared back. If old Peter Sandiford, whom he just remembered as a red-faced man with one gouty leg propped up on a small footstool, had not brought the place to the edge of ruin with his gambling, then he, Rowland, might be in a different position. In his grandfather's time the estate had been bringing in a good £5000 a year and its stables were one of the best in the county. Now, there were only a couple of hunters and the farm horses.

He looked around and sighed. The place needed a feminine touch. He had once hoped that Kitty would be the one to bring a touch of home to the place, to leave books lying round, to have bowls of flowers, her music open on the pianoforte... Lavinia could have told him that Kitty rarely read anything more demanding than the *Ladies' Fashion Magazine* and only practised her music under protest, but Rowland's dream held.

Rowland's mother, Mrs Sandiford, had parted from her husband in perfect amity when Rowland had gone to Eton. Her constitution would not support the rigours of the country, she said firmly. She would go to Bath for her health.

There was no formal separation. Mrs Sandiford came to stay during Rowland's school holidays. Her husband punctiliously visited her in January when the farming year was at its slackest. It was an arrangement that suited both of them.

'I am devoted to your father,' Mrs Sandiford had told her son on more than one occasion. 'But we do not rub well together. It is better as it is. When we meet we are pleased to see each other, and each of us is happy with our own lives. We are not really very well suited.'

However, Mrs Sandiford wrote her husband affectionate chatty letters of her doings in Bath and he responded with terse little notes about the state of the crops. Rowland had grown up accepting this state of affairs, but, as Mrs Heslop had frequently pointed out to her husband it meant that Rowland had a decidedly unrealistic view of women.

'I have always believed Elizabeth Sandiford to be a sensible woman,' she said. 'If she were here she would see through Kitty's wiles at once and be able to guide Rowland's affections in a more proper direction.' She gave an exasperated sigh. She had hoped that Rowland might one day look at Lavinia, but as her portion was small, and her charms beside Kitty's attractions only moderate, it did not seem likely.

Mrs Heslop was not the only person to be thinking about Mrs Sandiford. Never one to shirk an unpleasant duty, Rowland had written to his mother on his return from Hartfield and told her the terms of the will. Now, after a miserable evening by his own fireside, drinking far too much port and being

52

unable to get Kitty out of his mind, Rowland decided to write to his mother again and beg her to come down for a month or so. Either that, or he would go and stay with her. She would not be altogether surprised, he thought, by his cry for help.

Coincidentally, the following morning a letter from Mrs Sandiford arrived, but what it said was unexpected. She had not told him before, she wrote, but in November her friend, Samuel Bridges, had asked her to marry him and she had accepted. They had married very quietly a fortnight ago and were just returned from their honeymoon in Weymouth to find Rowland's letter waiting. She was so sorry for the trouble he was in and why didn't he come and visit them and have a change of scene? A short note from Mr Bridges added that he hoped Rowland would forgive the apparent hole-in-the-corner nature of the affair, but he knew what his mother was like about not wanting a fuss and he had given in to her wishes.

Rowland did know, and after the first shock was over he could even approve. He liked Mr Bridges, a retired lawyer of comfortable means, who for many years had been his mother's faithful admirer, but he was not sure that he wanted to go and stay so soon after their marriage. But neither could he stay at Merryn Park.

* * *

It was now a month since Mr Hartfield's death and those few weeks of unbroken sleep, good food and rest had had an astonishing effect on Merab's constitution. Babette, Amelia's French maid, remarked on it to her mistress.

'Mademoiselle's 'air is in much better condition now,' she observed one morning while pinning up her mistress's locks. 'It 'as more shine. If Mademoiselle would allow me to do it . . .' She shrugged. Merab refused to use the services of Amelia's maid through a combination of pride and an unwilling shame in the shabbiness of her clothes besides Amelia's.

'Her skin is better, too,' observed Amelia. 'Much clearer. She looked positively pasty-faced when she arrived, poor thing.'

Merab, too, was cautiously pleased with the improvement in her looks. And as the weather was mild, she was able to take some gentle exercise with Amelia in Sydney Gardens which touched her cheeks with a tinge of colour.

The ladies had discussed the question of mourning. The proper mourning for a grandfather was six months, but Amelia did not consider that at all necessary. Merab had visited Amelia in Bath before and her position was well known.

'Mr Hartfield treated you abominably,' said Amelia. 'If you go into deep mourning it may

54

look as though you are playing the hypocrite. I should have thought that half-mourning would be quite sufficient. Grey, violet, something of the sort. No coloured stones, of course.'

'All this is quite beside the point, Amelia,' said Merab with some asperity. 'I have no money to pay for any new clothes. As for jewellery, all I have are my mother's pearls.'

Later that evening Amelia discussed it with her husband. Babette had finished plaiting her hair and left, and Sir Thomas had come in from his dressing-room. Amelia patted the bed invitingly and poured out her concern. 'Merab might allow me to buy her some small token, a scarf perhaps, but she will not allow me to dress her. Oh, how worrying it all is!'

Sir Thomas kissed her cheek. 'You're a good friend,' he said, 'but one cannot help but applaud Miss Hartfield's spirit of independence.'

'But if only...' began Amelia.

'I know you,' said Sir Thomas indulgently. 'You would like to get her married off. But just remember, she's what, twenty-six now, and has no dowry worth speaking of.'

'I am not thinking of her marrying just anybody,' retorted Amelia. 'I am thinking of her marrying Rowland Sandiford. And, what is more, I heard in the Pump Room this morning that he is coming here to stay with his mother. Now do you see why Merab's clothes are of such importance?'

There was a pause. 'You'll never do it,' said Sir Thomas finally. 'Firstly, he's in love with the Parminster chit. Secondly, your friend, though delightful, is no beauty. And thirdly, Miss Hartfield seems to me to be a young lady of spirit. I hardly think she would agree to marry a man who has insulted her in the way you told me.'

Amelia threw him a look of affectionate scorn for his masculine mutton-headedness. 'We shall see,' was all she said.

Rowland was kept at Merryn Park for longer than he had hoped for his peace of mind by a number of urgent problems about the estate. Two men on the tramp up to Bristol had inadvertently set fire to a haystack in which they were sleeping and the resulting conflagration had threatened to spread to a nearby barn. Fortunately, the wind had changed direction and several of the farm-hands had rushed up from the village with rakes and buckets and limited the damage. But it all had to be dealt with.

Lady Parmister, of course, did not know this. She had never cared for the proposed match between Rowland and her daughter—Kitty, surely, could do better than a country gentleman of limited means? Lady Parminster had every intention of seeing that a further brilliant London season would ensure Kitty's future life with some far more desirable *parti*.

56

However, there was no doubt that Rowland was a man of considerable personal attractions, and moreover, was desperately in love with her daughter. She had assumed that Rowland would remove himself from Merryn Park as soon as possible. Unaccountably, he stayed on, looking white and strained in church while Kitty cried becomingly into her prayer-book and threw him anguished looks.

If Rowland would not go—tiresome man—then Kitty must. The London season was still some months away and she could not have her lovely daughter going into a decline before her very eyes. If Sir John had noticed that Kitty's distress seemed to be markedly assuaged by young Lieutenant Heslop's attentions and only switched on in church, Kitty's mother had not. And when Sir John pointed it out to her she was duly horrified.

'That settles it then,' she said. 'A match with Rowland is out of the question and the Heslops are as poor as church mice! I propose, Sir John, to send Kitty to her godmother for a couple of months, just until the start of the season.'

'What? To Bath? But isn't there a risk that young Sandiford will go too? After all, his mother lives there.'

'I don't believe so,' said Lady Parminster, after some consideration. 'So far as I can see all he wants to do is wander morosely round his estates. If he'd wanted to go to visit his mother, surely he would have done so earlier?'

'Will it not be too much for Mrs Banstead? She may not want a lively young girl to stay. One who has to be chaperoned everywhere.'

'Nonsense, she'll be delighted.' Lady Parminster summarily disposed of her husband's objections. Mrs Banstead, besides being Kitty's godmother, which was most suitable, was a sociable woman who much enjoyed the gaieties of Bath. Lady Parminster could not conceive but that she would be happy to have Kitty to stay. 'I could suggest that Lavinia Heslop went too,' she said, after a moment's thought. 'That way, the girls may chaperone each other during the day.'

Mrs Banstead wrote that she'd be delighted to have the two girls. Sir John raised no further objections and even gave Kitty ten guineas. 'Buy yourself some fripperies, puss.' Three days later the Parminster coach with Kitty, Lavinia and Kitty's maid set off for Bath.

CHAPTER THREE

Amelia sat in her morning-room engaged in smocking a baby's dress. She was four months pregnant and this time, she hoped, it would be the longed-for baby daughter. She loved her sons, naturally, but she had given her husband two and she felt that she was entitled to ask for a girl. But this pregnancy had not been altogether an easy one, and Merab's arrival had been a welcome diversion from her own state of health. She had begun cautiously to feel rather better, well enough, in fact, to be able to take a few gentle strolls with Merab around Sydney Gardens and to look forward to her daily trip to the Pump Room to drink the waters, which she did on her doctor's orders.

Merab was sitting in a chair opposite flicking through the pages of *The Ladies' Cabinet*, but it was plain that her thoughts were many miles away. At last she sighed, put down the book and said, 'Amelia, I've been here six weeks and I must consider what to do about my future. I ought to be looking around for a position of some sort.'

Amelia set a stitch or two before replying. They had had this conversation before and it worried her. Merab must not go and do anything silly before she, Amelia, had had a chance to see whether she could not organize Merab's life into a more satisfactory groove. However, she must tread carefully. Merab shied away from any notion of being on the marriage market and Amelia did not want to precipitate her into any hasty action.

'Some Queen's Square seminary?' she said. 'You know I'm willing to help in any way I can, but, have you really thought? They are such drudges, poor things. And all for twenty pounds a year.'

'I must do something,' said Merab firmly,

resolutely turning her eyes away from the comfortable fire and fixing them on the icy January scene outside. 'Though you may be right about the seminary. I doubt whether any Bath school for young ladies would be very impressed with my attainments at the Misses Goodison's! Perhaps I could be a housekeeper? God knows, I have had enough practice and I believe they are paid better too.'

'Never!' cried Amelia, sitting up and dropping the baby's smock. 'A housekeeper! At least a teacher is genteel.'

'I can't see that standing on my gentility is going to do me much good,' observed Merab, drily. 'I shan't get married now and surely it would be better to be a housekeeper on forty pounds a year than a "lady" teacher on half that?'

'I had hoped you would stay here,' said Amelia wistfully. 'At least until I have had the baby. You've no idea what a comfort you have been. I was suffering from all sorts of megrims until you arrived. In any case, you simply must stay for the Queen's visit! Rumour has it that she's coming in June and you wouldn't want to miss that!' Merab looked sceptical. Amelia stopped and shifted position before adding, 'You know, you're like a sister to me, Merab, and how can I bear to let you go and teach in some dreadful school? If only you'd let me buy you some decent clothes and take you about a bit.'

Merab eyed her suspiciously. 'I see! You want to marry me off! I know you.'

'But Merab, you're twenty-six and you haven't met anybody, apart from the odious Rowland Sandiford. Surely you'd like to make a few friends? And don't forget,' she added cunningly, 'that you might meet some suitable person who wants a governess. How much better will your chances be if you are well dressed! First impressions are most important, you know.'

Merab looked at her sceptically. 'Matchmaking,' she said firmly.

Amelia sighed as she thought over the conversation later. She'd mishandled it and now Merab was even more anxious to find herself some dreary post. Even now she was doubtless up in her bedroom writing to the Misses Goodison for a suitable reference.

However, the Fates, who up to this moment had seemed to mark Merab out for misfortune and a dreary future, with their usual unpredictability now decided to fling a small bonus her way. The following morning at breakfast Merab received a letter.

'If it's from the Misses Goodison, I don't want to know,' cried Amelia, pettishly.

'This is from Mr Camberwell,' said Merab, looking slightly stunned. 'And he's enclosed a draft for thirty pounds!'

'How wonderful! But where does it come from?'

61

'He managed to persuade the other executors that I am owed thirty pounds retrospectively for my work helping my grandfather with the estate business after his first stroke.'

'About time too, the old skinflint,' said Amelia, 'but does it mean that ...?'

'Yes, I'll be sensible and buy some clothes.'

Amelia sat up suddenly. 'Ah, now that's better. Let's make a list.'

'Wait a minute,' said Merab. 'I'm not putting myself on the marriage market, Amelia, that would be ridiculous. What I want are well-made clothes and sensible things like stout boots and a warm cloak that will last. And I'm not spending a penny over thirty pounds.'

'Have no fear,' cried Amelia. 'Leave it all to me.'

*　　　*　　　*

It was two o'clock in the morning and Merab was crouched on the mat in front of her bedroom fire trying to coax the embers into some sort of life. She took out a couple of curl-papers, poked them into the fire and blew gently. At last a wisp of smoke appeared and then a tiny flame. Quickly she fed it with another curl-paper or two and some of the twigs the maid had left for kindling. When the fire had caught and she was satisfied it was safe she sat back on her heels and huddled her darned and patched dressing-gown to her.

She had had a nightmare and was trying to shake off the disagreeable impression. She took a taper and lit a couple of candles, put them on the hearth and sat down on the mat. She had dreamt she was dressed up in the most preposterous, outlandish fancy dress, all padded out and with the bosom cut indecently low and she was in the Pump Room trying to get out and everybody was looking at her; the ladies giggling behind their fans and, worst of all, Rowland Sandiford was there, openly mocking. She looked a perfect quiz and when she awoke she was still blushing with mortification.

She hugged her shabby dressing-gown more closely around herself and thought. It was easy to see what had triggered off the dream. But why should she have been so anxious about some new clothes? She and Amelia had agreed on a list of essentials. There was nothing to startle in a serviceable cloak and a couple of daydresses, for example. And whilst thirty pounds would be ample for a basic wardrobe, it would hardly run to anything very extravagant.

So what was it? Perhaps it was fear of losing her invisibility after so long. She had not had a new dress since coming to Hartfield Hall. Shabby clothes were turned, old clothes were unpicked, and after her mother's death she had been forced to remake her mother's garments to fit herself, struggling to disguise the longer skirt with inserted bands of another material.

She had, she thought ruefully, gone straight from being a schoolgirl to being an old maid. There never had been a period when she'd been well dressed, young and pretty. She had never gone out into society and the only gentlemen she had seen on a regular basis had been her grandfather, Mr Camberwell and the vicar. Occasionally in church there would be a strange young man, guest of some neighbouring county family. But he never did anything other than look straight through her. And Cousin Rowland had made it all too obvious that as far as he was concerned, as a woman she simply did not exist.

And this was it. Merab acknowledged, staring into the glowing fire. She did not know why, because she loathed and detested him, but her first thought on reading Mr Camberwell's letter had been, Now I'll show him! And instead of bringing Rowland to her feet—and then spurning him—in her dream Rowland had mocked her pretensions and ridiculed her.

Merab rose and found the tortoiseshell-backed mirror that had been her mother's. She looked at herself carefully. Her unruly hair, which was already shedding more curl-papers—whatever could be done with it? It was far too thick and, in spite of her best efforts, curled wildly and would not be coaxed into proper ringlets. She was too pale. Her skin, a clear ivory, having outgrown its youthful tendency to spots, lacked colour. She would never have the pink and white complexion of a true beauty. Large dark-brown eyes fringed with long dark lashes stared back at her in the mirror and suddenly, unaccountably, filled with tears.

*   *   *

Major Bendick, recently sold out from his regiment, but who still prided himself on his military dash and way with the ladies, stood before the fire and surveyed his library with a certain amount of proprietory pleasure. His father had died recently, he had inherited a comfortable income, his sister was now safely married to the gentleman sitting with him and enjoying his port, and he had persuaded his mother that she would prefer to go and live with her widowed sister in Devonshire.

It had all been arranged with the precision of a military manoeuvre. The major hoped he had been a dutiful son, but on his return to his home in Bath after his father's death some six months previously, he had swiftly discovered that filial affection had its limits. His mother, who was of a romantic turn of mind, had swathed herself in yards of black crape and was obviously enjoying the role of inconsolable widow. His sister, who was practically on the

65

shelf at twenty-four, was showing an alarming tendency towards Evangelicalism, and the major decided that for his own peace of mind something had to be done.

A glance at the terrain informed him that the Reverend Clement Harcourt was best suited to removing his tiresome sister and that if he sold his father's rare 14th century collection of books—which he would never read and had no interest in—the resulting extra couple of thousand would enhance Eliza's chances and tempt the somewhat reluctant vicar into making the required moves. Mr Harcourt duly married Miss Bendick and the major turned his attention to his mother. At first it seemed unlikely that she would be amenable to persuasion: the widow had not enjoyed the easiest of relations with her late husband and had been looking forward to a number of years running the house according to her own, more genteel, notions. The major, having surveyed the battleground, as it were, decided on shock tactics. He invited a half-a-dozen raffish army friends to stay, had a number of hard-drinking and riotous card parties and followed it by inviting a lady of dubious propriety, whose hair was so improbable a shade of blonde that, after one horrified look, Mrs Bendick had unhesitatingly declared her willingness to take refuge with her sister, Augusta.

The major then generously offered her a further hundred a year on top of her jointure of £400.

The major was now ready to put his next plan of action into effect. He had lived a hedonistic bachelor life for thirty-five years, and what he now needed was a wife. He said as much to his brother-in-law.

'I'm thirty-five now, and it's time I settled down. I need a couple of sons, three to be safe. One as heir, one back-up and a spare. I should think that would do. The eldest, of course, will stay here and learn to administer the estate, the second can go into the army—or the navy,' he added generously. 'I am not fussy. And the third can go into the church.'

Mr Harcourt blinked. 'Supposing you had daughters?' he asked mildly.

The major waved this away as an irrelevance. 'I shall choose a good breeder, of course. And she must be a sensible woman. I don't care for these flighty misses just out of school. More hair than wit.'

'How do you propose to set about it?' asked the vicar, curiously. The major was a well-set-up man, tall, with a certain military bearing. He had straight brown hair, neatly trimmed, a cavalry moustache and very even white teeth. Such attributes would probably please the ladies, he thought, even though his wife had been less complimentary and called her brother 'a supercilious beast'.

There was a visitors' book in the Pump Room and anyone signing it could be sure of a visit from one of Bath's two Masters of Ceremonies. The major would consult this tome for potential future Mrs Bendicks. 'I shall go to the Pump Room tomorrow and make a list,' he said.

'A list!' echoed Mr Harcourt.

'Yes. Name, age, status. I don't mind a widow, though if she has any brats I'll pack 'em off to school. A respectable dowry, of course, but I'm not greedy. Three or four thousand would do.'

The vicar stared down at his port. He did not particularly like his brother-in-law and he now found himself wishing, in a most unchristian spirit, that the major would meet with a deserved check. 'Anything else?' he asked.

'Well, a reasonable share of good looks. And though I'd like her to be conversable—take an interest in my concerns, that sort of thing—I certainly don't want a blue-stocking. In my view female intelligence is best kept to household and children.'

'What about love?'

'Love?' the major laughed. 'Sentimental nonsense. I don't believe in it.'

* * *

The Pump Room the following morning was not particularly well attended, perhaps the inclemency of the weather had put people off. There was Mrs Bridges walking arm in arm

68

with her new husband and stopping every now and then to chat to friends. A group of giggling girls was indulgently watched by their mamas—the major looked them over briefly and then moved away. And there was pretty Lady Wincanton with a most pleasing roundness just beginning to show. The major liked to see women pregnant and he particularly liked Lady Wincanton who was not only pretty, but had also done her duty in giving her husband two hopeful sons and was, doubtless, preparing to present him with the spare. With her was a most attractive female he could not remember ever seeing before.

She was tall and slender and moved elegantly, the major noted with approval. She was wearing a dove-grey dress which bore all the marks of an expensive modiste. It was simple, there were no unnecessary frills, but the waist was slightly lower and the sleeves fuller than was fashionable in England. The major, whose career moves had included a bored vicomtesse when he was with the Army of Occupation in Paris, recognized a French creation when he saw one.

The lady turned towards him and the major could see pale creamy skin, pretty lips and a pair of large, almond-shaped brown eyes. Her hair was cut daringly short and rioted in becoming curls.

Whoever was she? He must find out.

No Pygmalion could have been more

pleased with the creation of his Galatea than Amelia was at Merab's transformation. The moment Merab had left the breakfast-table with Mr Camberwell's letter, Amelia, sickness forgotten, had summoned a chair, invented a library book that must be changed immediately and gone straight to Ariane's in South Parade. Madame Regnier, who ran it, had retired some years ago, but she kept on a few favoured clients and she was pleased to count Lady Wincanton as one of them (she was wealthy, she paid promptly and she trusted Madame Regnier's taste). In the carriage Amelia's mind had worked swiftly. She believed Madame Regnier would be happy to oblige so good a customer as herself, and Amelia did not doubt that she would have the eye to see that Merab had real style and elegance underneath those appalling clothes and dreadful hair-do.

She would take Madame Regnier into her confidence, she decided, Merab would be duped as to cost, if necessary, and any extra bills would go to Sir Thomas. It was perfect. That evening, as she was dressing for dinner, she confided in Babette.

'The hair of mademoiselle must come off, *naturellement*,' cried Babette, whose English tended to disappear when moved. She sketched airily with her hands. 'In Paris now, my cousin writes, it is short, short, short. All curls. Mademoiselle Merab will be beautiful. I shall cut and you shall see. The gentlemen will be wild for mademoiselle.'

'Well, for God's sake don't tell her that!' cried Amelia, who hid few secrets from Babette.

'Have no fear, *miladi*,' said Babette conspiratorially. 'She shall not suspect a thing.'

When her new clothes arrived some ten days later, and her hair cut amid vehement protests, Merab was astounded, pleased and alarmed at the change in her appearance in about equal measure. That evening Babette helped her dress for dinner. A black velvet ribbon was cunningly woven into her cropped curls and her violet dress served to emphasize the creaminess of her skin and to show off her enormous brown eyes.

'There, mademoiselle!' cried Babette, standing back to admire her handiwork. 'Now, that is how mademoiselle should look! *Miladi* will be pleased and Sir Thomas will be *bouleversé*.'

'I certainly don't want Sir Thomas *bouleversé*,' said Merab with asperity.

Babette smiled. 'He will be *bouleversé* in the most respectful manner.'

Merab laughed.

'Charming, my dear,' said Sir Thomas, when Merab came into the drawing-room that evening.

Merab looked across at Amelia, who was

standing with a smile of pleased satisfaction on her face. 'You don't think it's too—well, daring, for a governess?' she asked anxiously, looking down at what seemed to her to be a shockingly low neck-line.

'Nonsense, Miss Hartfield,' said Sir Thomas, answering for his wife and justifying Babette's good opinion. 'You look like the lady that you are, and I don't see that more is necessary.' He glanced across at his wife who raised her brows in a slight question. Sir Thomas gave her a suspicion of a wink. Amelia had been right, he thought. Miss Hartfield was a most attractive young woman. Not classically beautiful, her nose was a thought too aquiline for that and she was perhaps an inch or two too tall. But she would undoubtedly cause a stir in Bath society and might even, in spite of her lack of dowry, manage to find a husband. Though he would have to warn Amelia not to place her hopes too high.

Sir Thomas's admiration and Amelia and Babette's approval gave Merab the confidence to go with her friend to the Pump Room the following morning. Amelia took the waters on her doctor's advice, but on this occasion was more concerned that Merab should not go unnoticed. She finished her glass and looked around. Ah! The very man.

'Why, Major Bendick! How pleasant to see you.'

The major came forward with alacrity, bowed and kissed her hand. 'Lady Wincanton. Now don't tell me that you were drinking the waters.'

Amelia made a face. 'I must. But, Merab, allow me to introduce Major Bendick. Major, this is my friend, Miss Hartfield. We were at school together.'

'Miss Hartfield,' the major bowed. Egad, she was as lovely close to. What eyes! 'Do you make a long stay here?'

'A month or so, perhaps.' Merab admired his even white teeth as doubtless the major meant her to and glanced resignedly at Amelia.

'I hope longer,' said Lady Wincanton.

'I hope so too,' smiled the major. 'May I escort you ladies, if you are going to take a turn or two about the room?'

Amelia suddenly discovered that she was tired and sank artistically down on to one of the gilt chairs that were arranged round the edge of the room. But Merab would like a walk, she was sure. The major professed himself delighted.

Life at Hartfield Hall had not included a course in male gallantry and Merab was at first bewildered by the major's compliments. What on earth was she expected to say? He was far too pleased with himself, she decided, after listening to his civilities for some moments. Beneath the attentive exterior she sensed a man whose view of 'ladies' ranged between dolls

73

and angels and not much else. The major was walking slowly, bowing to right and left at various acquaintances as if showing off his prize.

'I see you do not care for my compliments,' he said when they had reached the end of the room and Merab had said virtually nothing.

'Major,' said Merab finally, 'I have spent the last eight years of my life living in retirement with my grandfather. Compliments have not come much in my way.' Indeed, she thought wryly, the only epithets that had been flung at her were 'whey-faced idiot' and the like. Her grandfather would have cut his tongue out sooner than compliment her.

Charming! thought the major. Such freshness. That would account for the half-mourning, of course. 'But now you are in Bath you must see the delights we have to offer. Music now, I am sure you like music. There are concerts in the Assembly Rooms on Wednesdays, you know. Nothing too serious, we always aim to please the ladies here.'

Merab looked at him, somewhat puzzled. 'May ladies not like serious music?' She had been brought up to take music very seriously and one of her earliest memories was of listening to her mama practise her scales.

'My dear Miss Hartfield!' he laughed indulgently. 'Do not tell me that you are a blue-stocking?'

'Indeed, no.' Merab thought fleetingly of the

Misses Goodison whose idea of female education was a little gentle perusal of one of Addison's essays, clear handwriting, with not too much regard for the spelling, and interminable sewing.

'I am very glad to hear it! Ladies' talents are best employed in charming us men, as you all know so very well how to do.'

Merab smiled politely. 'Major, this conversation is going round in circles. I can only repeat that I am not used to compliments. The school at which Lady Wincanton and I spent a number of happy years did not encourage female intellect, but we were all taught that a proper reticence was becoming in ladies. So I shall now ask you if you would be so good as to escort me back to Lady Wincanton.'

Delightful modesty, thought the major, and her remarks were not unintelligent—for a woman. He wondered what her dowry was.

'How could you!' cried Merab, when the major had left after a number of flattering remarks.

Amelia laughed. 'The poor man was longing to talk to you so I gave him the opportunity, that was all. Was it so very dreadful? He is very good-looking, you know.'

'Yes, I suppose he is.' Suddenly Rowland's cold grey eyes flashed into her mind. 'At least he has better manners.'

'Better manners than who?' asked Amelia.

But before she could pursue the question she was hailed by Mrs Tiverton who was talking with some friends by the window and Merab and Amelia moved across.

'My dear Amelia!' Mrs Tiverton kissed her affectionately and introduced her friends, Mr and Mrs Bridges. Merab was introduced and found herself standing by Mrs Bridges, a pleasant-looking woman in her fifties with greying hair, elegantly knotted, and a pair of smiling hazel eyes. She looked unaccountably familiar, but as Mrs Bridges did not remark on it, Merab felt that she must have been mistaken. Indeed, when could they have met? Certainly not any time during the last eight years.

The conversation turned for the second time to music. 'I must confess, my great love is Mozart,' said Mrs Bridges. 'Rather old-fashioned now, of course, but...'

'I do not believe that great music is ever really subject to the vagaries of fashion,' said Merab emphatically.

'Ah, so you agree with me?'

'Indeed I do. My mother, who sang beautifully, loved Mozart. She always taught me that one is there to sing or play the composer's work, not to show off oneself. "Mozart is far greater than we are", she used to say. And she was right.'

'So your first reverence is for Mozart,' said Mrs Bridges, smiling. 'I hope you will be able

76

to give us the pleasure of your company at some of the concerts, if Lady Wincanton can spare you.'

Merab accepted with far more pleasure than she had greeted Major Bendick's hopes of meeting again. She liked Mrs Bridges; a pleasant, unaffected woman, she decided. She would be happy to know her better. And her husband seemed courteous. At least there would be no tiresome major in tow.

Amelia returned home well pleased with the little expedition. She had launched Merab very successfully. The major was surely rather taken with her, she thought hopefully. Mrs Tiverton was undoubtedly one of the leaders of Bath society and she had quietly complimented Amelia on her 'charming friend.' And the Bridges were a pleasant couple who would extend Merab's acquaintance.

Mrs Bridges' reaction would have startled both Merab and Amelia if they could have heard it.

'So that was Merab Hartfield,' she said to her husband as they walked home arm in arm up the Gravel Walk. 'Not at all what I was led to expect. Rowland was so very vehement.'

'A very pleasant young woman,' said her husband. 'Intelligent and attractive too.'

'It was obvious that she had not the faintest idea who I was,' said Mrs Bridges, a slight frown creasing her brow.

'Shall you tell her?'

77

Mrs Bridges considered. 'No, I don't think so. Not for the moment at least. I should like a chance to become acquainted with her without prejudice, as it were.'

* * *

Lavinia Heslop had accepted Lady Parmister's invitation to accompany Kitty to Bath with gratitude bordering on rapture. Mrs Heslop was almost as enthusiastic. Mr Heslop's living was only a moderate one and he was unable to give his daughter a full London season. There were four expensive Heslop sons to be launched on the world and Lavinia's claims must come second. But whilst Mrs Heslop agreed with this, nevertheless she did not wish Lavinia to become an old maid simply through lack of opportunity. So the chance for Lavinia to spend a couple of months in Bath was not to be missed, even though she did not entirely approve of Kitty.

The Parminster carriage, containing Kitty, Lavinia and Kitty's maid, arrived at the Bansteads' house in Laura Place on a cold afternoon in mid-February. The girls were welcomed kindly by Mrs Banstead, Kitty's beauty was exclaimed over, numerous parties promised, and they were shown up to a pretty bedroom decorated with a delicate sprigged wallpaper and a number of Dresden shepherdesses on the mantelpiece. A couple of men-servants brought up their trunks, a maid brought them hot water and Mrs Banstead finally left them to themselves saying, 'Dearest Kitty, I shall take you to my very own modiste tomorrow! She has just come back from a trip to Paris and has all the latest fashions. I am sure you will be delighted with her. You too, Miss Heslop,' she added as an afterthought.

Any fears Lady Parminster might have had of Kitty going into a decline were soon laid to rest. She had indeed attempted to look pale and interesting on their first evening in the Assembly Rooms, but the sight of other girls dancing and looking pityingly at her proved too much for her resolution. Mrs Banstead, of course, knew a number of people, Kitty and Lavinia were introduced and in no time it seemed, when the next set was forming for a dance, both girls had partners.

Major Bendick was there, still intent on making his list. Merab's name was down, her friendship with Lady Wincanton vouched for her standing, but there was a worrying blank by the size of her dowry. There was no such blank by Miss Parminster's name. Mrs Banstead had discreetly advertised her god-daughter's forthcoming arrival and the major had pencilled in her £10,000. Lavinia did not figure on his list at all.

The major was well aware of his own attractions and he and Mrs Banstead understood each other very well. A tall, good looking man with all the assurance of a healthy bank balance and the indefinable air of a military gentleman, must always be acceptable, and the major soon found that Mrs Banstead had smilingly allowed a mutual friend to introduce him to Kitty.

But whilst her initial pretty deference flattered him, the major was not entirely won over.

'Shall you attend some of the concerts, Miss Parminster?' he asked, as they took their places in the set.

'Concerts?' echoed Kitty in horror.

'Yes, concerts. They are held here every Wednesday, you know. Are you fond of music?'

Kitty gave a trill of laughter. 'I must confess that although I can sing a song or two, as every young lady must, just the thought of sitting through a whole concert is enough to send me to sleep!' Seeing him look grave, she added, 'Are you, then, fond of music, Major?'

'Naturally—provided it has a proper tune. I don't care for all this modern stuff. Beethoven, now, most untuneful.'

A spirit of perversity took hold of Kitty. She gave him her prettiest smile. 'But I declare Beethoven's music is delightful.'

The major's brows snapped together. 'I am older than you, Miss Parminster. You must allow me to know best.'

'Oh, why?' asked Kitty, opening her eyes

80

wide.

Later, in the carriage going home, Mrs Banstead said, 'What have you done to put the major in a twitter, Kitty?'

Kitty shrugged.

'He's a most eligible man,' Mrs Banstead reminded her. 'Besides a very acceptable little estate, he has at least four thousand a year.'

Kitty didn't reply. Afterwards, when the girls were getting ready for bed, she said to Lavinia, 'He thought he had only to hint what he thought and I would instantly accept it.' She flounced on to the bed. In her book men deferred to her, not the other way about. Rowland had always been most deferential to her wishes.

Lavinia plaited her hair carefully and said, 'But he was very struck with you, Kitty. He still asked you for another dance.' Her voice was a little wistful, for the major was one of the most good-looking men she had ever seen and he had barely thrown her a glance.

'Yes he did, didn't he?' said Kitty complacently.

As the days went by Kitty had good reason to be self-congratulatory. The major might have withdrawn a little to pay attention to some lady in half-mourning, who, if not middle-aged precisely, was at least, in Kitty's opinion, too old to be claiming the attention of eligible men. However, she herself now had a new circle of admirers, the chief of whom was

Viscount Claydon, and he was a man Kitty was much inclined to take seriously.

Lavinia had come to Bath with every expectation of pleasure, but she soon found that her position as guest was no sinecure. At home, where their circle of acquaintances was well known to both of them, there was no sense of rivalry. Lavinia had always been Kitty's humble admirer and been grateful for any crumb that fell from her table. Moreover, she was known to have only a small portion and could not expect more than a modicum of male attention.

Here in Bath she attracted a fair amount of masculine interest and some of it Kitty felt rightfully belonged to herself.

'I don't know why Mr Corbett should dance with you twice,' she said one evening on the way home. He was a handsome young man, said to be the heir of old Mr Finch, who was his godfather, and worth some £5,000 a year. What did he want with poor Lavinia with her couple of thousand?

Lavinia, who was sitting in the forward seat, caught Mrs Banstead looking at her disapprovingly and said at once, 'I don't know I'm sure. Except that he obviously wanted to talk about you.'

It was not entirely true, but Kitty smiled and Mrs Banstead relaxed. Lavinia turned to watch the gas lamps out of the window. They shed an orange glow on the pavement and threw the surrounding dark into relief. She clutched her reticule tightly. For the first time she began to feel resentful of her friend. Was she, Lavinia, to be allowed no admirers of her own? She longed suddenly for her scruffy bedroom at home and the understanding company of her mama.

* * *

It was not until the end of February that Rowland finally arrived in Bath. He went to pay a courtesy call on his mother and her new husband in St James's Square but was resolute in declining their invitation to stay.

'No, thank you, Mama,' he said. 'I am putting up at the White Hart. I do not know how long I shall be staying and I would not want to inconvenience you.'

His mother, after a token resistance, said nothing more. Her remarriage, she knew, had been something of a shock to him, although he had known and liked her husband for years. But whereas he felt perfectly able to tolerate her Samuel when he was merely an elderly admirer, she quite understood that for her to marry him was another matter. She was ruefully aware that ladies of her advanced age—fifty-six—should not be poaching on the preserves of the young.

But she was a sensible woman. Instead of pressing him further she said, 'I hope you will stay to dine with us at least! Venison tonight. Samuel's brother has just sent us a haunch.'

'Thank you, I should like that.'

Rowland had, of course, learnt that Kitty was in Bath. Part of him knew very well that the gentlemanly thing to do would be for him not to go and risk upsetting her. But another part of him longed to see her and, perhaps, there was a small bit that hoped for some miracle. He pictured her being dragged reluctantly to the Assembly Rooms. Had he not seen her that last Sunday in church, weeping pathetically into a wisp of lace handkerchief?

In the end he told himself that courtesy demanded that he visit his mother and offer his congratulations on her marriage in person. After that he would see. He would stay in Bath for a few weeks, he decided. He would try to behave with a friendly, but distant, courtesy towards Kitty. If there were any chance that she would wait ... But no, that was hardly fair. He must come to terms with his altered prospects. He must realize that there would be no Kitty now and no Hartfield inheritance either.

Rowland had thought over the quarrel with Merab and come to the satisfactory conclusion that he was well out of it. What, marry a dowd, an old maid with no accomplishments, singularly lacking in beauty? She was probably a shrew into the bargain. If she had been even passably acceptable then surely Cousin Julian would have made them acquainted long ago? His ill manners were an aberration, due to shock about the will: nobody could possibly blame him for being overset at such a time.

He went to the Assembly Rooms the following evening. It was a Monday and there was a Dress Ball. He would be sociable, he decided. The Master of Ceremonies would doubtless introduce him to a number of attractive ladies and he would strive to relax and enjoy himself.

He walked in rather late, and was moving across the floor to pay his respects to the Master of Ceremonies when he came face to face with ... who was she? Surely he knew her?

Rowland stared. In front of him was a tall slender woman with a riot of dark-brown curls which framed a charming face. Her skin was a very pale olive with a becoming flush just staining her cheeks as she stared at him. Her eyes were dark brown, large and lustrous, and she was wearing an elegant silk evening gown in a deep violet which set off her creamy skin to perfection.

Rowland's heart gave a sudden leap. Who was she?

The lady was as startled as himself. 'Mr ... Mr Sandiford ...'

'Miss Hartfield!' Anger swept over him. 'What the devil are you doing here?'

85

CHAPTER FOUR

Bath society was not so exclusive as the fashionable London world. There was enough camaraderie among the genuinely ill and convalescent to ensure that. Those who took the waters for their health or embarked on a course at the Queen's Baths soon found that fellow sufferers were welcoming and notes were swapped on favourite doctors and cures and this friendly feeling extended itself to the Pump Room and Assembly Rooms. A lady who would not be tolerated among the *ton* in London would be welcomed in Bath, provided she made herself agreeable—and was wealthy enough to afford it.

Accordingly there were many who invested their savings in visiting Bath in the hopes of finding an entrée to society and none more assiduously than Mrs Dinah Harrison, a wealthy widow in her early fifties. With her was her son, Joseph.

Mrs Harrison was a well-set-up woman with dark hair, now liberally streaked with grey, dark eyes, and a somewhat mulish disposition. She was the widow of a minister of a well-to-do nonconformist chapel and had been used to deference as the minister's wife—an invitation to one of Mrs Harrison's teas was an honour, nay, almost a royal command. Unfortunately, her bossiness and air of rigid propriety had not helped in her quest for a more refined society.

Bath was very much a public world: you arrived in the city, you wrote your name in the Pump Room book, you were visited by the two Masters of Ceremonies and, if you could pay the not inconsiderable subscriptions to the Assembly Rooms and the various public venues where the Polite World went to see and be seen, then Society would allow you in. What happened then was up to you. And Mrs Harrison was tolerated, but no more. Lady Mandersby and the honourable Mrs Tiverton, the two doyennes of Bath society, might bow politely if they happened to meet her in a doorway, but she had not been introduced and she was not part of their circle.

Joseph was a stocky young man with elaborately curled and pomaded dark hair. He had all of his mother's mulishness added to a small-mindedness of his own. By profession he was an attorney, working mainly for a sugar merchant in Bristol, where his cold grasp of the minutiae of business made him very useful. Nobody got the better of Joseph Harrison, he liked to inform his colleagues.

He, too, was angered by their lack of social success in Bath. Joseph saw well enough that a wife out of the top drawer would enhance his prospects considerably. A touch at his superior's daughter having been unaccountably spurned, he had come to Bath to try his luck.

He formed one of the outer satellites of Miss Parminster's circle.

'Now, there's a girl worth looking at,' he said to his mother as they sat in the Assembly Rooms' ballroom waiting for the music to begin. He nodded in Kitty's direction.

'Worth a pretty penny, too, I have no doubt,' added Mrs Harrison, pursing her lips. 'Not but I think that her gown is most immodest. Why it's practically transparent. You might almost see her ... limbs.' She had been going to say 'legs', but changed it as being too indelicate.

Joseph looked at Kitty complacently. She was on the catch, doubtless, and her clinging dress was meant to emphasize her charms. After marriage, of course, she would wear something more sober. Joseph had no intention of allowing his wife to be the object of every ogling male eye.

He eventually obtained his dance with Kitty and flattered himself that he had made something of an impression. He was just about to risk his luck a second time and ask for her hand in the Boulanger when he saw his mother gesticulating wildly.

'Whatever is the matter, Mother?' he asked irritably as he reached her side.

'You see that woman with Lady Wincanton?' hissed Mrs Harrison.

Joseph looked; a tall elegant woman, he

noted. Attractive too.

'Well, what of her?'

'I heard Lady Wincanton call her "Merab"!'

'What of it?'

'My sister was called Merab.'

'My dear Mother, you call me over to tell me that?' He began to move away again.

'Joseph!' He turned. 'Don't you understand? Could she be Abby's daughter?'

'Abby?'

'Abby, you dolt. My disgraced sister, the opera dancer. Said she had married into the gentry. Can't remember his name, something like Hartshorn. Of course, we all knew better. Married indeed! Was that likely?'

Joseph looked at the woman again. She was part of an animated group with Lady Wincanton and Major Bendick. Well dressed, self-assured ... money. His mind ran along well-oiled grooves. His eyes narrowed. 'You mean...'

'Of course. If she is Abby's daughter then we are made. Look at her. It is plain *she* isn't short of a penny—and she moves in the right circles.' Just like Abby, she thought savagely, to do so well for herself and care nothing for what became of her sister. Not a word had they had from her all these years.

'But I thought you had cast her off,' said Joseph.

'Of course we cast her off when she became an opera singer. Showing her legs in the chorus—and a lot more I don't doubt. And I never believed in that "marriage" for a moment. But if she did pull it off then it was her duty to apprise her sister of the fact.' Mrs Harrison did not allow the logical inconsistencies inherent in this statement to bother her. Instead she sniffed and glared at Merab across the room.

'She may not want our acquaintance.' Joseph's attorney's mind moved swiftly.

'I don't intend to give her the choice,' snapped his mother. 'Go and find out who she is.'

* * *

Merab stared incredulously at Rowland. For a moment she quailed. She was back again in Hartfield Hall with her cousin looking disdainfully at her—her shabby clothes, her pallor, her general inadequacy. Then she rallied. She was here as a friend of Lady Wincanton's and accepted in Bath society. Lady Mandersby, whose exclusivity was proverbial, had complimented her on her style. Major Bendick found her not unattractive. Why should she quail?

She raised her chin and surveyed him coolly. 'I am staying with my friend, Lady Wincanton.'

Rowland glared at her. 'Fortune-hunting, no doubt.'

Merab lifted an eyebrow and glanced across at Kitty Parminster briefly before replying, 'I might say the same of you, sir.'

For a moment Rowland was speechless. 'How dare you?'

'Mr Sandiford,' said Merab icily, 'I owe you no explanations. I am as fully entitled to be in Bath as you are.' She saw out of a corner of her eye that several people including Mrs Bridges were watching them with interest and added, 'We are occasioning some remark.' Rowland looked round impatiently. 'I think we had better part, don't you?' She dropped him a slight curtsey and moved away.

Rowland was left staring angrily at her retreating back.

Amelia listened to her friend's disjointed account in dismay. She had glimpsed Rowland earlier but had said nothing. She had hoped, romantically, that he would take one look at Merab and be bowled over. Instead, he had quarreled with her practically in public and if all eyes hadn't been on them, there were certainly enough curious ones.

'Oh dear,' she said at last, realizing that it sounded woefully inadequate. 'I suppose he's come here after Kitty Parminster.'

'I suppose so.' Merab, who had been feeling exhilarated at having turned the tables on her tormentor, now suddenly felt unaccountably depressed. 'What shall I do, Amelia?'

Amelia shook her head. 'You cannot cut

him. He is a cousin, after all. And you certainly don't want any hint of that disgraceful will to come out.'

Merab shuddered. The humiliation of that moment was still strong. 'He will hardly come in my way now,' she said after a moment. 'I suppose a distant bow and the merest commonplaces will do.'

Men! thought Amelia.

*   *   *

Kitty was careful to drop no hint of her involvement with Rowland Sandiford to her godmother and had enjoined Lavinia to silence on the subject. Her one worry was that her mother would have mentioned his name to Mrs Banstead, but fortunately Lady Parminster's sense of decorum was too strong. Kitty had recovered from her disappointment with surprising swiftness but saw no reason why Rowland should not be kept dangling, at least for a while. He was one of the most good-looking men in Bath and his attentions could only add to her consequence.

'But poor Mr Sandiford,' cried Lavinia, who had a kind heart. 'If you treat him like that won't he be terribly upset? And he loves you so much, Kitty.'

'Then he should be richer,' said Kitty unsympathetically.

'But it's not his fault if his cousin leaves his

money elsewhere!'

'Of course it is,' snapped Kitty. 'He should have danced attendance on his cousin. Written him little notes, that kind of thing. He knew how important this Hartfield money was to our marriage.'

'What did happen to the money?' asked Lavinia curiously.

Kitty shrugged. 'Some charity, I believe. Well, he's had his chance.' She looked at herself complacently in the glass. Lord Claydon had compared her to a fairy queen— and he was right. Only ... Lord Claydon had not yet come up to scratch.

'What shall you do?'

'I shall be very nice to Mr Sandiford,' said Kitty sweetly. 'I shall dance with him, let him pay me compliments, fetch me a glass of wine, that sort of thing. And I shall take care to do it when Lord Claydon is there.'

'And what about the others? Mr Harrison and ... Major Bendick,' asked Lavinia, with an air of studied indifference.

'Are you interested in Major Bendick?'

Lavinia diligently plaited the fringe of her dress. 'I am sure he doesn't think of me. He only dances with me when he can't dance with you.'

'Major Bendick is my second string,' said Kitty, watching Lavinia's downcast face with satisfaction. With £4,000 a year he deserved her serious consideration. And she certainly wasn't going to see Lavinia snaffle him. 'You may have Mr Harrison, if you like.'

'Thank you,' said Lavinia tonelessly.

* * *

Rowland found Kitty both tantalizingly encouraging and maddeningly elusive. Over the next week or so he pursued her assiduously. She would dance with him no more than twice in an evening and yet the intimate glances she gave him seemed constantly to promise more. When he caught her behind a display of potted palms and kissed her she reacted angrily.

'What do you think you're doing?'

'But Kitty...'

'Don't "Kitty" me!'

'But Miss Parminster then...'

'That's better.' She dimpled prettily and gave him her hand.

Rowland kissed her fingertips. 'Now, Kitty...'

'No, I'm serious, Mr Sandiford. You have no right to call me by my Christian name. It would not do. Whatever would people think?'

'Have you forgotten me so soon, then?' said Rowland bitterly.

Kitty saw that he needed some encouragement. 'I have not forgotten,' she said softly, glancing up at him with wistful blue eyes. 'But if we are too intimate, my godmother will write to Mama and Papa will come and

94

take me home. And that would be unbearable.' She thought of the possibilities of Viscount Claydon.

'I, too, found it unbearable not being allowed to speak to you at home,' said Rowland quietly.

Kitty smiled. 'So you see I must observe the proprieties.' She glanced around. Her godmother and Lavinia were at the far end of the room. Lord Claydon was nowhere to be seen. She stepped behind the palms. 'Very well, then,' she said. 'One kiss.'

She allowed him a few seconds then pulled away. 'Now, Mr Sandiford,' she said brightly, 'I trust you are going to offer me a glass of ratafia.'

Frustrated, yet dazzled, Rowland allowed himself to be led towards the refreshment room.

* * *

The day after Merab's unexpected meeting with Rowland proved to be wet and miserable. The two ladies decided to stay at home and were happily sitting in Amelia's boudoir discussing Kitty Parminster.

'I cannot see what men see in her,' said Amelia crossly. She was still put out not only by Merab's account of her meeting with Rowland, but also by watching him subsequently dancing attendance on Kitty.

95

'She's very pretty,' offered Merab, determined to be charitable.

'Like a wax doll!'

'Men like dolls. Look at Major Bendick.'

'Nonsense, Merab. Why, only last night he was extolling your intelligence.'

'He might *extol* it,' said Merab, 'just so long as I don't *show* it. What Major Bendick means by female intelligence is that they agree with him.'

'I thought you liked him,' faltered Amelia in dismay.

Merab flashed her a sceptical glance. She knew very well that Amelia had him marked down as suitable husband material.

'Certainly I like him,' she said coolly. 'He is a pleasant well-mannered man, why shouldn't I like him? Besides, he's decided to have a *tendre* for me. I am sure you will agree that that argues a high degree of intelligence as well!'

'You're impossible,' said Amelia, shaking her head fondly.

At this moment the butler appeared with two cards on a tray which he offered to Merab. Merab picked them up slowly. Whoever was paying calls on her? *Mrs Eli Harrison* she read on one and *J. Harrison, Esq.* on the other. She turned them over. On the back of Mrs Harrison's were two pencilled words, *née Cooper*. Merab went white.

'What is it?' Amelia flung down her sewing.

Merab handed her the cards. 'Cooper was

96

my mother's maiden name.' She indicated that Amelia should turn the cards over.

'Where have you put them, Gregg?' asked Amelia.

'In the yellow drawing-room, my lady. Sir Thomas is in the library, and I did not think he would wish to be disturbed.'

'I'll have to see them,' said Merab despairingly. She had been thinking fast. This was undoubtedly her Aunt Dinah and from what her mother had told her she had been a spiteful, envious child with whom she, Abigail, had had little in common.

'Inform Mrs Harrison and her son that we shall be down shortly,' said Amelia, 'and offer them some refreshments.'

'Certainly, my lady.' The door closed behind him.

'I don't like it,' said Merab. 'Why does she want to know me now? She cast off my mother when she took up her singing and teaching. And she never answered the letter Mama wrote to announce that she was marrying Papa. What can they want?'

'Why should they want anything more than to make your acquaintance?'

'Mama used to say that Dinah was a self-centred little piece and as hard as nails.'

'Merab,' said Amelia gently, 'that must have been thirty years ago. All this is singularly unprofitable. Let us go down and see. Unless you'd prefer to meet them alone?'

Merab shook her head emphatically.

Mrs Harrison had dressed carefully, for the occasion had presented her with something of a quandary. She wished to enter the social circles her niece moved in and therefore a certain discretion and deference were necessary. On the other hand she did not feel that she owed Abigail's daughter—the product of a *mésalliance* between an opera dancer (to put it no worse) and the ne'er-do-well Jonathan Hartfield—any particular civility. And she was anxious to emphasize her own absolute respectability. It was a tricky tightrope. She wanted the advantages an acquaintance with Merab would bring, but she was in no mind to thank her for them.

Accordingly, she wore a carriage costume of sober black merino trimmed with black seal-skin with a high neck-line. On her head was a turban, known as a Prussian helmet, which added to the austere affect. A parasol with a telescopic steel stick completed her wardrobe.

Joseph had also dressed with care. He wore fawn pantaloons with black Hessians, a double-breasted morning-coat and, after several unsuccessful attempts, had tied his cravat in the American style which, he felt, gave him that necessary touch of modernity. He had observed Merab carefully and approved of what he saw and the thought had flashed through his mind that, although he would prefer Kitty Parminster to wife, nevertheless his new cousin would also make an up-and-coming lawyer a not unsuitable helpmate. She knew the right people, she had a certain quiet elegance and her dowry would be useful for a man on his way up in the world.

The moment Mrs Harrison saw Merab she knew how much she disliked her. She was taller than her mother but had those same eyes, eyes that could beguile any man. She had the same carriage too; Joseph might call it 'elegant', but to Mrs Harrison it was evidence that this Merab was playing off superior airs exactly as her mother had done. Merab's courteous enquiry as to where she was staying in Bath seemed to her impertinence, and her friendship with Lady Wincanton was surely mere toadying.

Her eyes snapped. 'And do you make a long stay in Bath yourself, Niece?' she asked ungraciously.

'Not too long, ma'am. I must look for a teaching post soon.'

'A teaching post!' echoed Joseph, horrified.

'Why, yes,' said Merab. Her cousin was a hard-featured man, though well enough, and if he and his obnoxious mother thought to come sponging off her, then the sooner they were disabused of that notion the better. 'My grandfather left me no money, you know. I must earn my own living.'

Mrs Harrison looked at Merab's soft grey merino morning dress and had her doubts. 'I

99

am sure Lady Wincanton won't let you do that,' she suggested.

'I prefer to be independent.'

'But whilst you are here you are going to the Assemblies, are you not?' put in Joseph who, no more than his mother, believed in his cousin's poverty and now saw his chance slipping away from him. 'I hope I may stand up with you for a dance or two, Cousin.'

'I do not dance, Mr Harrison. I am still in mourning for my grandfather.'

Mrs Harrison could bear it no longer. 'Hoity toity, miss,' she said. 'Less of those airs, if you please. Your mother was just such another, playing the fine lady. You think you're so high and mighty now that you cannot dance with your cousin? Well, let me tell you...'

'Mother!' Joseph's voice rose.

She stopped. 'Perhaps I should let bygones be bygones,' she said with an effort. 'Though things have come to a pretty pass when a niece sees fit to sneer at her relations.'

Merab glanced at Amelia who had turned away and was staring, expressionless, out of the window.

'I am not putting on airs, ma'am,' she said quietly. 'Nor am I repudiating my relations. But my grandfather, with whom I have been living for the last eight years, only died in December, and it would be most unbecoming in me to dance.'

'Eight years! And you expect me to believe

that he didn't leave you provided for? Why, he owned as snug a little estate as anyone could wish for!' Mrs Harrison had taken care to look up Merab's circumstances in *The County Families of the United Kingdom.*

'Mother!' implored Joseph. 'This is none of our business.'

'Nonsense, Joseph. Am I not her aunt? And her mother was the same, never giving you a straight answer.'

No wonder, thought Merab, such prying was enough to make anybody close up.

'Grandfather was eccentric,' she said at last. 'He chose to leave his money to charity.' She paused and added with a touch of irony, 'He appeared to hold similar views on my mother and me to those you hold yourself.'

'I do apologize for my mother,' said Joseph desperately. 'This meeting has upset her.'

Mrs Harrison rose to her feet. 'I shall say goodbye, niece Merab,' she announced. 'I can see that filial affection means nothing to you. But as a Christian I still offer the hand of reconciliation. Come Joseph, we must go.'

Merab and Amelia rose and saw them out, waiting politely on the doorstep until the carriage was out of sight.

'What a dreadful woman!' cried Merab. 'Dearest Amelia, I only trust that you won't repudiate me now!'

Amelia kissed her cheek. 'We all have dreadful relations,' she said. 'You should see

101

my cousin Caroline. Ghastly woman. She's part of the rackety Prince of Wales set: drinks, gambles, has lovers by the score. Always teetering on the verge of bankruptcy. Don't tell me about relations.'

'At least she's not in Bath!' She gave an anxious smile. 'Was I really so rude?'

'Of course not. You were perfectly polite. If she chooses not to believe you, that is not your fault.'

'I shouldn't have bought these clothes. They give the wrong impression.'

'Nonsense. Your aunt, if I mistake not, is socially ambitious. She couldn't stand the idea of that coming to nothing,' said Amelia robustly.

Amelia had spoken forcefully, but she was more worried than she wanted Merab to know. She was concerned about what her husband would think. It wasn't that Mrs Harrison or her son were vulgar precisely, but they were certainly not the sort of relations Merab needed hanging about. They would do nothing for her consequence. Major Bendick was cautiously expressing an interest in Merab and Amelia thought that at so delicate a stage in the proceedings the last thing the affair needed was Mrs Harrison's intruding ways.

Would a sensible man, such as she knew the major to be, really want this overbearing aunt? Even if Mrs Harrison now believed in Merab's lack of dowry and lost interest, that interest would surely revive if she thought Merab was to become the wife of Major Bendick!

Sir Thomas, when his wife dared to broach the subject, was not sanguine either. 'Scuppered her chances,' he said firmly. 'I have seen the woman. A damned canting Methodist. I know the type.'

'Surely it's not as bad as that?' pleaded Amelia. 'She didn't try to convert me or take to praying.'

'Humph. But she'll have strict ideas about the theatre, gambling and God knows what else. The best Miss Hartfield can hope for is that they go back to Bristol before news of their relationship gets out.'

Amelia sighed. 'I fear that Mr Harrison is one of Kitty Parminster's court. I doubt whether they will be leaving just yet.'

'What Miss Hartfield needs is for someone else to take her up,' said Sir Thomas eventually. He still thought his wife was over-optimistic in finding a husband for her friend, but he was touched by her downcast face. He would not allow his wife to take up these Harrisons, but so long as Miss Hartfield managed to keep them off he would not interfere.

As if in answer to Amelia's prayer an invitation arrived the following morning for the Wincantons and Miss Hartfield to join a party given by the Bridges for the forthcoming concert in the Assembly Rooms.

'Should you like it, Merab?' asked Amelia.

'Very much.' Merab had liked Mrs Bridges.

The guests had been invited to partake of refreshments in the Tea Room before the concert. Mr Bridges had arranged a buffet supper for half past six and the concert began at half past seven.

Merab dressed with care. She wore one of her two new evening dresses, a grey silk, and draped a delicate black lace shawl which Amelia had given her over her shoulders. There was an ebony comb in her hair and she carried a black lace fan. Her skin would always lack colour, but its creaminess was set off by the shawl, thought Amelia with approval.

There was, however, a shock awaiting Merab at the Assembly Rooms, for there standing beside Mrs Bridges, who was waiting for her guests in the Tea Room, and chatting easily with her husband was none other than Rowland Sandiford!

'Mr Sandiford,' gasped Merab, clutching her shawl tightly to her. 'How do you come to be here?'

Rowland raised an eyebrow. 'Why should I not be?' he asked coldly. 'Mrs Bridges is my mother.'

'Your mother!'

'So that's where I have seen you,' said Amelia, coming forward and shaking Mrs Bridges' hand. 'I knew I had seen you before, but I did not recognize the name. Do forgive me.'

Mrs Bridges smiled, allowing Amelia to break in, which she guessed was as much to save Miss Hartfield from embarrassment as anything. 'I only married Mr Bridges in November,' she said. 'I believe we had met before Mrs Tiverton introduced us, but I think it was at a garden party and some years ago.'

'Of course,' said Amelia. 'I remember now.'

Mrs Bridges turned to smile at the stupefied Merab. Rowland had moved away, so she said, 'My son can be too tiresome sometimes, Miss Hartfield. I hope that his coming here won't spoil your evening.'

'No! no!' Did she know everything then? Wild thoughts whirled round Merab's head.

'And I hope that I shall be able to further my acquaintance with you a little.' Mrs Bridges saw that Merab was still looking stunned, so she pressed her hand briefly and then let her go. 'Mr Bridges,' she called to her husband, 'I am sure Miss Hartfield would like a drink.'

Rowland's first reaction was to accuse Merab of deliberately engineering an acquaintance with his mother in order to ... what? Trap him? But fortunately this time his good angel stopped him from saying the hasty intemperate things that rose to his lips.

He knew very well that she was virtually penniless, but he also saw, with unease, that there were a number of men in Bath who found the new Miss Hartfield not at all unworthy of their attentions. Rowland found himself unaccountably put out by this. Who would have thought that that scrawny female could have turned out so well?

He found himself edging nearer to where Merab was talking to Mr Bridges.

'I sing sometimes in the evenings,' Merab was saying. 'Sir Thomas likes the old songs, "Early One Morning" and so on. They have a beautiful pianoforte. Such a tone!'

Merab sing, thought Rowland. God forbid! Kitty now, she had a sweet voice and warbled away prettily. But then she'd been properly taught. He dreaded to think what his cousin's squawking would sound like.

'I am looking forward to this concert so much,' Merab continued. 'It is such a long time since I heard proper music.'

'Who is your favourite composer, Cousin?' Rowland found himself saying.

Merab turned slowly. 'Mozart, without a doubt.' He had spoken in his usual cynical tone, and yet she had noticed that he called her cousin. 'For me Mozart says it all. When I was little my mother used to sing me to sleep with *"Se vuol ballare, signior contino"*, and I've loved Mozart ever since.'

Her Italian accent was good, Rowland noticed, disconcerted. 'You must have had an unusual childhood, sung to sleep with Mozart. Most children would get "Hush a bye baby".'

Merab smiled. 'Oh, I had that too. I just

106

preferred the Mozart.'

Rowland could think of nothing whatsoever to say. A thousand questions sprang up. What sort of childhood had she had? What had happened to her before she came to Hartfield Hall? And, unbidden, came a new notion: why had Cousin Julian been so hostile towards his granddaughter?

Merab put down her glass and looked a little doubtfully at him. 'It is very kind of your mother to invite me,' she said hesitantly. 'I hadn't realized that she must know all about me.'

She had meant no more than to express her sense of obligation at being accepted by Mrs Bridges when she had been the means (though innocent) of doing her son out of a fortune.

Rowland, however, decided to misunderstand her. 'You mean you think my mother has thrown us together deliberately?' he asked angrily. 'Doubtless you are considering that perhaps you were somewhat overhasty in throwing away a fortune.'

Merab went white. Was he actually daring to suggest that she was trying to manoeuvre a proposal out of him? For a moment she was so angry that she reached for her glass with the intention of hurling its contents in his face. Then sense prevailed. 'If that's what you think then you had better warn your mother against me, hadn't you?' she said. 'Who knows, she might have been considering that the will was not my fault and wishing to get to know me for my own sake.' She gave a falsely sweet smile and added, 'I cannot think why you have this inflated idea of your own attractions. Excuse me, I see Major Bendick has arrived.' She moved away.

The concert was impeccably played, but Merab found it difficult to concentrate. How dared he? Had he really thought that she would ever accept him? Why, she would be mad to do such a thing. One thing that Merab felt she had learnt during the long years of living with her grandfather was that the experience of being negated and belittled was not one she was ever willing to endure again. To teach in a Queen's Square seminary might be drudgery, but it would also be independence and she might reasonably hope to have the respect and even affection of her pupils. Better far a life as a spinster teacher than one as the despised wife of some arrogant male.

Rowland's view of the affair was, however, not so far off the mark as Merab had imagined. His mother expressed her exasperation to her husband that night.

'I despair of Rowland sometimes. I find Merab Hartfield delightful. Intelligent, attractive, with excellent manners, what more could he desire?'

'Kitty Parminster, perhaps,' said her husband, removing his cuff-links and placing them carefully on the mantelpiece.

'Kitty Parminster!' echoed his wife scornfully. 'Why, she'd bore him within six months.'

Mr Bridges could see why his stepson found Kitty so attractive: those adorable dimples, the enchanting way she had of looking up at you from under her lashes. But he was a sensible man, and he said nothing.

* * *

Lord Claydon drew a deep breath and knocked at the front door of the Bansteads' house in Laura Place. He was dressed as befitted so momentous an occasion. His hair was pomaded, his valet had gone through at least a dozen cravats trying to achieve the perfect *Trône d'Amour* and his new morning coat had just arrived from the tailors.

Inside, Kitty was dressing feverishly. Her maid had done her hair three times and Lavinia, who had been sitting on the bed assuring her friend that she looked beautiful, was trying not to feel envious. For last night, Lord Claydon had asked Mrs Banstead if he might call this morning on a very important matter. Neither Kitty, nor Lavinia, nor indeed Mrs Banstead had doubted his intentions for a moment. Only a day or so before Mrs Banstead had written to Lady Parminster with the encouraging news that Lord Claydon was growing particularly attentive.

At last Kitty was satisfied. The maid left.

'Does he love you very much?' asked Lavinia wistfully.

'Lord, yes.' Kitty gave her reflection a satisfied smile. 'He's wild about me—and I haven't even let him squeeze my hand.'

'Poor Mr Sandiford will be devastated.'

'Won't he though!' said Kitty, pleased.

*　　*　　*

Rowland did not hear of the engagement for a further week. Lord Claydon had immediately posted off to Wiltshire to obtain Sir John's consent and Sir John had then sent a notice to *The Morning Post* and *The Times*. Rowland had not bothered to scan the papers very clearly and as Kitty had been particularly encouraging the previous evening, allowing him a stolen kiss behind the curtains of a small ante-chamber, he had no suspicion that an engagement was even imminent.

It wasn't until he met his mother in the Pump Room that he learnt the news.

'I am so sorry, dear,' she said. 'I know what a blow it must be to you.'

'What blow?' asked Rowland, his eyes scanning the crowd for Kitty. But as he turned and saw her face, he already knew.

CHAPTER FIVE

Sir Thomas and Lady Wincanton were in the breakfast parlour when Sir Thomas gave an exclamation and pushed his copy of *The Morning Post* over to his wife.

'There!' He indicated with a finger.

Amelia put down her cup of coffee and looked. *A marriage has been arranged between Lucius, Viscount Claydon and Miss Catherine Mary Parminster* ...

'I thought that would interest you,' observed Sir Thomas.

Amelia read it again and smiled. 'It does, very much. Well, that's her out of the way.'

'You cannot still be thinking of Sandiford and Miss Hartfield making a match of it? Why, they never meet but they quarrel.'

'Exactly! They are not indifferent to each other,' Amelia explained, impatient at his masculine obtuseness.

Sir Thomas laughed indulgently, 'You're impossible, my dear. I grant you it would be a tidy ending and the Hartfield money and estate would be back with the family where it belongs, but I cannot see it happening.'

The news affected Merab differently. She had barely exchanged two words with Kitty but had instantly disliked her. How far this was due to Rowland's adoration of the young lady

111

would be hard to say, but whereas most people thought Kitty exceedingly pretty and found her playful wilfulness enchanting and were prepared to be indulgent towards her youth, Merab, unaccountably, felt a most unladylike urge to slap her face and shake her until her teeth rattled.

Her first reaction was a lightening of spirits. Why, she didn't know, and the second was a certain grim satisfaction in the thought that surely now Rowland must see what a vain, self-seeking little minx he had set his heart on.

She was entirely unprepared for what happened next.

It was raining. There was a sodden March sky and scurrying clouds. Merab was sitting in the library, and outside the rain fell monotonously. She was reading *Moll Flanders*, a book she was sure she shouldn't even be looking at, and she was thoroughly absorbed in the heroine's racy adventures. She did not hear the front door knocker and she jumped when, a few minutes later, Gregg came into the room.

'It's Mr Sandiford, miss,' he said. 'Begs for a few moments of your time.'

'Mr ... Mr Sandiford?' Merab dropped *Moll Flanders* and stared at him in dismay, a wave of colour mantling her cheek.

Aha, thought Gregg.

Merab tried to collect her thoughts. Whyever did he want to see her? It must be something to do with Hartfield. Had there been a fire, perhaps? Or another, later, will found?

'Show Mr Sandiford up, Gregg,' she said at last. The moment he had gone she thrust *Moll Flanders* under a cushion and rushed to the glass to pat her hair. When Rowland entered a few moments later, Merab was sitting, a model of ladylike decorum, one hand resting gracefully on the arm of the chair.

'Cousin Merab.'

Merab's eyebrows rose and something like panic seized her. 'Cousin Merab'? Why was he now acknowledging their relationship when only last week at the Bridges it seemed he had repudiated it?

'Sir.' It was all she could manage. 'Pray sit down.'

Rowland ignored this and instead began to pace up and down. Merab watched him in increasing bewilderment.

'I imagine you know why I am here?' he said at last, his voice sounding unnaturally harsh.

'I? No.' Merab's own voice trembled. 'Have you had news from Hartfield, perhaps?'

'News from Hartfield?' repeated Rowland, thrown.

'I ... I thought that might explain why you are here.'

Rowland turned. 'You know perfectly well why I am here.'

'Indeed, I do not.'

113

'Let us stop beating about the bush, Miss Hartfield. You know that Miss Parminster is engaged to be married to Lord Claydon?'

Merab inclined her head. 'I am sorry for the pain the notice must have caused you.'

Rowland waved this aside. 'It's a honeyfall for you, however,' he said.

'For me?'

'Stop putting on airs, Cousin,' said Rowland coldly. 'It doesn't suit you. There's nothing now to prevent our marriage. Whilst Kitty remained free I couldn't bring myself to ... but that's all over now. Once we're married I daresay you'll want to return to Hartfield Hall and that's agreeable to me. I'll settle a third of the estate on you, that's fair enough, and that will still leave me enough to stand for Parliament.' He turned and looked at Merab. She did not seem to be reacting as he'd imagined.

'Come now,' he said impatiently. 'You've made your stand. And if you want I'll apologize for my behaviour over the will. I admit I was over-hasty.'

'You mean you don't think I manipulated Grandfather into making that will so that I could get a husband?' Merab's voice was dangerously quiet.

'I was overwrought,' said Rowland shortly. He still felt uncomfortable about his behaviour that day and didn't want to remember it too closely. 'And you look quite different now.

114

Quite presentable.'

'Thank you.'

'Of course, you are twenty-six and on the shelf. At least you would be if you weren't going to marry me. But you are more, well, attractive than I thought. And I have no objection to the match.'

'But I have!'

'Of course, it will have to be private ... what did you say?'

Merab rose and faced him. 'Mr Sandiford, let there be no possibility of a mistake here. I am not marrying you under any circumstances whatsoever.'

Rowland gave a short laugh. 'Oh, come now ...'

'What you are offering me is an insult. You want that fortune and you now think that I am just about presentable, so you are attempting to bribe me with a third of the estate so that you shall have the rest to fulfil your political ambitions.'

'I cannot see what is so insulting about it.' Rowland resumed his pacing. He was aware that something was wrong, somewhere, but decided that it must be Merab. 'Just like a woman,' he said at last. 'Illogical, emotional. For Heaven's sake, I'm offering you respectability, financial security, what more do you want? All right then, half the estate.'

'Get out!' shouted Merab suddenly. 'I don't want your rotten business deal. As far as I am concerned this whole inheritance has been nothing but a humiliation and a misery and the sooner the lot goes to the destitute orphans or whatever, the better. I wouldn't marry you, Rowland Sandiford, if you were the last man on earth. Now get out!'

The moment Rowland had gone Merab sat down and burst into tears. Had she been mad to throw away £7,000? But what sort of life had Rowland offered her? A wife and not a wife? Living deserted in that dreadful old place? If she came up to Bath—a deserted wife—she would be the subject of whispers and perhaps ostracized.

But there was something else that lurked half-hidden in her mind. It wasn't that she loved Rowland, good God, any female would be insane to give her heart to a man so self-centred, but that the life he was proposing for himself was one she thought would suit her very well. Mistress of a forward-looking estate, wife to a Member of Parliament and one who was on the side of Reform, too.

Merab read the papers, she knew that there were great inequalities and injustices. To be a small part of trying to remedy that would be a not unworthy ambition. She knew she could run a household and she could learn to entertain. If she couldn't aspire to being a great political hostess at least she could have had a wider life, be in touch with the currents of opinion in the world.

116

If Rowland had offered her a proper share in his life as mistress of his house, would she have accepted him? But he would have had to have been a very different person, one who had the imagination to see things from her point of view. A man who felt that she might have something to offer in his life would not have approached her so arrogantly, expecting her to fall in with his plans. Merab blew her nose firmly and mopped at her eyes. Moll Flanders would not have put up with Rowland Sandiford for a moment! And Moll would have been right.

*　　*　　*

Joseph Harrison stared at *The Morning Post* in dismay. Why, the underhand little vixen, was his first thought. Kitty had been very gracious to him at the Assembly ball last week, granting him two dances and even allowing him to kiss the tips of her fingers. And this was what it had all been for. Joseph remembered now that Lord Claydon had been there in the background and, at the time, he had felt a glow of satisfaction in receiving favours the viscount had not. But now he could see it all. She had been playing a double game—encouraging him in order to make Claydon pop the question. And, the artful little piece, it had worked.

Well, who wanted an arrant little flirt like that? Doubtless she'd be extravagant too, and that would be no good for business. His mind wandered to Merab. They had not met since that disastrous afternoon, they had bowed politely across the Pump Room and that was it. And his mother's animadversions on the ingratitude of nieces had been long and vocal.

Joseph, however, had had second thoughts. He had gone over the matter several times in his mind and decided that his mother had allowed her indignation to overcome her judgement. In the main he was inclined to agree with her that Merab must have been well provided for, but he decided that she did not wish to be wooed for her money. It might have been wiser to have accepted Merab's story at face value and to have allowed a further acquaintance to get at the truth.

Whilst Joseph professed the greatest respect for his mother, nevertheless he felt that on this occasion a man needed to act for himself. Accordingly, he wrote a careful missive to his cousin, apologizing for his mother's hastiness and suggesting that he must always be honoured by their relationship. *As you know, dear cousin*, he finished, *I am a lawyer and any help I can give you over your grandfather's estate, for example, please do not hesitate to ask. It would be a pleasure to be of service to you. Your affectionate cousin, J. Harrison.*

Merab showed the letter to Amelia over breakfast.

'Humph,' said Amelia, regarding the

118

profusion with scepticism. 'He wants to know what your expectations are.'

'I have already told him,' objected Merab.

'But he doesn't believe it.'

'Oh dear, what should I do?' Merab had not mentioned Rowland's visit to her friend, and now it seemed as if she were going to have problems with Joseph as well. 'Mrs Harrison seems such an unguarded woman. I would rather not antagonize her further if I can help it.'

'Drop him a courteous note thanking him for his concern—you can mention Mr Camberwell—and add that you will always hold his mother and himself in the deepest respect.'

'What on earth does that mean?'

'Why nothing!'

'To tell you the truth, Amelia, I would rather Mrs Harrison didn't make our relationship known.' For some reason, though Merab did not say this, the thought of Rowland knowing was almost harder to bear than anything.

'I agree. I confess I was hoping that they would both leave Bath.'

'It's odd,' Merab reached out to take an apple. 'For most of my life I have had virtually no relations, now suddenly, I have them from all sides—and none of them agreeable!'

'Come now. You like Mrs Bridges.'

'True, but she is only a relation by marriage. And her son is perfectly obnoxious.'

Joseph received Merab's reply and saw at once that it was a politely worded evasion. Miss Hartfield did not want him to know the extent of her fortune, he thought. It must be large then. The Hartfield estate was a good one. Merab might be worth anything up to £20,000 and that warranted his very earnest attention.

His mother, he realized, would be no help in this matter. She was all too inclined to speak her mind when she would do better to button her lip. He would have to lime this twig very carefully indeed. Mrs Harrison took the hot baths twice a week and then spent the afternoon in the Pump Room restoring her system with tea and toast with friends. He would make a point of finding out what Merab did on those days and pursue his acquaintance with her. There would be nothing too obvious, a quiet attention to her wishes, a small posy perhaps, some little trifle that pleased the ladies, and he was sure that she would come to confide in him.

*   *   *

Rowland was so put out at Merab's refusal that he did what he would never normally have considered doing: he consulted his mother. He told his story, he thought, rather well: his generosity in offering Merab half the estate, his

120

permission for her to live at Hartfield, and he ended with her really unhinged refusal.

Mrs Bridges sat in her pleasant drawing-room with a worried frown on her face. At one point she raised her eyes to the ceiling. Finally, Rowland stopped talking. 'What more could I have offered, Mama?' he finished.

Mrs Bridges could have thought of several things. Instead she said, 'I notice that Major Bendick is becoming rather particular in his attentions towards Miss Hartfield.'

'That booby!' Rowland flushed with annoyance.

'Nonsense, he's an intelligent, cultivated man. He could offer Miss Hartfield a very comfortable home.'

'I've offered her Hartfield.'

'From what you tell me Hartfield is the sort of place one cannot wait to get away from,' observed Mrs Bridges.

'Well, of course, for me it would be. Depressing place, uncomfortable too.'

'I cannot see why Miss Hartfield should like it any better. And there is the added impression of many years with a cantankerous old grandfather as well. Personally, I'd never want to see that place again.'

Rowland shifted uncomfortably.

'Major Bendick could offer a proper home,' Mrs Bridges went on, taking up her sewing again. 'I understand that he feels that the time has come to settle down with wife and family. I daresay Miss Hartfield would like a proper husband and children.' Her voice was deliberately expressionless. She picked up the scissors and snipped carefully at a stray thread.

'Children!' echoed Rowland, thunderstruck.

'Most women do,' said his mother calmly.

Rowland got up and took several agitated turns around the room. For some reason he found his mother's statement most unpalatable. No, the major would never marry her, he thought. No money. On the shelf. A dowd. But try as he might he couldn't bring back to mind the skinny creature who had first greeted him when he'd arrived at Hartfield Hall; a scrawny woman in a badly-fitting black dress and with hair scraped back in a tight bun.

Instead, he saw a laughing woman with liquid brown eyes walking with Major Bendick in the Pump Room, her slim figure admirably set off by a clinging grey silk dress.

A sudden picture came into his mind of Merab at Merryn Park putting a bowl of flowers on the table. He shook his head violently. It was Kitty he wanted, Kitty who he had hoped would grace his home, not Merab. Whatever could he be thinking of? If he couldn't have Kitty, he didn't want anybody.

'How could you think I'd want anyone other than Kitty ...' he began.

'Kitty is an unprincipled, manipulative little baggage, and I pity Lord Claydon being saddled with her.'

'Mama!'

'And you,' went on Mrs Bridges calmly, 'are an addle-pated fool, my son.'

*   *   *

Having switched his attentions from Miss Parminster, Joseph found himself watching Merab carefully, and he was not pleased to note the assiduity with which Major Bendick was pursuing her acquaintance. He was unaware that the major was in something of a quandary. The major liked Merab and admired her grace and dignity, but he had the unaccountable feeling that she was laughing at him. Everybody knew that women's brains were just pieces of fluff, but he couldn't help thinking that Merab was more intelligent than any lady ought to be.

The previous evening, for example, he had informed her of the correct view on the nonsense about extending the franchise to working men. 'Absurd, of course,' he said. 'Why, next the ladies would be demanding the vote!'

'Ridiculous,' agreed Merab, casting down her eyes to hide the ironic gleam. 'Why, if women had the vote they might demand that taxes be spent on who-knows-what? Safer cities, street lighting, a lowering of the tax on corn and other absurdities.'

The major looked at her. She couldn't be

123

serious, could she? 'The farmers need the price of corn to be kept high. It would be grossly irresponsible to lower it.'

'Especially as it is their vote that keeps the Tories in power.'

'Good Heavens, Miss Hartfield.' The major's eyes began to pop. 'I shall think you are a Radical next!'

'I am concerned, certainly, that the poorest in our society should get enough to eat,' Merab replied. 'Whilst the price of corn is high that is difficult, you know.'

The major dismissed the poor with a wave of his hand. 'You are far too attractive a lady to bother your pretty head about such matters, Miss Hartfield.' He offered her his arm. 'Now, may I get you a glass of lemonade?'

Merab saw Joseph staring at her from across the room. 'Why, thank you, Major,' she said.

It was not until later that Joseph was able to claim Merab's attention. The major had stayed long enough (he thought) to convince Merab of the error of her ways with regard to the Corn Laws and was content to leave her sitting next to Amelia and her husband.

'The man's a bore,' announced Merab the moment the major was out of earshot.

'Then why have you been encouraging him?' asked Amelia crossly. She had just been admiring the fine couple they made and was put out.

Merab gestured to where Joseph was

making his way towards them.

'Oh dear!' said Amelia inadequately. 'Such an impossible man.'

Sir Thomas looked at Merab in some amusement. Gone was the drab creature who had arrived out of the blue. The new Miss Hartfield, fashionably gowned and poised, looked as though she could cope with any number of unwanted suitors.

Joseph had now arrived in front of them. He bowed punctiliously to Sir Thomas and his wife, then turned to Merab. 'I know you don't dance, Miss Hartfield, but may I persuade you to take a turn with me?'

'Certainly, Mr Harrison.' Merab resigned herself.

'I was most gratified by your letter,' observed Joseph next.

'Oh?'

'I said to my mother, "Cousin Merab shows herself truly the lady".'

Merab raised her eyebrows.

'My mother finds it difficult to understand, although generally her understanding—for a female—is most superior, how things have been left with you.'

'Mr Harrison.' Merab thought quickly. 'As you are a cousin and have been kind enough to interest yourself in my affairs I am sure that you will keep my confidence if I tell you of my grandfather's will.' Merab was certainly not going to explain the humiliating conditions, but she did hope that by telling him something she might be able to persuade him to lose interest.

'I am all attention.' Joseph's eyes lit up. She was coming to trust him.

'You probably know already that my grandfather cut my father out of his will when he married my mother.'

Joseph bowed. 'I had heard something,' he said cautiously. 'But surely he thought better of it?'

'Alas no. Even when my father's elder brother died, who would have inherited everything, they were not reconciled. Instead, my grandfather decided to leave the estate to a second cousin.'

'But surely, as his granddaughter, you had some claim?'

'None that he acknowledged. But it is worse than that. My grandfather was a very irascible man and in the end he quarrelled with the cousin, too, and left everything so tied up that it all goes to charity.'

God, thought Joseph, what a narrow escape. 'But you are not penniless, are you?' he asked, with a decent show of concern.

'Not quite as bad as that, thankfully,' said Merab. 'I have about seventy pounds a year of my own.'

Joseph dropped her arm. 'But this is dreadful, Miss Hartfield. Cannot the will be disregarded? Your grandfather's mental state, perhaps?'

'I can assure you, Mr Harrison, that Grandfather was *compos mentis* until the end of his life. As I mentioned before, I shall stay with Lady Wincanton until after her confinement and then I shall seek a post as a teacher.'

'You seem very calm about the prospect.' Joseph looked at her with a sudden suspicion.

'I was at my grandfather's beck and call for eight dreadful years, Mr Harrison. I can assure you that the humiliations of so dependent a position have not been lost on me. I am hoping that my small inheritance will enable me to keep some independence.'

Back in his lodgings Joseph thought over this conversation. Somehow he could no longer disbelieve Merab; he had heard tales in the family of old Mr Hartfield's intransigence. But now another thought occurred to him: Merab might have only seventy pounds a year, but she had something more, and that was social standing. If he lowered himself to overlook the lack of dowry then might it not be considered that the acquaintance of the Wincantons and her friendship with the Bridges and others made up for it?

If a man comes from nowhere then it is connections he should look for and Merab's connections were good. He explained as much to his mother the next day.

'Thinking of marrying Merab Hartfield with

only seventy pounds a year!' she exclaimed. 'Why, she's a pauper. Even Alderman Mills's Sarah has more than that.'

'But Sarah Mills isn't acquainted with the Wincantons.'

'She's after you, that's what it is,' went on Mrs Harrison unheeding. 'Sees that she won't get Major Bendick, I daresay, knows that you are making a pretty penny and thinks she'll have a go. Oh, the artful hussy.'

'But Mother...'

'Don't "Mother" me! I can see it all. She softens you up with stories of her grandfather and now she's got her claws into you. It was one thing to make a push for that twenty thousand, but to offer for Abby's girl with no more than a thousand or so, never!'

'Come Mother, my mind is by no means made up.'

'I should hope not,' sniffed Mrs Harrison.

*   *   *

The weather, which had been cold and wet, now suddenly decided to turn spring-like and for nearly a whole week it was warm and sunny. In Sydney Gardens all the daffodils came out and Mrs Tiverton invited Sir Thomas, Amelia and Merab to a luncheon party. The Tivertons lived a mile or so outside Bath in Widcombe, and as they drove there Merab suddenly became aware of time

128

passing.

'It's three and a half months since my grandfather died,' she said, looking around her as the carriage bowled along. 'The weather has been so depressing for so long that I'd quite forgotten that spring was on its way.'

'It always rains in Bath,' sighed Amelia. She pressed her hand gently over her stomach. The baby was kicking strongly now and she found the movement of the carriage uncomfortable. Three and a half months, she thought, and still nothing settled about Merab. Silently she cursed Julian Hartfield. Even the meanest legacy to his granddaughter—a few thousand—would have transformed her prospects. What was in store for her now? For the moment Amelia could persuade her to stay with the excuse of the coming baby, but by the end of summer the baby would be here and any chance of the Hartfield inheritance gone. Merab would be left facing an uncertain future and with all the miseries of being a badly paid, overworked teacher.

Merab too was feeling uneasy, but not because of the passing of time. She had made the decision to seek a post as soon as the baby was born and resolutely refused to let herself think further about it. What was the point? No, she felt uneasy because she was sure that the Tivertons had invited the Bridges and probably Rowland to their luncheon and she had not been in his company since that

129

dreadful proposal.

A handsome pair of ornamental gates announced that they had reached the Tivertons' estate. The carriage turned right into a park with grazing fallow deer. The Tivertons had bought the estate some dozen years previously and had at once set about improving it. A lake was created, complete with rustic bridge and a pagoda, and under Mr Tiverton's enthusiastic direction trees were planted and vistas opened up.

Mrs Tiverton liked her gatherings to be informal and the moment they arrived she told them cheerfully that she would not stand on ceremony with them and that perhaps the company would like to wander round a little before luncheon. They might like to view the shrubbery, and the walk through the wood down to the lake was very pleasant. For those who preferred to stay put there was the orangery. 'Lady Wincanton,' she finished, 'I have had my mother's sofa brought down for you. I thought you might like to rest yourself.'

Amelia accepted gratefully. Her back was aching and the jolting of the carriage over the ruts had not improved it.

'Mr Sandiford,' went on Mrs Tiverton, and to Merab's horror Rowland appeared from a side room. 'Why don't you take Miss Hartfield down to the lake? The view is really very pretty from there and you may see the pagoda.'

Merab, who had opened her mouth to say

130

that she would stay with Amelia, now found herself outmanoeuvred by her determined hostess and rather weakly accepted Rowland's arm and allowed him to lead her from the house.

For a few moments they walked in silence. Merab did her best to appear at ease: after all, she told herself firmly, it was not she who had behaved badly, she had nothing to reproach herself with. Then Rowland said, 'Mrs Tiverton is perhaps a little bossy, but she is very kind-hearted and I am pleased that my mother has such an agreeable acquaintance in Bath.'

The topic was unexceptionable and Merab took it up. 'Bath is not a large place,' she managed, 'I imagine one might be very much at the mercy of a small circle. Uncongenial people could affect one's happiness far more than in, say, London.'

She felt understandably pleased with herself. They had exchanged a couple of perfectly innocuous platitudes without either of them coming to blows.

Rowland had obviously decided to be on his best behaviour. 'Do you miss London, Miss Hartfield?'

'I miss my parents and the happy life we had.' Merab stared at the lake with sight suddenly blurred. 'And yes, I suppose I do miss the excitement of it. My father encouraged me to read the newspapers and to have views on

131

current affairs, and I miss that.'

'He did?' Rowland was astonished.

'Papa believed that women have brains and should be allowed to exercise them,' said Merab a trifle acidly. 'We would argue about the war in the Peninsula. Papa believed that Lord Wellington should be supported.'

'And you didn't?'

'Oh, I agreed with Papa,' she smiled. 'But he did so enjoy the argument so I tried to provide the opposition!'

'Did your grandfather ever mention my own political ideas?' asked Rowland hesitantly. And then, as if he'd said too much, exclaimed, 'Ah, there is the pagoda.'

Merab threw the pagoda a cursory glance and Rowland a more searching one. They seemed to be getting on to dangerous ground and she had no wish to provoke another quarrel with him. But when she ventured to look at him she saw a glint of humour in his eyes.

She laughed. 'Certainly. You must know that they were poppycock, balderdash and the sort of half-witted ideas only to be expected from Radicals.'

'And if they were adopted the country would go to the dogs?'

'Naturally. Grandfather knew of no half measures. He wouldn't even set up a school in the village. He didn't believe in teaching working men to read and write. He thought it led to sedition.'

'And what do you think?' asked Rowland, curiously.

'I? I am only a woman, Mr Sandiford, what does it matter what I think?' Her tone was ironic.

'But your father had the greatest respect for your opinion, so surely I may ask?'

'Grandfather was right, of course; give working people access to ideas and argument and they will almost certainly want change. Whether that is sedition or not depends on your viewpoint.'

'And in your view?' Rowland pressed.

'I believe we need change,' said Merab quietly. 'Too much power in the hands of an oligarchy leads to stagnation and corruption.'

Oligarchy, thought Rowland. He couldn't imagine Kitty even knowing the word. Unwillingly, he acknowledged a dawning respect for his cousin.

They had now reached the lake and stood gazing down at their reflections for a moment. The reflections were turned towards each other, Rowland bending down a little to catch Merab's words. Suddenly embarrassed, they both looked away and automatically turned their steps back to the house.

On their return they found that other guests had arrived, among them Kitty and Lord Claydon. Kitty was looking adorable in soft pink with a small spray of silk roses in her hair.

On her left hand was a magnificent sapphire ring which every now and then she held out to admire.

'We shall have a house in the best part of London, shall we not, Claydon,' Kitty was saying.

Lord Claydon smiled and looked besotted.

'I shall go to all the balls and dance the night away and have a new gown for each of them.'

What on earth did Rowland see in her, wondered Merab. She noticed that he had retreated to the window and was looking out over the lake they had just visited.

'Why, Mr Sandiford, I didn't see you,' Kitty trilled.

Rowland set his shoulders and moved to greet her.

'You know Lord Claydon?' Kitty was enjoying herself and looked from one to the other. Rowland looked grim and Lord Claydon polite but uncomprehending. 'This is Rowland Sandiford, darling. An old beau. I think I may call you that, don't you, Mr Sandiford? His estate marches with Papa's and I have known him all my life.'

Lord Claydon bowed. Rowland, Merab noticed, had turned pale. A muscle twitched at the corner of his mouth. Kitty put her arm through Lord Claydon's and mouthed him a kiss. 'Claydon is taking me home next week, so that he and Papa can discuss settlements— horrid things—but one must live after all. Shall

I send Papa your regards?'

Rowland didn't answer. Merab, looking covertly at him, saw that his eyes held a look of shock, anger and something else—could it be relief? And at that moment the gong went and Mrs Tiverton came forward to shepherd her guests into the dining-room.

Merab had been so taken up with watching Kitty that she had failed to see another new arrival and it wasn't until Mr Tiverton touched her arm and begged leave to introduce him that she realized that Joseph Harrison was standing behind her.

'Mr ... Mr Harrison,' she stammered.

'Oh, you know each other?' said Mr Tiverton genially. 'Harrison has been doing some work for me about my West Indian property, you know. When I saw he was in Bath I invited him to join us.'

'I am delighted to see Miss Hartfield looking like Ceres the goddess of spring,' said Mr Harrison. 'May I escort you in?' He indicated the dining-room.

Merab forebore to tell him that Ceres was not the goddess of spring and unwillingly put her hand on his arm. Joseph was obviously feeling in a good mood. He had never expected to be invited to the Tivertons and indeed, if Mrs Tiverton had had anything to do with it he would not have been. She always complained that her husband was too lax. But Mr Harrison was well enough, she supposed, and, thank

God, he had not brought his dreadful mother.

'Jolly place, this,' said Joseph, looking round. He had mentally priced the furniture and the silver. 'I expect Hartfield Hall is much larger, though?'

'Not at all,' said Merab. 'It is smaller and certainly shabbier. My grandfather didn't believe in redecorating rooms he rarely entered.'

'Do you know Hartfield Hall, then, sir?' Rowland had come up behind them. Who was this man, with his over-pomaded hair and his flashy waistcoat? How did Merab know him?

Merab hastily introduced them, cursing the chance which had brought them together. She didn't stop to analyse it, but her one thought was that Rowland must not know that Joseph was her cousin. But it was too late.

'I've never been there myself,' said Joseph. He looked at the man in front of him and smelled danger. How well did he know Merab that he presumed to butt in on the conversation? Joseph didn't want anybody else muscling in on his territory. 'But I've heard of Hartfield Hall of course. Miss Hartfield is my cousin, so naturally, I'm interested.' He gave Merab's arm a squeeze.

'Her cousin!' Rowland was stupefied.

Merab felt ready to drop. 'I have only just become acquainted with Mr Harrison,' she managed to say. 'We are related on my mother's side.'

'First cousins. Pretty close,' said Joseph.

136

CHAPTER SIX

Mrs Harrison sat at the breakfast-table in a mood of barely concealed anger. Joseph had not told her about his lunch at the Tivertons', but she had heard of it from her maid who was friendly with the Tivertons' groom. And why had she not been invited? The Tivertons knew Joseph had a mother in Bath. And to cap it all that hussy Merab Hartfield had been there as well.

Mrs Harrison had nourished a life-long dislike of her sister Abigail, and the thought that Abby's daughter was a welcome guest in a house where she herself was not invited filled her with such anger that she could hardly bear it. Abby had been the pretty, younger sister, whilst she, Dinah, was the 'homely' one. It was Abby who had gone off to London and had a glamorous career in the opera—and was probably no better than she should have been—whilst Dinah had stayed at home with Mother. Abby had married into the county whereas she had had to settle for snuff-taking old Eli Harrison.

She poured herself another cup of coffee and stared with dislike at her devilled kidneys congealing slowly on her plate. The door opened.

137

'Morning, Mother.' Joseph, wearing a startling new waistcoat in red and yellow, came in, bestowed a dutiful kiss on his mother's unyielding cheek and sat down. 'Ah, coffee! Just the ticket.'

'You seem cheerful this morning,' observed Mrs Harrison, her displeasure deepening.

Joseph gave a condescending smile. 'I believe I am.'

'May I ask why?'

'I hope to be able to make a happy announcement in due course.' Joseph gave a satisfied sigh. He'd seen off the opposition at the Tivertons'. This Mr Sandiford had left him a clear field and Merab had listened attentively to him. He knew he had impressed her. He had mentioned his business dealings and made sure that she realized that he was a man who was going places. He intended to pop the question as soon as possible. If he was going to use Merab's connections—Sir Thomas Wincanton could surely throw a little business his way?—then he wanted Merab to know that he had something to offer in return. 'My client, Sir Thomas Wincanton', yes, he liked the sound of that very well.

'I hope you are not thinking of offering for Merab Hartfield?' cried Mrs Harrison, pushing her plate from her.

'And why not?' Joseph's smile faded.

'She's penniless for a start.'

'She has about fifteen hundred pounds,' corrected Joseph. 'She also has connections.'

'Connections!' Mrs Harrison could barely hide her rancour. 'Mother an opera dancer, to put it no worse. Father a ne'er-do-well clerk. And if they really were married why were they never acknowledged in the family, tell me that?'

'In the end Mr Hartfield did acknowledge Merab and Aunt Abby.'

'As what?' spat his mother. 'Merab was working as a housekeeper there! Have some sense, Joseph!'

'Mr Hartfield was eccentric,' snapped Joseph. 'I am asking her and that's flat. I'm sorry you don't like it.'

'Like it!' Mrs Harrison shrieked. 'Abby was a slut and I don't suppose your dear Merab's much better. I see what it is, you've been seduced by that fancy luncheon party. Yes, I know about it, and those fine-sounding people. Have you thought why you were invited, Joseph? You hardly know them, but Merab does. She wangled an invitation for you so that she could trap you! That's what it is!'

Joseph sat back in his chair and stirred his coffee thoughtfully. Of course! Now that made sense. She'd seen that this major fellow wasn't going to come up to scratch, so she set out to indicate that an offer from himself would not be unwelcome. A slow smile spread over his face. He would pay a visit to the Wincantons that very afternoon.

*   *   *

After the Tivertons' luncheon, Rowland left with his mother and her husband. They had got into the Bridges' carriage with Rowland taking the forward seat. Mrs Bridges watched him unobtrusively as he fiddled with the window strap and stared blindly out of the window. Surely he hadn't quarrelled with Merab again? She had followed their progress to the lake with a certain quiet pleasure and exchanged a conspiratorial glance with Amelia who was sitting on a day-bed near the window. Neither lady had said anything.

Could it be Kitty? Her behaviour had been ill-bred in Mrs Bridges's opinion. She had been unable to hear the conversation but the way Kitty had made eyes at Lord Claydon and done everything possible to flaunt her betrothed state at Rowland was surely enough to disgust any sensible man. The only question in his mother's mind was whether her son could be accounted a sensible man.

But when Rowland spoke it was not about Kitty.

'Did you know that Harrison fellow was Miss Hartfield's first cousin?'

'Harrison?' put in Mr Bridges. 'The chap with the loud waistcoat? Surely not?'

140

'Well, he said so and she did not deny it.'

'Oh dear,' said his mother. 'Poor Miss Hartfield. How awkward for her.' Trouble, she thought, never comes in small battalions. 'I suppose Mrs Harrison must be her mother's sister.'

'She's an appalling woman,' stated Rowland. 'Pushy. No wonder Cousin Julian wouldn't acknowledge them.'

'Miss Hartfield isn't like that, though,' Mr Bridges pointed out. 'I think she is charming and I cannot believe that her mother wasn't likewise. After all, we know Mrs Hartfield ran away from her family, don't we?'

'What sort of female would do that?' Rowland tugged savagely at the window strap as he spoke and suddenly the window fell open and a blast of cold air entered the carriage. By the time he'd apologized and pulled the window up his spurt of temper had disappeared. He'd come back from his walk with Merab feeling a curious sense of happiness. Even the unexpected meeting with Kitty had not entirely dispelled it. But Mr Harrison's cool assertion of kinship had killed it stone dead.

'Your father met Jonathan and his wife in London once,' said Mrs Bridges suddenly.

Rowland turned to her. 'When?'

'About ten or twelve years ago, I think. He bumped into Jonathan somewhere in the City and went back to dine. Miss Hartfield was

141

away at school at the time. Mark said that Mrs Hartfield was delightful. Rather Italian-looking, petite, somewhat delicate and very pretty. If she'd been remotely like Mrs Harrison I'm sure he'd have mentioned it.'

Some of Rowland's depression began to lift. 'Miss Hartfield seemed very thick with this Harrison. Allowed him to take her in to luncheon.'

'What else could she have done?' asked Mrs Bridges reasonably.

* * *

Joseph, hair carefully pomaded and his person liberally scented, presented his card to Gregg. After a few moments during which he surveyed himself with some satisfaction in the hall mirror, he was shown upstairs to where Merab was sitting in the yellow drawing-room. She had not really wished to see him and said as much to Amelia.

'Probably just a courtesy call,' said Amelia, who had missed most of the previous day's happenings. She had been feeling a little queasy and been content to remain on the day-bed. 'You won't mind if I leave you for a few minutes, will you? Nurse wants to talk to me and I'll be back shortly.'

'Of course not.' Merab suppressed an urge to beg her to remain and awaited her unwanted visitor with resignation.

Joseph entered the room and gave a swift satisfied look around. Alone! Doubtless carefully contrived. He bowed over her hand.

'Cousin Merab.'

'Sir. Please be seated. Lady Wincanton offers her apologies. She will be here shortly.'

'It is not Lady Wincanton I have come to see,' said Joseph playfully.

Merab's heart sank.

'You must know by now why I am here.'

'Indeed I do not, sir.'

'Ah, the ladies!' Joseph wagged a finger at her reproachfully. 'Come now, I beg you, do not be so coy.'

'Coyness is far from my intention,' said Merab with asperity.

'Come, Cousin, you have made your wishes very clear, I believe, and I am here to answer them. Did you not persuade Mr Tiverton to ask me to luncheon? Confess!'

'I certainly do not know Mr Tiverton well enough to do any such thing!'

'But you dropped a hint, perhaps, of a partiality?' said Joseph, smiling archly.

'Mr Harrison,' said Merab firmly, 'I will no longer pretend to misunderstand you. But you are mistaken in thinking that I have a "partiality" for you.'

'You'll never hook Major Bendick, you know.' The sweetness of Joseph's tone had begun to slip.

'I am sure you are right, sir.'

'Then, dammit, why won't you marry me? I can support you. And your connections will be useful to me.'

So that's it, thought Merab. Connections. I should have guessed. Well, all she could do now was finish the conversation as soon as possible and in such a way as left Joseph in no doubt as to her answer.

'I believe it is customary for there to be some affection between husband and wife. I have none for you and you have none for me.' She rose as she spoke and reached out her hand for the bell-pull.

Joseph forestalled her. 'Isn't there, by Jove?' he shouted. He jerked her into his arms and tried to reach her mouth.

'Stop it!' cried Merab, twisting and trying to free herself. 'Mr Harrison! Let me go this instant!'

'Like a bit of rough stuff, do you?' said Joseph thickly and set his teeth at her neck.

Merab screamed.

There were hurried footsteps and the door opened.

'Thank God!' Merab pulled herself free.

Amelia came into the room. 'Mr Harrison!'

'Get out!' Merab's voice was beginning to shake. 'Get out, Mr Harrison. And please don't come again.'

Joseph reached up to straighten his cravat. 'You'll regret this,' he snarled. 'Luring me on and then playing the prude. There's a word for

women like you. Slut! Just like your mother.'
He gathered up the shreds of his dignity and
left the room.

* * *

It wasn't until a week or so later that Amelia
began to realize that there were rumours. If
fewer people came up to greet them in the
Pump Room she assumed that they hadn't seen
them. Besides, she was not feeling very well this
pregnancy and it was sometimes a relief not to
be sociable. But when Lady Mandersby, who
with Mrs Tiverton was the undoubted leader of
Bath society, cut Merab then Amelia began to
realize that something was wrong. Even Mrs
Tiverton, whilst she didn't go as far as cutting
them, was nevertheless coolly vague about a
proposed drive up to Lansdown.

Reluctantly, Amelia confided in her
husband that night. She didn't want to, but she
knew from experience that it would be better if
he heard it from herself. Sir Thomas listened
thoughtfully and then said, 'I'll find out for you
what they're saying. But if it's really damaging,
Amelia, then I'm sorry, but your friend will
have to go. I cannot have my wife associated
with anything unsavoury.'

Amelia picked up the candle and took it to
the bedside table. 'Poor Merab, it's not her
fault. It can't be anything she has done.'

'Very likely not,' said Sir Thomas, picking

up his own candle. 'But these Harrisons are unpleasant people to be associated with anyway and a really damaging story coming from them would be ruinous. I'm afraid you'd better start trying to find Miss Hartfield a teaching post. What about your cousins in Dublin?'

'I suppose so.' Amelia got into bed, blew out the candle and burst into tears.

Amelia was not the only one to have noticed the sudden coolness. Mr and Mrs Bridges discussed it one afternoon over their tea tray.

'Mrs Tiverton's hints were most unpleasant,' said Mrs Bridges.

'Mrs Harrison has been talking with a vengeance,' agreed her husband.

'It comes from her?'

'Who else would say that Abigail Cooper had run away from home to be a chorus girl in the opera? And then become the mistress of Jonathan Hartfield?'

'She said that!' cried Mrs Bridges. 'Mrs Tiverton was not so explicit. She merely hinted that she'd heard that Miss Hartfield's parentage was "irregular" was I think the word she used, and she was reluctant to continue the acquaintance.'

'Does she know of your relationship to Miss Hartfield?'

Mrs Bridges shook her head. 'Rowland has chosen not to acknowledge it, so I felt in honour bound to support him. Of course, I hoped he'd come round...'

'I expect he was terrified lest any rumour of this atrocious will came out.'

Mrs Bridges sighed.

'What shall you do?' asked her husband.

'What can I do? Whilst Rowland is so set against Miss Hartfield I can do little. I shall continue to acknowledge her, naturally, but I don't see what other course I can take. If I acknowledge her as a cousin and Rowland does not that would only make the situation worse for her.'

Rowland himself had been feeling vaguely uneasy about Merab ever since the Tivertons' luncheon. Several times he'd almost decided to pay a call on the Wincantons but had backed down at the last minute. He found the fact that half of him wished to pursue his acquaintance with Merab profoundly alarming and it led him to spend several mornings galloping over Lansdown in an attempt to divert his mind.

He also stopped going to the Pump Room. He had no wish to meet Kitty during her remaining days in Bath. As his mother had hoped, it was the episode at the Tivertons' luncheon which had finally enlightened Rowland as to Kitty's true character. Her behaviour had been both cruel and unnecessary, he now realized. She had chosen Lord Claydon freely, nobody was forcing her to marry him, and there was no reason for her to flaunt Claydon in front of him. She had, he now saw, played with him, taunting him with her eligible betrothal and Rowland had been at first hurt and shocked and then angry and resentful.

Kitty knew very well how upset he'd been at their parting and yet, in Bath, she had deliberately kept him hanging on; encouraging him with secret hand squeezes and stolen kisses behind pots of palms. He found himself thinking that Merab would never have behaved in such a fashion.

He took out the conversation by the lake and examined it carefully. His cousin had shown herself to be both intelligent and thoughtful. Had Julian Hartfield ever known that she held those views? He would like to ask her.

His thoughts turned reluctantly to Joseph. How the devil did Merab come to have such a fellow as a first cousin? He was something of a tuft-hunter too! Rowland had disliked his obsequiousness towards Mrs Tiverton. Merab seemed to be remarkably thick with the man, he thought crossly. He saw her again, hand on Joseph's arm, allowing him to lead her into the Tivertons' dining-room.

His fists clenched involuntarily. Then he relaxed. What the devil was it to him that Miss Hartfield was pursuing some ill-bred Bristol attorney? Did he care?

Rowland's mood was so unpropitious that he snapped the head off the inn servant who had dared to ask whether he would be going

148

out that evening, and snubbed the pretty maid who ventured to wish him, 'Good day, sir', when she met him on the stairs.

He spent several very unpleasant evenings gambling in the Orange Tree coffee house where he punted recklessly, won several hundred pounds the first evening and lost it again the following two nights.

On the third day he met Joseph by chance in the Orange Tree. Joseph was sitting by the window, newspaper in hand and studying the commodities market. He looked up as Rowland came in and smiled to himself. Rowland saw him and inclined his head curtly, 'Harrison.'

Joseph was pleased to have his name remembered. He'd done his homework since meeting Rowland and now knew that he had a very pretty little estate in Wiltshire. 'Sandiford. May I offer you a cup of coffee?' Without waiting for a reply he clicked his fingers at a waiter. Rowland shrugged and sat down.

'May I ask how you met Miss Hartfield,' asked Joseph after they had drunk their coffee. 'Another cup?'

'No thank you. I met Miss Hartfield through Lady Wincanton,' said Rowland mendaciously. 'I had no idea that you were related. Lady Wincanton, as you know, was at school with Miss Hartfield and I'd gathered there were few relations on either side.'

'Miss Hartfield is no relation of mine any

149

more,' said Joseph calmly. 'My mother has informed me of the true state of affairs.'

'Which is?' Rowland's eyes narrowed.

'Her mother, Abigail Cooper, was no better than she should have been. She was in the opera chorus, calling herself Rosalba Bersanelli, and you may imagine what that meant! Scores of lovers I have no doubt. And then she took up with Jonathan Hartfield. But marriage? Oh no! There was no marriage, you can be sure of that. Why, his own father disowned him. So Miss Prissy Hartfield has no right to the title. Plain Merab Cooper is what she ought to be.'

Rowland's cold grey eyes looked him over contemptuously. The fellow had been all over her the previous week. 'Refused you, did she?'

Joseph's face turned purple. 'Refused me! I'd like to see her get a chance. No, she tried to get her claws into me. Saw the opportunity for an advantageous marriage, I daresay.' Joseph glanced at himself in the mirror and tweaked his cravat. 'I soon told her what I thought of that idea.'

Poor Merab must have had quite a week, thought Rowland with sudden rueful amusement. But this creature in front of him! 'Why are you telling me all this?'

Joseph recovered himself. 'Oh, I don't want to ruin her,' he said smoothly. 'I just thought I should put you on your guard. You can keep it to yourself, I daresay?'

He had advised a number of people to keep it to themselves and the results had been most gratifying.

*   *   *

It took Merab some time to coax Amelia into telling her what the rumours were saying. In the end it was only by threatening to ask Sir Thomas that Amelia gave in. They were in Amelia's boudoir, a charming room papered in watered silk in a soft green with comfortable furniture and a number of cosy cushions. Amelia sat by the fire, her feet on a small beaded footstool. Merab was sitting opposite her, holding out her hands to the blaze. She suddenly felt cold.

'It must be Cousin Joseph or Aunt Dinah,' she said wearily when Amelia had finished.

'Not Mr Sandiford?' Amelia had heard discreetly from Gregg of Rowland's visit and, as Merab had not confided in her, she had feared the worst.

'Cousin Rowland? Well, I don't altogether like him,' said Merab judiciously, 'but I doubt whether he'd do anything so ungentlemanly.'

Amelia raised her eyebrows. 'He appears to have gone up in your estimation.'

Merab flushed. 'He is, at least, a gentleman,' she said evasively. 'Joseph is not.'

Amelia sighed. What was the use of Merab finding Mr Sandiford less objectionable if, as

151

Sir Thomas was quietly urging, she had to go?

'I must go back to Hartfield,' said Merab after a moment's silence.

'No!' cried Amelia. 'Oh, Merab, you must not! Why, that would be an admission of guilt, don't you see?'

'How can I stay here? Do you think I cannot see what is happening? I cannot have you tainted by the slurs on me. I am sure Sir Thomas agrees with me.'

Amelia sighed again.

'Of course he does,' went on Merab. 'What husband would not? But I need to go back to find some evidence of my parents' marriage at any rate. Do you think it's easy for me to bear the thought that my father might have so wronged my mother?'

'Of course I understand, dear Merab.' Amelia's eyes were full of tears. 'And I don't believe your father was anything but honourable. As for the other...'

There was a knock at the door and Gregg entered. 'Mr Sandiford requests a few moments, my lady.'

Amelia glanced at Merab who had paled suddenly. 'Show him up, Gregg,' she said. 'And we shall not be at home to other visitors.'

'Very good, my lady.'

Rowland strode in looking pale and determined. He was also, Amelia noted, looking singularly handsome in a dark-blue, double-breasted tail coat, which suited him admirably. The more she saw him the more she thought that he and Merab were well matched, and she cursed the fate that brought them together in so perverse a fashion that they were unlikely ever to recognize the fact.

Rowland started without preamble. 'I have come about these rumours,' he said, accepting Amelia's indication of a seat. 'I know exactly where they are coming from and I was wondering if there were anything I could do to help?'

Amelia looked at Merab and rose to her feet. 'We are most grateful for your support, sir,' she said, smiling at him, 'and I will leave you to talk to Merab about it. I am promised up in the nursery.'

Rowland opened the door for her. When he sat down again he gave Merab a brief résumé of his conversation with Joseph. 'I suspected that you had turned him down,' he finished.

'I did.' Merab flushed. She suddenly remembered that she had also turned Rowland down, though not, thank God, in this very room. 'He ... he was most obnoxious. He was after my "connections", as he termed it. I suppose he is now making sure that I don't have any.' She added that she thought she should now go back to Hartfield Hall, at least to find her parents' marriage certificate. 'I think it will be in Mama's trunk,' she finished. 'After she died I couldn't bear to go through it, so I just left it.'

Rowland had no doubt that the marriage would prove to be genuine; it was the other accusation that concerned him more. He could understand that Merab had been brought up to think that her mother had been a singing teacher. That was bad enough, though it was respectable—just. But the rumours of Mrs Hartfield having been an opera chorus girl were far more damaging and, as Rowland knew very well, those rumours had been extant in the family for years. But how could he suggest to Merab that her parents had lied to her about her mother's profession?

'How do you propose to travel?' he asked eventually.

'I hadn't thought. The stagecoach, probably. Perhaps if I write to Mr Camberwell he could arrange for Farmer Willett to collect me in Cirencester after market.'

'It won't do. A lady cannot hang about the King's Head!'

'Perhaps the Mail? I really do not want to ask Sir Thomas.' Merab thought worriedly about the cost. The Mail was more expensive.

'No, I'll take you.'

'You!' Merab looked at him aghast.

Rowland raised an eyebrow. 'I have been thinking for some time that I ought to check what's happening about the estate.'

'But it would not be proper,' Merab blurted out. Go in a travelling coach alone with a man! Why, no lady would do such a thing and keep a

154

shred of reputation.

'I promise not to propose,' said Rowland dryly.

Merab flushed scarlet and was silent. Just then Amelia returned. 'An excellent idea,' she said warmly, when she heard. 'And there will be no problem about propriety for Merab can take Lottie.' Lottie was the maid who had been designated by Amelia to help Merab. Lately, the housekeeper had reported that Lottie was showing a most unsuitable interest in a young corporal, so to give her a change of scene could only be beneficial. And anything which threw Merab and Mr Sandiford together was surely to be encouraged? She sat back and beamed at them.

Amelia and Merab parted amid tears. 'Of course, you'll be back soon,' wept Amelia. 'I know everything will be all right.'

Merab kissed her. 'Of course.' But she knew she would not. Sir Thomas had been polite, even consolatory, but there was no doubt he'd been relieved too. Merab would not return without an invitation and she was well aware that Sir Thomas would never allow Amelia to issue one. She couldn't blame him. What man would willingly let his wife be ostracized?

Rowland said nothing to his mother, save that he would be leaving Bath. She assumed that he would be returning to Merryn Park and it was only a remark of Amelia's, when she met her by chance a day or so later in Milsom

155

Street, that led to the truth.

'He's escorting Miss Hartfield home!' she exclaimed.

'Yes, didn't he tell you?'

'No.'

Both ladies were silent and both decided that the omission was interesting in the extreme, but neither felt they knew the other well enough to comment on it.

Rowland collected Merab and Lottie very early, barely seven o'clock, for it was a full day's journey. Merab's trunk and Lottie's portmanteau joined Rowland's luggage on the carriage roof. Lottie, weeping silently, climbed in and then with a wail threw her apron over her head. Merab raised her eyes to heaven and Rowland gave a slight smile.

'Get in, Cousin,' was all he said. He climbed in after her, tapped on the roof with his cane and they set off.

The journey was initially uneventful. Merab, who had been dreading Rowland's undiluted company for a whole day, cautiously began to relax. Possibly Lottie's presence inhibited him, or perhaps he had mellowed towards his cousin, whatever the reason they found themselves talking about the improvements Rowland was attempting at Merryn Park and Merab was making interested comments.

'I was reading about the benefits of fish manure somewhere,' she said. 'Though I suppose you will be too far from the sea for that to be easily available.'

Rowland looked at her and raised an amused eyebrow. 'And what do you know about fish manure, Cousin?'

Merab laughed. 'Nothing. Except that it enriches the soil. But I confess I don't understand why the soil should need it. Surely nature does not intend fish to land on fields naturally?'

'Nature doesn't allow one crop to be used exclusively either, and it's well known that any crop used year after year diminishes the fertility of the soil.'

'Nature prefers variety?'

'It would seem so. Of course, we don't understand this yet...'

The conversation was terminated abruptly by a sudden jolt which sent Lottie sprawling, followed by a shot and the whinny of frightened horses. Lottie gave a shriek. Rowland's hand went to the carriage pistols.

'I wouldn't if I was you, cully.' The carriage door was wrenched open and a burly man, mask over his face, pushed a pistol in Rowland's chest.

'Come on, sharp, hand over the goods.'

'What makes you think we have any?'

The pistol prodded his chest. 'Stop playing. Your purse. And the lady's.' He jerked his head. 'Get out.'

Reluctantly Rowland did so. In the moment that his bulk filled the doorway Merab,

157

without pausing to think, reached out for the carriage pistol. Pray God it was loaded! She cocked it and took aim. She could see the highwayman clearly. Rowland was still protesting and the man, impatient, grabbed his arm and pulled him roughly down the carriage step. Rowland fell and in that split second Merab fired. Lottie screamed. The highwayman fell back and the horses, terrified, started plunging.

Merab, frightened lest the carriage should go over Rowland, leapt out of the carriage and shouted to the coachman, 'For God's sake hold them!'

At that moment there was a second shot and Merab felt a sudden stinging sensation in her arm. She dropped the pistol. A red patch appeared and quickly spread. A second highwayman, gun steady, had ridden up and was aiming at her. But before he could do anything Rowland, who was still on the ground, picked up the fallen pistol and fired the second barrel. Cursing, the man clutched his leg, turned his horse and fled.

There was a short silence broken only by Lottie's shrieks and the first highwayman's groans. Rowland rose slowly. He and Merab looked at each other. Then Merab turned white and fell.

She was only dimly aware of what followed as she drifted in and out of consciousness. Her dress was ripped unceremoniously off her shoulder and the wound laid bare. 'Only a flesh wound,' she heard someone saying. Could it be Rowland sounding so concerned? Her one thought, incongruously, was that thank God she was wearing one of her old dresses for travelling. Her world clouded over again.

When she came round she could not work out at first where she was and what was happening. She felt confused and muzzy. The top of her arm hurt abominably and she was lying against someone's chest. With a start she sat up. Rowland removed his arm. He was holding her bonnet in one hand together with a small clutch of hairpins.

'I never knew how many hairpins women needed,' he said, with a tolerable assumption of normality. 'You've been shedding them all the way.'

Merab stared at him for a moment, frowning, then suddenly colour surged up over her face.

'We were held up,' she said.

'We were indeed,' agreed Rowland.

'Oh miss, you was ever so brave!' put in Lottie who had been jerked out of her misery and now seemed quite animated.

'Was I?'

'You shot him, miss. Serves him right, I say.'

Merab turned to look at Rowland.

'You shot one of the highwaymen,' he explained. 'There was a second one though who winged you. And I shot *him*.'

'I didn't kill him, did I?' It had all come

flooding back now.

'No. Fortunately, we were quite near a village. I reported it and the local magistrate has taken the fellow into custody. I made a statement on your behalf and there is no need to trouble yourself about it further.' He spoke calmly.

Merab sat quietly and then she said, 'It might have been one of my new dresses.' Then suddenly she started to cry. Rowland put his arm round her again and handed her his handkerchief. After some moments Merab disengaged herself, sat up and blew her nose firmly.

'I'm sorry. Crying over a dress that I wasn't even wearing. It's so silly.'

'Reaction,' said Rowland.

'Were you hurt?'

Rowland shrugged. 'Maybe a bruise or two. And you'll be all right, it was a flesh wound only, thank God. You'll be a bit stiff for a week or so, but it'll heal.'

He turned and looked out of the window. He had ripped the dress from her shoulders without a moment's hesitation, but now the remembrance of that white shoulder with the red bullet wound scored through it affected him profoundly. Merab, lying there on the carriage seat, had seemed fragile and vulnerable. If Lottie had not been there he would have felt an irresistible urge to . . .

He shook himself. Lottie had been there.

Merab, his cousin, whose existence had robbed him of his expected inheritance, had suffered a small wound, that was all. Why should he feel that it changed anything?

CHAPTER SEVEN

Their arrival at Hartfield was inauspicious. Most of the servants had been paid off and there remained only Mary and Jenny and one outdoor man. They had been told of Merab's arrival and her room had been prepared, but there was the problem of Rowland. Propriety demanded that, without a chaperone, he himself could not stay at Hartfield Hall and originally he had intended to put up at the inn in the village and come over when necessary.

But he could not, in all conscience, leave his cousin to the inexpert ministrations of two flighty housemaids and Lottie was just as useless. Merab had fallen silent the last half-hour of the journey. He guessed her wound was painful and when he touched her forehead briefly it was hot. A slight fever would be normal, but it made it impossible for him to leave her.

He would have to stay that night, he decided. Lottie could sleep in Merab's room on a truckle bed, that would at least observe the proprieties, and he would consult Mr

161

Camberwell the following day. Perhaps some respectable older female could be found who would stay a week or so.

The coach turned up the Hartfield drive and a few moments later had drawn up at the house. Rowland leapt out and let down the carriage steps. But it was obvious that Merab was in no condition to walk. Ignoring her muffled protests, he picked her up and carried her into the house and tried not to hear Jenny and Mary's giggles behind him. He took Merab up to the drawing-room, pushed open the door with one shoulder and called to Lottie to make herself useful and remove the dust sheets from the sofa.

Merab opened her eyes and said faintly, 'I feel hot.'

'You have a slight fever,' said Rowland shortly. 'I'm going to redo your wound properly and then you're going to bed. Lottie will bring up some laudanum and mind that you take it. Are you hungry?'

Merab shook her head.

Rowland laid her carefully on the sofa and went to organize the dressing. When he returned it was with Mary, who was carrying a tray on which were some lint, a roll of bandage, some scissors, a bowl of hot water, a flannel and a steaming poultice. He turned to Mary. 'Squeamish?'

'No, sir.'

'Very well. You'd better stay. I may need

162

some help.'

'If you'll wait a moment, sir,' said Mary as she watched him unwrap the makeshift bandage and begin to ease the bloodstained dressing away. 'I'll get a dust sheet. No point in making a mess over everything.'

Rowland picked up the flannel and began to moisten the bandage where the blood had dried and stuck. Merab gripped her underlip firmly between her teeth.

'I'll be as gentle as I can.'

'I'm all right,' said Merab shortly.

The wound, when exposed, was a long score. It had begun to bleed again in places, but, to Rowland's relief, it did not look inflamed. He washed it carefully, patted it dry and said to Mary, 'Bring the poultice over here, would you.'

'What's that for?' Merab eyed the mixture uneasily.

'Just in case there's any inflammation. It's only bread and water.'

'Hm.'

'My dad uses it on horses,' put in Mary hearteningly. 'It's ever so good, Miss Merab, honest.'

Merab started to laugh, then winced.

Rowland smeared the mixture over the wound. 'Lint,' he said. Then, 'Bandage.' He wrapped it expertly. 'Not too tight?'

'No, it feels all right. Thank you,' she added after a pause.

'Lottie,' said Rowland. 'You go with Mary and see that Miss Hartfield's bed is ready. I'll bring her up in about ten minutes.'

'Very good, sir.'

Left alone the cousins sat silent. Rowland made a few adjustments to the knot and then took hold of Merab's wrist to feel her pulse.

Merab, suddenly aware of her bare arm and shoulder, flushed. Her pulse, which had been reasonably steady under Rowland's ministrations, now began to race. Rowland looked up and their eyes met. For a long moment neither spoke. The world stopped turning. All Merab could hear was the clock ticking preternaturally loud in the silence. She noticed that his eyes, though grey, had tiny dark flecks in them and his eyelashes were long and dark. Then Rowland released her wrist and said in a voice from which all emotion had been drained, 'I daresay Lottie will have your room ready by now. I'll carry you up.'

Merab said nothing, but as they went up the stairs she could hear that his own heartbeat was quite as unsteady as her own.

* * *

Merab woke late the following morning. For a moment she couldn't remember where she was; the window was in the wrong place, the bed curtains unfamiliar, then everything flooded back. She sat up cautiously and felt her shoulder. It was stiff and sore, but otherwise seemed all right.

She allowed her thoughts to drift to Rowland. He had bandaged the wound himself, she remembered, and he had been very kind and gentle. There had been nothing of the brusque, overbearing man she had loathed on the day of that dreadful will-reading. And then last night, in the quiet of the drawing-room, there had been that moment ... But here Merab's thoughts shied away. No, she had been delirious, she had been mistaken.

She pulled herself further up the bed and looked round. There was a truckle bed in the corner with Lottie's bag next to it, so at least the situation had some semblance of propriety. Merab was well aware that this episode might easily be seen to compromise her utterly if ever it should become known. Then she shook herself. She had precious little respectability left in any case.

There was no point in thinking any more about her cousin, she decided with resolution. She must bestir herself. She must look in her mother's trunk and discover the truth. She rang the bell for Lottie.

Rowland was in the library when Merab came downstairs. She thought she noted a touch of constraint in his voice, but he asked her civilly enough how she had slept and how she was feeling.

'Better,' said Merab shortly. She then forced

herself to add with a tolerable assumption of ease, 'I must thank you for your ministrations. I doubt whether poor Lottie would have known what to do.'

Rowland waved it aside. 'I'd better have a look at it. Have you breakfasted?'

'Lottie brought me up some coffee and toast.'

Rowland rose and went to the bell. 'I'll get Mary.'

The wound, he saw, was clean and healing as it ought. This time Rowland did not deal with the wound himself, but directed Mary and watched her carefully while she washed, cleaned and rebandaged.

'There!' he said. 'Mary can look after it for you. I can see no reason why you should not be as right as rain in a week or so.'

'Thank you.' Merab smiled rather wanly at Mary and was glad to lean back for a moment in the leather armchair.

'With your permission, Cousin,' said Rowland, 'I shall go and visit Mr Camberwell this morning.'

'Of course. But, Mr Sandiford, before you go, could I ask you to organize about Mama's trunk? I should like it brought down to my old sitting-room. I need to look through it.'

'Are you sure you are up to it? You look very pale.'

'I'm sure. There are things I must know.'

Rowland looked at her intently for a

moment and then said, 'Very well.'

Some half an hour later Rowland, greatcoat on and hat in hand, came into the library where Merab was still sitting and said, 'The trunk is in the sitting-room and the fire has been lit.'

Merab opened her eyes. 'Thank you, Cousin.'

He smiled briefly and left.

The trunk was a haircord one, bound with hoops of iron and studded with brass. Merab kept the key in her jewel box and she now knelt in front of the trunk and opened it. Someone, on Rowland's orders probably, had oiled the hinges and lock, so it was not difficult to open and lift the lid.

On top were those of her mother's clothes that Merab had not been able to bring herself to throw out: an evening cloak in ruched velvet that had seen happier days, several pairs of gloves too small for Merab herself, and her mother's beaded evening reticule. These she took out reverently and laid them on the sofa. Underneath were boots and slippers, her mother's parasol, a couple of enormous old-fashioned muffs, one in a yellowing swansdown, and a somewhat crushed hat, which Merab recognized as her mother's Venetian bonnet, with its artificial flowers now sadly flattened. These too she removed.

At the bottom of the trunk were her mother's Bible and prayer book, various small boxes and a pile of papers wrapped in oilskin

167

and carefully tied with ribbon. One of the boxes, of inlaid mahogany, she knew contained her mother's papers. Carefully, she lifted it out, wincing as she did so, for she needed both hands.

It was not locked and Merab took it to the sofa and, pushing aside the muff, sat down with the box on her lap and opened it. On top was a letter from the vicar written to Merab herself on her mother's death. 'A gracious lady' he had written and it was true. Even in her last illness her mother had kept her gentle dignity. There was the certificate of death and burial. There were certificates relating to her father's death. There was a copy of Merab's own christening entry in the parish register and underneath that a folded piece of paper. Merab opened it with trembling hands.

It was her parents' marriage certificate. The wedding had taken place in St Pancras' Church on April 14th, 1789. The witnesses were Theodore Barnfather, organist and a Mrs Eliza O'Riley.

Mr Barnfather she just remembered as an old man who had died when she was about six. He would greet her parents after church on Sunday and there was always a twist of barley sugar for Merab tucked into his waistcoat pocket. Perhaps it had been he who had given her mother away?

But Eliza O'Riley? The signature was a flamboyant one, the E and R curling wildly.

168

But who was she? Merab's own second name was Eliza. Could she have been named after this Eliza? Merab knew she had been named after a beloved sister of her mother's who had died young, and she had always assumed that the sister had been Merab Eliza like herself. But was this true?

She sat for a long while in silence. The rest of the box was empty and she didn't feel like tackling anything else. She was legitimate. That surely was the most important thing? In her heart of hearts, she realized, she had never doubted it, but it was strange how malicious rumours could so undermine one. She had never thought otherwise, and yet Joseph had made her so mistrustful that she needed to see the evidence with her own eyes.

She would leave the other boxes for the moment, but the clothes must be dealt with. They must go. Most were unwearable now, but Lottie might be able to make use of something. The reticule and parasol she would keep. She rang the bell.

Lottie seemed to have recovered from her disappointment over the corporal with gratifying speed. She had enjoyed the drama of the hold-up—once it was safely over—and Jenny and Mary were an admiring audience. Now she drew in her breath at the treasures in front of her. Cast-offs were a maid's rightful perquisites and every maid knew where such things could be sold if she did not want them herself.

'Thank you, Miss Merab,' she said, her eyes sparkling. 'Oh, and it's nearly luncheon, Miss. Mr Sandiford has just returned.'

'I'll be down in a moment.'

The luncheon was somewhat meagre; some ham, some cheese, a loaf of bread and half a plum tart.

'Cousin?' Rowland indicated the ham.

'Yes, please. And a small slice of bread and cheese.'

Rowland did as he was asked and then cut up the ham and cheese for her into manageable portions. 'There,' he said as he buttered some bread soldiers and offered them, smiling.

'Thank you.' Merab smiled back. 'I haven't had these since I was a child. What's the news from Mr Camberwell?'

Rowland shrugged. 'Not much of interest, save that he considers that we should be able to make a hundred or so on the furniture. He says that it is not specified in the will and therefore is legally ours. He asked me if there was anything either of us wished to keep.'

Merab shook her head. Most of the furniture was dark and heavy and belonged to the beginning of the previous century. Even in its heyday it had never been anything other than solid country furniture. The carpets, which might once have been valuable, were worn and shabby. Anyway, where would she keep them?

170

'I suppose the silver might be worth something?' she said hopefully.

Rowland held up his fork and examined it for a moment. 'I doubt it. This is silver plate. We might get somebody to look at the books.' He then added, 'I called in on Mrs Barden on my way there. She has agreed to come and stay for a week or so and solve the vexed question of propriety.'

'Mrs Barden!' cried Merab, her eyes lighting up. 'Dear Mrs Barden. But she must be over eighty by now. Is she well enough?'

'She seemed extremely spry to me. She told me that she has a couple of noisy grandsons of about twelve and fourteen and a bit of peace and quiet wouldn't come amiss. I shall go and collect her about four o'clock.' Rowland finished his ham and offered Merab some of the plum tart. 'It looks good. Tell me, how has your morning been?'

Merab reached into her pocket and handed him a folded piece of paper.

Rowland scanned it rapidly. 'I never doubted that your parents' marriage took place. Your father would hardly have been disinherited for merely mounting a mistress! By all accounts your Uncle Edmund never lacked those.'

Merab looked up sharply, doubt in every feature. 'B ... but you said...' Merab remembered every word: *I never knew old Julian had any by-blows.*

171

Rowland chased a piece of pastry around his plate for a moment. 'I am aware,' he said slowly, 'that I owe you an apology, Cousin. I behaved extremely badly to you when we first met. The ill manners were all on my side. I have no excuses.' He spread his hands. 'Cousin Julian mentioned only once about eight years ago that you and your mother had come to live at Hartfield. I confess I scarcely believed him. I felt that you had been "invented" so that I should toe the line. Your presence here came as a most unwelcome shock and I'm afraid that I instantly jumped to all the wrong conclusions.'

'You are apologizing?' asked Merab warily.

'I am. Most sincerely.'

Merab looked down at her plate in some confusion. Rowland apologizing? Did he really mean it, or was this a ploy to get her to accept his proposal for a marriage of convenience? Convenient, at least, for him.

'Why?' She was unable to keep the suspicion out of her voice.

'Because I was wrong. And because, Merab, I can see that I must have hurt you unwarrantably to have made you so suspicious of me now.'

There was a pause. 'I must say it will be a most unusual sensation to have a relative with whom I am on normal speaking terms,' said Merab, striving for a light tone to cover her embarrassment at hearing him call her by her Christian name.

172

'The will will not be wanting on my side, I assure you.'

They divided the remaining piece of plum tart between themselves in cautious amity.

*   *   *

If Mrs Harrison heard the news of Merab's departure with undisguised glee, Joseph's reaction was very different. As a schoolboy he had enjoyed bullying smaller, weaker children and always looked forward to playtime when he could pick on one of the little ones and torment him. He liked the feeling of power when a child cringed as he came near, the profferings of sweets and marbles in propitiation and their abject gratitude when he accepted their offerings and left them alone. Of course he was glad that Merab had paid the price for her refusal of him—but the pleasure of seeing her squirm was now gone.

However, one couldn't have everything and what he now had to do was consolidate his social position. Merab, he realized with anger, had been well liked and too open a reference to her was looked on askance. He therefore cultivated a spurious sympathy.

'Ah, my poor cousin,' he sighed to Mrs Tiverton. 'It really is not her fault and one cannot blame her for wishing to keep it all hidden...'

'My mother is so upset about it,' he

173

informed Lady Mandersby.

'It does her credit, I'm sure,' replied that lady, surveying him through her lorgnette with a marked lack of enthusiasm. 'Bath society is far too lax nowadays, and one must draw the line somewhere.'

Joseph was not so pleased with this response that he wished to pursue it.

Mrs Harrison was not so sensible. She was delighted that Merab had gone and lost no opportunity of expanding on the disgraceful details of Abigail Cooper's career. A dancer in the opera chorus, champagne parties in various unsavoury nightclubs, mistress to a dozen lords, the stories grew wilder and wilder.

As Mrs Bridges remarked to her husband after meeting Mrs Harrison in the Octagon Room one evening, 'One wonders whatever will be next? A secret marriage to the Prince of Wales, perhaps?'

'At least,' replied Mr Bridges comfortably. 'You know, my dear, I don't think you should worry too much. Already people are beginning to disbelieve it. And if Miss Hartfield can at least produce a birth certificate then I see no reason why she may not be reestablished.'

'But those dreadful Harrisons will still be her cousins. If only they would go.'

* * *

Merab and Mrs Barden greeted each other

with unaffected pleasure.

'Miss Merab! Why, don't you look a picture! I always said you'd be beautiful one day, just like your sainted mother. And your poor shoulder. Villains, these highwaymen are, villains.' Mrs Barden surveyed Merab with delight. She's a real lady now, she thought. Surely this Mr Sandiford would come to his senses? The stories of his rudeness had got round and were not lost in the telling, though Mrs Barden was bound to say that he had behaved like a proper gentleman with her, making sure she had a rug to put over her knees in the carriage.

'Mrs Barden! How pleased I am to see you!' Merab stepped forward and kissed her cheek. 'How well you look.'

'Now don't you worry about a thing, Miss Merab,' said Mrs Barden when she had taken off her bonnet and cloak. 'We stopped at the butcher's on the way here and Mr Sandiford bought a nice side of beef. I shall make sure that you don't starve.'

'But Mrs Barden,' cried Merab, 'you're not to put yourself out. I'm sure my cousin explained that it's this ridiculous propriety...'

'And quite right too,' said Mrs Barden, beaming at them. 'But it'll do me good to be here, Miss Merab, don't you fret yourself. My daughter's very good to me, but she hasn't let me lift a finger and between ourselves I do get a little bored. Now, my dear, how about tea?'

'Yes, please,' said Merab, giving in. 'Cousin Rowland, will you join me? I am still in the process of going through Mama's things, but if you don't mind the mess it is at least warm up there.'

'You don't object?'

'No,' said Merab after a small hesitation.

Later, when Jenny had brought up the tea, she confessed, 'It's stupid, I know, but I'm reluctant to open these packets.' She indicated the oilskins. 'It seems like a violation of my mother's privacy.'

Rowland looked at the packets and then said carefully, 'I cannot believe that your mother was anything other than a sensible woman. She had time to destroy things had she wished to. That she chose not to must mean that you are free to see them.'

'Yes, you must be right. I hadn't thought of that. But what if ... what if ...?'

'You mean what if the obnoxious Joseph was right?' Merab could say nothing. 'Merab, there are opera dancers and opera dancers. Whilst it is true that their reputation is not high, it would be foolish to suppose that there are no virtuous girls amongst them.'

'Th ... thank you, Cousin.'

'Come then, be brave. Which shall you open first?'

'The small packet?'

'Here it is.'

'Oh!' Inside were two packets of letters. One

176

tied with a red ribbon, the other with a blue. 'My parents' writing.' Those in her father's hand were addressed to Miss A. Cooper.

Rowland smiled. 'Love letters?'

'I imagine so. I shall read them later.' For that she must be alone. 'I'll have the big packet please, Cousin.'

Rowland handed it to her.

Slowly Merab untied the string and unwrapped the oilskin. Inside were a number of playbills, programmes and opera posters. Quickly Merab scanned them. Eliza O'Riley was a name that occurred a number of times, but no Abigail Cooper.

'Thank God! My mother's name is not here!' she cried, and paused to mop her eyes. 'But this Eliza O'Riley who was at my parents' wedding, who was she?'

Rowland had been sitting in a chair to Merab's right. He now came over, sat down on the sofa beside her and took hold of her hand. 'Merab,' he said, gently, 'your mother sang under another name.'

'Another name!' Merab stared at him with large tear-filled eyes. 'H ... How do you know?'

'The egregious Joseph.'

'What ... what was it?'

Rowland pointed slowly to the playbill. 'Rosalba Bersanelli.'

The playbill was somewhat tattered. A couple of winged putti held up a swag of roses at the top and underneath was written:

The Kings Theatre, Haymarket, presents:
La Finta Principessa
by Signior Luigi Cherubini

At the bottom of the cast list under *Ladies in Waiting* was the name *Signorina Rosalba Bersanelli*. The date was April, 1784.

'Your mother must have been very young,' observed Rowland. He was still holding her hand comfortingly.

'Nineteen.'

The next poster was dated the following year and was another Cherubini opera: *Giulio Sabino*. This time her mother's name was higher up the playbill. *Elena ... Signorina Rosalba Bersanelli*.

'You know, Cousin,' said Rowland, looking at Merab with concern, 'these show that your mother was good. I mean, they only perform opera at the Kings Theatre and Covent Garden, and to get a named part at twenty years old surely says something for your mother's professionalism?'

'You are kind,' said Merab tonelessly. She stared blindly down at the two playbills, then withdrew her hand from Rowland's and stood up. 'If you'll excuse me, Cousin, I'd like to be alone.' She inclined her head briefly and left the room.

Rowland wrapped up the posters and
178

replaced them in the trunk, then, after a few moments' thought, went to the bureau where he found quills, ink and paper, sat down and wrote.

* * *

Mrs Bridges sat in her pleasant drawing-room overlooking St James's Square and looked down with a proprietorial pleasure at the copper beech in the middle of the square's garden, which was just coming into leaf. She liked being this high up; the air was clearer, and if they didn't have the spectacular views of the Royal Crescent then they didn't have the Royal Crescent's noise either. They had all the benefits of the Upper Town's amenities and few of the inconveniences.

It was, of course, a longish walk down to the Pump Room, and something of a toilsome one coming back, but the exercise kept them both healthy and they could always hire a chair if the weather was inclement. Anyway, she was convinced that the walk helped her husband's tendency to gout. At this point her reverie was broken by her maid coming in with a letter on a silver salver.

Rowland, it was from Rowland. Eagerly, she broke the seal. She scanned it twice, carefully, and then went in search of her husband.

'It's awkward,' said Mr Bridges some twenty

minutes later. 'I agree with you that Miss Hartfield's legitimacy does help, but this opera business ... I don't see how we can get round that.'

'Deny it,' said his wife roundly. 'What proof does anybody have, after all? I grant you it would be impossible if Abigail Cooper hadn't used another name, but as she did, who's to know? For Heaven's sake, it's all over thirty years ago!'

'Do you think you could convince Mrs Tiverton and Lady Mandersby?'

Mrs Bridges considered. 'Rowland is at least acknowledging Miss Hartfield as kin—though if he'd done it earlier he would have saved us all a lot of trouble—could we use that?'

'Lady Mandersby will want to know why she wasn't acknowledged earlier.'

'The will?'

'Good God, Liz, you cannot tell her about the will!'

'Not the real will, naturally. It was mislaid, some technical problem. It is only now that the truth has come to light. Mr Hartfield did acknowledge Miss Hartfield, but being a cantankerous old soul, left the estate to neither of them: it all goes to charity.'

Mr Bridges, a lawyer, could see several objections, but raised none of them. He was shrewd enough to see that Merab's rehabilitation would depend more on Lady Mandersby's whim than on hard facts. And

Lady Mandersby was decidedly tired of the Harrisons.

'But will Bath look kindly on a young lady who may be legitimate, but now has no fortune?' worried Mrs Bridges.

'She has what her father left her. There is no need to say how much that is. In any case, my dear, since I presume you want her to marry Rowland, her fortune is immaterial. If they marry then the Hartfield estate becomes theirs.'

'If,' said Mrs Bridges, gloomily. 'Rowland can be so quixotic. He falls for that silly chit, Kitty Parminster, and ignores a delightful cousin right under his nose. Sometimes I despair of him!'

'His letter at least sounds more positive.'

'Yes,' said his wife more hopefully. 'There is that.'

* * *

Merab made no reference to her mother's singing that evening, nor for several days following. She read her parents' love letters and wept over them in the quiet of her bedroom. At first, her mother had been adamant that they could not marry; she feared for her dearest Jonathan's prospects. Jonathan pleaded; he would not ask her to be his mistress, he insisted, she was worth more than that. Eventually—the letters spanned nearly a

181

year—Abigail had given in and they were married. The letters ended with a brief note in her mother's handwriting attached to the bundle from her husband.

So my dear Jonathan and I were married and now we have a sweet child. But how harshly he has paid for it and God preserve him for his goodness towards us.

It was dated the month of Merab's birth.

Was it worth it, Merab wondered? Yes, for they had been happy. Perhaps it was better that both had died quite young. They would never know the creeping poverty that might otherwise have been theirs. Merab now knew that her grandfather would never have been reconciled.

But for her mother to have been an opera singer! To have lied to her daughter. That was a different matter. Merab had heard of opera singers at school. Women who were no better than they should be, who were willing to exhibit themselves, frequently scantily clad, on the public stage! How could her mother have done such a thing? It was one thing to teach singing, or even to give a recital at a private party, but to act scenes of passion and violence for every Tom, Dick or Harry to see!

Merab took to walking in the garden. Her thoughts went round and round. Mama! Her gentle, modest mama acting on the public stage. Merab had never been to the opera herself, but she knew the librettos well. Her mother had explained the plot of *The Marriage of Figaro* and others. To sing Cherubino! To be seen in breeches! To sing Susanna and be made love to on stage! She blushed with mortification to think of the lascivious looks, the catcalls, maybe the importunities of the bucks and beaux in the dressing-room afterwards ... How could she have done it?

She couldn't eat and only pushed the food around her plate. She couldn't sleep either and lay wide-eyed and exhausted whilst Lottie snored on her truckle bed in the corner.

Finally, one evening after dinner, Rowland said, 'Merab, this cannot go on.'

'What do you mean?' Merab was defensive.

'It's your mother, isn't it?'

Merab didn't reply.

'Come up to your sitting-room. I think it's time we talked.'

Listlessly, Merab followed him.

Rowland opened the trunk which had been pushed against the wall and took out the oilskin packet and removed the various playbills and programmes and carefully spread them out on the floor in chronological order. He then led her to the sofa and made her sit down beside him.

'Look,' he said, 'you must stop thinking of your mother as some sort of whore—yes! I know I shouldn't use the word in front of a delicately nurtured female, but it's important that you understand. She was not a whore. Look here, and here,' he pointed. 'Your mother plainly worked extremely hard. Look at this!' He opened a small leather-bound book. 'This must be her work diary. "Singing lessons" it says. "Practice." "Teaching the Misses Blackstone." "Singing lessons" again.' He turned to March 1784. 'Rehearsal' was written right the way through. 'Merab, this is not the diary of a harlot. This is the diary of a young woman who is dedicated to her work.'

'But...' stammered Merab. Tears were pouring down her face and she couldn't stop them, 'It's not the singing, it's the acting. Exposing herself in public, where everybody— the most vulgar tradesman—could look at her. How could she do it?'

Rowland thought for a moment, then he said, 'I'm sure I remember you saying once that your mother believed that if she sang Mozart she was there to glorify Mozart and not herself. Am I right?'

Merab nodded. She groped for her handkerchief.

Rowland looked down at the playbills. 'I do not know Cherubini's operas,' he said, 'nor what your mother's parts entailed, but I am sure that she acted as a professional, and in order to do her best for the composer. It was not Abigail Cooper who was on stage, or even Rosalba Bersanelli, it was *Elena*. Do you see?'

Merab was silent. Suddenly she remembered at the Misses Goodison's Academy they had acted a little play. It was a moral interlude, written by the elder Miss Goodison, and Merab had been chosen as the villain because she was tall. She had worn a pair of breeches and strutted around the makeshift stage and terrified the heroine, a winsome little girl with flaxen curls known to Merab and her friends as 'Dimity Dora'.

'I ... I think so,' she said at last. She had enjoyed being the wicked Sir Rodrigo, but she had always known that it was just a part. 'Thank you. You are very kind.' There was a pause. Rowland bent down and gathered the papers together, put them back in the oilskin and placed them in the trunk.

Merab sat staring into the fire. He was right. He must be right. She didn't think she could bear it if he wasn't. And wasn't her mother everything that became a virtuous and modest lady? Had she ever seen or heard anything which suggested otherwise? Merab might not like it, and she didn't, but she would have to learn to accept it.

She became aware of Rowland sitting next to her. He acknowledged her as kin. This did not seem to have made any difference to him. She had no doubt that he was genuine. Unaccountably, her spirits rose.

There was an old spinet in the corner of the room. It had belonged to her great-grandmother and Merab had had it tuned shortly before her grandfather died. She turned to Rowland.

'I want to thank you,' she said with resolution and stood up. Rowland looked slightly alarmed. 'Don't worry,' Merab smiled. 'It's quite painless.'

There was some music in a canterbury beside the spinet. Merab leafed through it, took a branch of candles from the mantelpiece and sat down at the spinet. She was glad that her back was to him, for she felt self-conscious.

She had chosen Cherubino's aria, *Voi, che sapete che cosa a amor*, and the notes soared out pure and liquid. Rowland listened in amazement. Involuntarily, he rose to his feet and moved over to the spinet so that he could see her face.

CHAPTER EIGHT

The next few days passed quietly. Merab's wound continued to heal as it ought and the cousins kept up a wary peace. Indeed, somewhat to her surprise, Merab found herself liking Rowland. If he was occasionally acerbic, it was no longer directed towards herself. He treated her with courtesy and even warmth. He took to discussing his political aspirations with her and they found themselves in agreement on

186

wanting a wider franchise, though Merab, rather naughtily, declared that she saw no reason why this should not be extended to women as well.

In fact, she had never so much as considered such a thing before, and had initially set out simply for the fun of provoking an argument. But as she argued she began to convince herself. Was there any rational argument against it? So far as she could see there could be nothing but the weight of custom. Did she not consider herself quite as intelligent as her cousin Joseph? Or Rowland himself come to that?

'But, surely, Cousin, you do not want to be up there rubbing shoulders with the grocer? The rough and tumble of politics is not for delicately nurtured ladies.'

'If the votes were cast in private I shouldn't have to be,' countered Merab. 'In any case, what is wrong with the grocer?'

'And this from the lady who worries about the grocer seeing a female singer acting on the public stage?'

'That's different.'

'Oh, the illogical female mind. How, pray?'

Merab was nonplussed. 'Well, the singer may be being professional but the grocer watching her may be having very different thoughts,' she said at last, awkwardly. She meant something much cruder, but felt embarrassed about saying so.

'You mean her thoughts may be pure but his may be lascivious?'

Merab blushed. 'Yes.'

'So this singer is responsible for the grocer's thoughts? They are her responsibility?'

'No, of course not!' Merab paused, turning it over in her mind. Then she said, 'So you agree, Cousin, that people, whether male or female, are responsible for their own thoughts and actions? That an adult, of either sex, is a rational human being?'

'Yes.'

'Then,' said Merab triumphantly, 'why are you hesitant about women also getting the vote? If we, too, are rational human beings, then I cannot see that logically you can deny us similar rights to what you have or want for your own sex.'

Rowland began to laugh. 'Oh, Merab! Why didn't we meet before? I should so much have enjoyed arguing with you when I was up at Oxford. Tell me, did Cousin Julian ever know that you had these Radical ideas?'

'Of course not! I don't believe he ever asked me what I thought about anything. But you haven't answered my question.'

'I daren't,' said Rowland, spreading his hands in a gesture of surrender. 'You have driven me into a corner, and you know it! You are quite right, and I have no argument but prejudice.'

'Ah!' said Merab. She sat there and grinned.

She felt extraordinarily pleased with herself.

'You look like the cat that's got the cream,' said Rowland.

They both started to laugh and then Rowland said, 'It seems to have cleared up outside, would you like a walk?'

*　　*　　*

This happy accord, however, was not destined to last. The following day Mr Camberwell came while Rowland was out riding. He had obviously decided that as far as was legally possible he would see that Merab got every penny she could out of the estate. Mr Sandiford, he informed her, had renounced any claim on the books or furniture.

'That's very good of him,' said Merab. How could they so have mistaken each other that first meeting?

'He's arranging for a book-dealer from London to value and possibly buy the books.'

'He did mention it.'

Mr Camberwell looked at her over the top of his spectacles. The months in Bath had done her good, he decided. She looked well and far more attractive than he had foreseen.

'I wonder, Miss Hartfield, if you have—er—considered whether a marriage with Mr Sandiford might not suit you both? Forgive me for mentioning it, but as you know, I am loth to see the property so ill disposed of.'

'Has Mr Sandiford said anything?' Merab's colour rose.

Mr Camberwell looked down at his fingers. 'Obliquely only. I gather that he did make you an offer which you declined. I only wondered whether you might not have been a little hasty?'

Merab's blush deepened, but this time with anger rather than embarrassment. 'Mr Sandiford offered me a third of the twenty thousand, provided I kept out of his way and lived here. I declined.'

'I'm sorry.' Disgraceful, he thought. And how gratuitously rude. 'He did not make that clear to me. I apologize for mentioning it.'

After Mr Camberwell left Merab went into the garden to cool her temper. All her dislike of her cousin came flooding back. How dared he make her that insulting proposal and then add insult to injury by allowing Mr Camberwell to think that he had done the decent thing and put the blame for the refusal squarely on to her shoulders? The fact that he then allowed the sale of the books and furniture to profit her was probably due to an uneasy conscience.

Much though Merab would have liked to, she could not afford to fling it back in his face. A few hundred pounds extra would make a great deal of difference to her and very little to him. She would have liked to have challenged Rowland with it, but, of course, it was impossible. He might take it as a signal that she wanted a renewal of his offer. The very thought made her blush with mortification.

It would be wisest to hold her tongue and pretend that the conversation with Mr Camberwell had never taken place. It took her half an hour's solid tramping up and down the somewhat overgrown shrubbery to regain the tone of her mind. It did not make her like her cousin any better.

*　　*　　*

There was a small knot of gossiping ladies in Crescent Fields; Lady Mandersby, Mrs Tiverton, Mrs Bridges and Lady Wincanton. Lady Mandersby and Mrs Tiverton had met in the library in Milsom Street and were taking a short stroll before going on to the Assembly Rooms. They were discussing Mrs Harrison.

'I declare I am sick and tired of hearing about poor Abigail Cooper's iniquities,' said Mrs Tiverton. 'The stories get wilder and wilder. And I cannot help wondering why Mrs Harrison is spreading such tales about her own sister?'

'One can scarcely blame Miss Cooper for wanting to get away,' said Lady Mandersby. 'Of course, if she didn't marry Mr Hartfield that was very shocking...'

'But she did,' put in Amelia. 'As you know, Lady Mandersby, I was at school with Miss Hartfield, I cannot believe that the Misses

191

Goodison, two very strict ladies, would have taken on a pupil whose credentials they were not sure of.'

Mrs Bridges saw her opportunity. 'Miss Hartfield is legitimate,' she said firmly. 'I should know. Miss Hartfield is a cousin of my late husband.'

The small gathering was duly astonished.

'But why did you say nothing of this before, dear Elizabeth?' asked Mrs Tiverton. If she had not snubbed Miss Hartfield directly, she had certainly been cool enough.

'A difficult family circumstance, I'm afraid. Nothing to do with the Harrisons, whose existence I, for one, was unaware of. No, to do with old Mr Hartfield's will.'

'You will have to explain, Mrs Bridges,' said Lady Mandersby. She, too, was feeling slightly uneasy and like Mrs Tiverton, somewhat guilty.

Mrs Bridges, with a show of candour, gave the assembled group a brief, mendacious, rundown of the story. Merab and her mother had been living in perfect amity with Mr Hartfield. They had never heard of Rowland Sandiford, a mere third cousin of Miss Hartfield's. Rowland, for his part, had always understood that he was the heir. He had heard, of course, of Jonathan Hartfield's unfortunate marriage (the word was emphasized) but had no idea that there was a reconciliation. But old Mr Hartfield had lived up to his reputation as a difficult man. He had left the estate to neither of them. It had all gone to charity instead. 'My son was very angry,' ended Mrs Bridges. 'He felt it was Miss Hartfield's fault, which, of course, it was not, and refused to recognize her.'

There was a pause while the ladies digested this. 'So Miss Hartfield is penniless,' said Mrs Tiverton at last. She had liked Merab, and now felt sorry for her, but she wasn't sure how far she wanted an acquaintance with a penniless girl.

Amelia, who had been sitting on a bench at the edge of the group and listening with the liveliest interest, said, 'Miss Hartfield's fortune is certainly modest, but she is by no means penniless.' She exchanged a look with Mrs Bridges. Quite what that lady had in mind Amelia didn't know, but she missed Merab sorely and anything which might help to rehabilitate her was to be encouraged.

'How much did you know of this, Lady Wincanton?' asked Lady Mandersby, reassuming her role as doyenne of society.

'Most of it.' Amelia mentally crossed her fingers. 'But Miss Hartfield, naturally, felt wary of discussing her private affairs. She did not know whether her Hartfield connections wished to acknowledge her and was reluctant to appear a toady.'

This brought an approving smile from Mrs Tiverton. 'A proper modesty.'

'And one we have seen very little of from the Harrisons,' put in Mrs Bridges, dryly.

'But why are you bringing this up now, Elizabeth?' went on Mrs Tiverton, turning to her friend. 'I take it that you wish the girl to be acknowledged?'

'I think she has done nothing to deserve the Harrisons' calumnies,' said Mrs Bridges carefully. 'I do not know her very well, but now my son has come to his senses and is willing to acknowledge her, I was thinking of inviting her to stay. What do you suggest, Lady Mandersby? I shall be guided by your advice.'

This was a shrewd move and Lady Mandersby, who had been going to veto the idea, now took a more conciliatory tone. 'Certainly,' she said. 'Why not? Miss Hartfield is a very pretty-behaved young lady. Furthermore, I can see no reason why we should be forced to take our lead from Mrs Harrison of all people!'

There was a general consent and Mrs Bridges gave an inward sigh of relief.

'And the best of it is,' said Amelia quietly to Mrs Bridges as the gathering broke up, 'that it will put the Harrisons in their place.'

The two ladies exchanged a conspiratorial glance. Then Mrs Bridges said, 'Lady Wincanton, forgive me, but you do not look well. Allow me to call you a chair.'

'Thank you,' said Amelia. 'It's this worry over Merab. I feel I let her down. But indeed,

194

Mrs Bridges, I couldn't help it.' Amelia was too loyal to say that several times she had nearly quarrelled with her husband about it. Her eyes filled with tears and she looked away. 'Forgive me. It must be my condition.'

'Of course, my dear.' There was a chair rank on the Royal Crescent and Mrs Bridges raised a hand. 'A chair for Lady Wincanton, please.'

*   *   *

The Harrisons remained in their rooms in Queen's Square. Mrs Harrison was enjoying what she felt to be her enhanced consequence: Bath society now knew who she was. If she was not invited to private dinners—well, Bath was a public place and anybody wealthy enough to take out subscriptions for the various social activities was welcome to attend. She was acknowledged by all and Lady Mandersby had once even offered her hand on parting.

Joseph was not quite so content. Life was sadly flat once he had ruined Merab's reputation and she had left Bath. Kitty Parminster had gone and he really could not be expected to be more than polite to Miss Heslop who was as good as portionless. Joseph was seriously considering returning to Bristol.

One morning, however, something happened to make him change his mind. His mother had been for her usual turn in the Pump Room. Joseph had escorted her there, dutifully walking by the side of her chair, and left her drinking the waters. He had spent the morning riding on Lansdown and did not return to Queen's Square until mid-afternoon.

He was greeted by Mrs Harrison in a state of considerable agitation.

'Joseph! Thank God you've come! She's back!'

'Who's back? Miss Parminster?'

'Miss Parminster!' echoed Mrs Harrison, sinking down on one of the chairs and fanning herself agitatedly. 'No, that creature, Merab Hartfield!'

'What!' Joseph spun round.

Mrs Harrison surveyed him with a sort of gloomy satisfaction. 'I saw her in Milsom Street with Mrs Bridges. They were just coming out of the library.'

Joseph's eyes narrowed. For a moment rage made him speechless. Back! And taken up by Mrs Bridges! It was not to be borne.

'Are you sure?' he said at last.

'Do you think I don't know my own niece?'

Joseph chewed his lip and considered. His look was so dangerous that Mrs Harrison said, 'You won't do anything foolish, now, will you Joseph?'

'Foolish, no,' said Joseph curtly. 'Effective, yes.'

*　　*　　*

196

Mrs Bridges had been an exemplary mother in that whilst she sincerely loved her son she had resisted the attempt to push him in any way. Throughout his stormy adolescence she had listened to his outpourings on the iniquities of church and state, read the pamphlets he pressed on her, supported him with affection, but made it clear that she expected his championship of equality and democracy to be applied as much to the various tedious elderly ladies of their acquaintance as to the labourers on the estate. She had no patience with ill-mannered young men who preached democracy whilst seducing housemaids and being rude to their parents' friends.

The current situation, however, had her in something of a quandary. If Rowland was to reconsider his cousin's eligibility then he would have to stay in Bath. What was the use of Merab being a delightful and charming companion if Rowland were not there to appreciate her? And how could his mother see that he did so without alienating him by demanding that he stay? If she cultivated a sudden illness then Merab would be obliged to leave. It was all very awkward.

Rowland brought Merab to Bath on Thursday (dropping Lottie off at the Wincantons' on the way) and left for Merryn Park the next morning. However, to Mrs Bridges' relief he returned the following week, took a couple of rooms in Gay Street and proceeded to escort them to various lectures and concerts with gratifying regularity.

Mrs Bridges longed to ask why, but decided not to risk it. Even if she had done so it was doubtful whether Rowland could have told her: he was in that curious state of mind where he did things without allowing himself to know why he was doing them.

He'd arrived back on his estate at one of the busiest seasons of the farming year. They were in the middle of lambing and fields were being sown and crops planted. Normally he would be out from dawn to dusk, seeing what needed to be done, following progress with interest and helping where necessary.

This year, though he had gone out the day after his arrival, it did not have the same savour. He was pleased, naturally, that so many of his ewes had twinned, but his thoughts were elsewhere.

Merryn Park, too, felt different. The hall had an unused, lonely look when he came in that evening, his footsteps echoed in the quiet. Even a bottle of his father's best claret failed to raise his spirits.

Sunday was worse. Rowland went to church only to be confronted by the sight of Lord Claydon and Kitty sitting in the Parminster pew, heads bent together over the same prayer book. Whether Kitty loved Lord Claydon Rowland rather doubted. What was undeniable was that, given the opportunity, she would dart Rowland a soulful smile whilst turning to pass the collection plate or retrieve a fallen glove.

Rowland was not the only person to notice this. Mrs Heslop did. And Sir John Parminster who was sitting in the pew behind his daughter, decided that young Sandiford would be a fool to hang around while Kitty remained unmarried. Sir John himself was delighted, as any father must be, that his daughter would be a viscountess, but he'd always liked Rowland and there was no doubt that Kitty's behaviour was exasperating.

The weather had turned wet and chilly. Rowland stayed behind in church to greet some of his tenant farmers and give the Parminsters time to go. When he finally reached the church porch the rain had set in. His spirits which had been low ever since he'd left Bath sank lower and he braced himself for a cold and wet walk home.

'Mr Sandiford, how nice to see you.' It was the vicar's wife.

Rowland raised his hat. 'Mrs Heslop.' He looked around, 'Is Lavinia not here?'

'No. Mrs Banstead kindly offered to keep her. She will bring Lavinia home when she comes for the wedding. Lavinia is to be a bridesmaid.'

Rowland pulled himself together. 'I am sorry that I did not know,' he said courteously. 'I only stopped in Bath for one night on my way here, otherwise I would have asked Lavinia if she wished me to carry a letter for you.' There was a pause and then he added, 'And when is the wedding to be?'

'In June.' Mrs Heslop looked at him covertly. The relationship between them was good, but not close, and normally the rectory did not make overtures to Merryn Park. But on this occasion something in Rowland's face, a lost quality she had not seen there before, made her add, 'Mr Sandiford, won't you come home and have some luncheon with us? A cold collation only—Sunday you know—but you could give us the Bath news and wait till this horrid rain passes. I am sure my husband would be delighted to see you.'

'Why, thank you. I should be glad to.' Rowland looked surprised, but pleased.

During luncheon Rowland relaxed. The Heslops were good hosts and saw to it that their guest enjoyed himself. The talk ranged over the parish, Lavinia's enjoyment of Bath and kind enquiries after Mrs Bridges. Mrs Heslop allowed herself to hint that this must be a trying time for Rowland with the Parminster-Claydon marriage so close.

'I have received an invitation,' acknowledged Rowland. 'But I really do not want to go.'

'Go! Good Heavens no!' exclaimed Mrs Heslop. 'But why do you not return to Bath? Surely that would be best?'

'The estate...' began Rowland.

'Come now, Sandiford,' put in Mr Heslop. 'You have a good steward, I know. And ewes will lamb and plants grow whether you are there or no.'

'Go back to Bath, dear,' said Mrs Heslop in her motherly way. 'My husband is right. The estate will manage well enough without you this once.'

Rowland's face lightened. 'I'll think about it.'

Two days later he was back in Bath.

* * *

Mrs Banstead's invitation to Lavinia to extend her stay in Bath was not so delightful to that young lady as she had led her good mother to suppose. Whilst Kitty was there she had felt very much the poor relation and useful only in that she was a foil to Miss Parminster's triumphs and a sort of supernumerary maid to Mrs Banstead, to run upstairs to fetch a shawl or read to her until she fell asleep for her afternoon nap. Mrs Banstead was anxious that Kitty should make a good match under her aegis and any hopes that poor Lavinia might have she swiftly learnt were to be hidden away in her own heart.

There were disappointments too. She had allowed herself to become too interested in Major Bendick. Just to see that tall military figure with the well-clipped moustache and even white teeth had made her feel quite faint. But it had not lasted long. The major barely acknowledged her. And then Kitty, perhaps seeing her friend's interest, had maliciously repeated the gossip: 'He's wife-hunting, you know. He has it all planned. A wife with money and in due course, three sons.'

'What about love?' Lavinia asked wistfully.

'Love!' Kitty laughed. 'Love comes with the dowry.'

At first Lavinia didn't believe her. But she was a sensible girl, and as she watched him she noticed that he did indeed talk only to girls with substantial dowries. She listened too, and she couldn't help reflecting that the major (though he was still very handsome) had an annoying habit of talking down to ladies and was inclined to tell them what to think.

There were a few tears shed in the privacy of her room, but she decided that the major could not be so very special after all and was able to meet him without those tell-tale blushes to give her away. But it was an upsetting time for her and there was nobody with whom she could share it.

Things were rather easier after Kitty had left, for although Mrs Banstead was entirely self-centred, it was the sort of comfortable selfishness that likes everybody around itself to be happy. Mrs Banstead liked to see Lavinia dancing and even bought her a length or two of muslin and had them made up for her by her own mantua-maker.

When Rowland called shortly after his return to Bath, bearing a letter from her mama and two guineas from her father, Lavinia was pleased to see him. He was somebody from home, and to talk about her parents and how things were at Merryn was a real luxury. Rowland was touched. He had, of course, known Lavinia all his life, but while Kitty was staying with Mrs Banstead, he had been circumspect and hardly seen her.

Perhaps it was that he now had rather more understanding of the position of a young woman with a small dowry and few prospects, but he saw, with a new knowledge, that her situation was not ideal. During his half-hour call he noticed that twice Lavinia was sent out of the room on some small errand. He had always had a fondness for her and now took the trouble to talk to her and expressed the hope that, if she were going to the Cotillion Ball on Thursday, he might have the honour of standing up with her.

When he had gone Mrs Banstead cross-questioned Lavinia. How large was his estate? How much had he a year? Did he have any dependants? Any younger siblings who must be supported? (Such a drain on the purse.) The answers were satisfactory and Mrs Banstead was pleased.

Just the husband for Lavinia, she thought.

Not so wealthy that it would show Kitty up and no title. The income was moderate, but as Lavinia had only £2,000 it would be an excellent match for her. She would promote it. Lavinia saw, of course, where the questions were leading, but she could hardly say that until recently Rowland had hoped to marry Kitty.

One result, however, was that Merab and Lavinia became acquainted. Rowland asked his mother to introduce them during the Cotillion Ball. Lavinia had seen Merab from afar before and had admired her elegance— such style that she herself could never aspire to, she thought. But Miss Hartfield was a cousin of Rowland's? She was astonished.

'Third cousins once removed,' said Merab with a smile. 'We only met at my grandfather's funeral, so you see, I scarcely know him.'

'What is a third cousin once removed?' asked Lavinia cautiously.

'It's rather complicated,' Merab laughed. 'Cousin Rowland explained it to me, and I assure you that I understood it perfectly while he was saying it! But, of course, it's now gone completely out of my head.'

'I know what you mean,' Lavinia nodded wisely. 'One of my brothers tried to explain the principles of electricity to me, and it was just the same. But it's odd though, that you should be cousins, I mean, and not have met. And I have known him all my life.'

A sudden, unaccountable pang went through Merab.

*   *   *

Mrs Bridges watched the growing relationship between Merab and her son with a mixture of amusement and exasperation. Of her guest's emotions she was a little in doubt; Merab had cultivated a calm friendliness and it was difficult to see what else—if anything—lay underneath. Of her son's feelings she was more certain. Though he, too, had a mask of courteous amiability, she noticed that his eyes would move round the room until he found Merab before he relaxed.

If Merab sang, as she now sometimes did in the privacy of St James's Square, Rowland's eyes never left her, though if she glanced towards him he immediately looked away.

'He's in love with her,' she told her husband one morning.

'Is he, my dear?'

'You don't believe me?'

'Frankly, no. Does he send her flowers, make up to her in any way? If he does, I haven't seen it. He doesn't even invite her out to drive with him, which he might, you know, with perfect propriety.'

'It's that that's worrying me,' responded his wife. 'I was so pleased when he came back to Bath. I thought ... well, you must admit that

205

we see him every day. And he watches her all the time when he thinks nobody is looking.'

'Then why doesn't he do something?' demanded her husband reasonably.

'I don't know,' cried his wife. 'And I certainly cannot ask him.'

Merab herself was aware that Rowland was watching her, but interpreted it differently. He was anxious, she thought, that she should not be cold-shouldered by anybody. He was making up for his former behaviour by demonstrating at every possible opportunity that he accepted her as kin. She was being given the Sandiford seal of approval.

She wondered why it depressed her.

He would escort them most evenings to the Assembly Rooms for balls or concerts and seemed happy to take part in the social whirl. Whenever the Master of Ceremonies introduced him to a young lady, Rowland asked her to dance. In no time at all, it seemed, there was a bevy of eager girls, watching him from behind fluttering fans, whose eyes lit up as he approached. And none more so, Merab felt, than Lavinia Heslop.

He danced well, Merab noticed, as she sat on her gilt chair beside Amelia or Mrs Bridges, and tried not to mind that she was with the chaperones. He was tall and good-looking and moved with an easy grace, and whenever Merab saw those grey eyes shining down at some well-born and eligible damsel, she forced herself to look away.

It made her feel uncomfortable and she neither liked nor understood it. You're being stupid, she told herself. What's the matter with you? He comes and talks to you and takes you in to tea. You take a turn about the room with Major Bendick, the Tivertons are pleased to see you. Count your blessings, Merab.

It made no difference.

She remained in a curious state of agonized indecision until one Wednesday. They had all met, as usual, in the Octagon Room, and there had been a concert, followed by tea. Mr and Mrs Bridges had gone home early and Rowland promised to escort Merab back later.

At eleven o'clock the Rooms closed, cloaks were collected, chairs called for and goodbyes said. The night was pleasantly balmy and the cousins decided to walk. The moon was full and sailed out from behind a cloud just as they reached the Royal Crescent. The sky was studded with stars, with the great arc of the Milky Way throwing a spangled belt across the sky. Below them lay the city of Bath, silhouetted against the night sky.

'It's beautiful!' Merab stopped to admire it.

'Yes,' said Rowland. But he was not looking at the sky.

Merab's senses froze. The air around them seemed tangible with something unspoken. 'Whatever is that noise?' she asked at random.

'What noise?' Rowland sounded distracted.

'A sort of crunching.'

'Cows. They're still eating.'

Merab peered. Cows grazed on the grassy slopes below the Crescent and she could now see them. 'At this time of night?' She sounded scandalized and Rowland laughed.

The atmosphere lightened and all might have continued as before when suddenly, behind them, came a cry and the sound of breaking glass. They turned round to see a man running off into the night. Another man with a broken lantern was sitting dazed in the gutter. Merab and Rowland ran over.

'Are you all right?' Rowland helped the man up. This was not one of the throng from the Assembly Rooms, he saw. This was a shabby man, probably from one of the poorer areas round the canal. What was he doing up here? Bath owed its success to successful policing of the fashionable streets. A vagrant with no good reason to be here was probably up to no good. Rowland kept hold of his arm in case he took it into his head to try and accost Merab.

The man was drunk and glared at him. 'Mind your own business,' he shouted. He staggered to his feet and pushed past them, giving Merab an angry shove as he did so and lurched off.

Merab gave a cry and clutched at her arm. Rowland turned. She was quite white.

'Merab!'

'I ... it's all right. He knocked my wound,

208

that's all. I shall be all right in a moment.'

Her cloak had come off. Rowland picked it up. He pulled her gently into the darkness of a doorway and put his arms round her. For a while neither spoke. Rowland stroked her hair and made reassuring noises. Merab was content to rest her head against his shoulder. So this is what I wanted, she thought, with a sense of dreamy wonder.

'Your sweet arm,' Rowland murmured. He eased the dress off her shoulder, exposed the scar and set his lips to it.

It was not a light make-it-better kiss.

What would have happened then was given to Merab to ponder on later in the privacy of her room. There were voices behind them and Rowland gently released her. She pulled up the sleeve of her dress with unsteady fingers. Rowland put her cloak around her shoulders and offered her his arm.

They walked back to St James's Square in silence.

*　　*　　*

Joseph could not immediately hit on a suitable plan which would disgrace Merab and at the same time humiliate Rowland. He had thought back to the conversation with Rowland in the Orange Tree coffee house and realized that that gentleman must have been aware that he, too, was a cousin of Miss Hartfield's and known quite as much, if not more, about her as Joseph. The fact that Merab had now returned flaunting proof of her legitimacy seemed to Joseph, in some obscure way, to be Rowland's fault.

Joseph was furious with his mother for setting the rumours in motion, furious with Rowland for allowing him, Joseph, to carry it on, and furious with Merab for being legitimate and returning in social triumph. He tried to cover himself by saying everywhere that he was delighted things had turned out well, but on the one occasion when he had called on the Bridges in hopes of seeing Merab, he was told that 'Miss Hartfield is not at home'.

If Rowland had not been there, Joseph might have considered wooing Merab again, this time more carefully. He allowed himself a brief pleasurable fantasy of teaching Merab a sharp lesson in obedience and humility once they were married. Rowland, however, had constituted himself something of a watchdog and kept a close eye on his cousin, especially where Joseph was concerned, and Joseph did not choose to risk a public rebuff. The one point that gave him any satisfaction was that Merab appeared not to have been lying when she said that she had no fortune. He saw that, whilst she enjoyed social standing, she did not have many suitors. Sandiford seemed polite rather than interested, though Major Bendick was still attentive.

He chewed his lip and pondered. One potential avenue of revenge, he thought, might be through Merab's fondness for Lady Wincanton, who was plainly not well. Joseph ran through various possibilities. If a message came to Merab purporting to be from Lady Wincanton, would she not rush at once to her friend's assistance? What would she do? Take a chair probably. And if, whilst in that chair, somebody overpowered her with chloroform, what then?

Yes, he saw the glimmerings of an idea, but it needed more. A really clever plan would utterly humiliate Sandiford as well. Now, how might it be managed?

* * *

Major Bendick paced up and down his library lost in unaccustomed thought. His emotions were in turmoil and so unused was he to this state of affairs that all he could do was pace up and down the carpet, every now and then aiming a swipe with an imaginary sword and shouting, 'Damme!'

The worst had happened. The major had fallen in love. He had not done what any sensible man would do, find a suitable lady of birth and breeding and allow himself to express the sort of affection that her handsome dowry required. No, he had found that he could not stop thinking about Merab Hartfield. Even

211

when Mr Harrison had assured him (in confidence) that she was a penniless interloper, with a mother little better than a whore, the major found that this information had little or no effect.

He had even done the unthinkable and confided in his brother-in-law, the Reverend Clement Harcourt.

'I tell you,' he shouted, 'I find I don't care! Damme, what's the matter with me? I'm told that she's base-born and all I can do is think that she's gone!'

'Perhaps,' suggested Mr Harcourt mildly, 'you've discovered that you love somebody better than yourself?'

'What!' trumpeted the major. 'Love her! But how can I? Didn't you hear what I said? She's penniless and a bastard.'

'How else would you describe it?' asked his brother-in-law.

The major glared at him.

When Merab returned the major was thrown into a fresh quandary. All his life he had given orders and had them instantly obeyed. His batman did what he told him; his orderlies scurried at his command; at home his servants did his bidding at once, but he could not fling orders at Merab. Reluctantly he realized that this was one area where the rules were reversed and if Miss Hartfield expressed a wish, it was the major who instantly obeyed. And found that he wanted to do so.

He began to see that something hitherto unknown had entered his life and he must follow it, whether he would or no.

Mr Harcourt watched all this for some weeks and cautiously observed to his wife, 'You know, I do believe your brother is not quite the obstinate blockhead I always thought him.'

'Pshaw!' retorted his wife. 'He's a pig-headed buffoon and always will be.'

'Even buffoons sometimes fall in love,' said Mr Harcourt.

*   *   *

One of the very real pleasures of Mrs Bridges' society, Merab decided, was that both ladies could sit in the drawing-room, Merab reading and Mrs Bridges sewing and neither of them felt obliged to talk. She could be alone with her thoughts. Even if Mrs Bridges noticed that she hardly turned the pages of her book, she was never pursued with concerned enquiries. She might be as private as she wished.

Merab had need of it. She had realized the previous night that, not only had she fallen in love with Rowland, but that he, too, was not indifferent to her. But to go over those precious moments was a sort of sweet torture, for if he truly loved her, why did he not say anything? They had been back in Bath nearly two weeks now, it was well into April, and though he had been attentive she could not see that he had singled her out at all.

Looking back, Merab could see a number of little moments, strung like glowing pearls on a necklace, which she now felt to be significant: conscious silences, tender looks hastily withdrawn and, since their return, his unobtrusive care for her welfare.

But could she be wrong? Could that kiss, which she still seemed to feel burning on her arm, the way he held her so tenderly, have been a mere aberration, brought on by a spot of romantic moonlight and a minor episode with a drunk?

Merab had not been in love before—how could she have been isolated as she was?—and the wonder of the new world she inhabited where colours were brighter and emotions heightened, might not be shared by him. Perhaps men felt differently about these things? Rowland had spoken openly of her uncle Edmund's mistresses, he had seemed to know all about the world of *chères amies* from the opera or theatre.

A thought struck her. Oh God, perhaps he had felt, in spite of his protestations, that she, too, was such a woman? That he might kiss and fondle her with impunity? For a moment she went cold with horror. Dear God, let it not be so! Let Rowland not think that she was the sort of easy woman Joseph had implied her mother to be.

'Merab,' Mrs Bridges' voice broke into her thoughts.

'Yes, Mrs Bridges.' Merab drew a deep breath and closed her book.

'How about a walk down to the Pump Room? My husband should have finished his letters by now.'

It was the fashion to visit the Pump Room during the morning to see friends, drink the waters and make arrangements for the day.

'Yes, of course, Mrs Bridges.'

The Pump Room was less crowded than it had been a few weeks earlier, for it was getting near the end of the winter season and many families would be going up to London for the season there or returning to their country estates. Mr and Mrs Bridges went down to take the waters and indulge in a little pleasant gossip and Merab, feeling restless, decided to look at the arrivals book. This tome rested on a table near the window and was signed by any visitor who wanted to inform friends of their arrival or to signal to one of the two Masters of Ceremonies that they wished for a visit and were willing to take out subscriptions for the various social events.

Merab glanced at it idly. She did not expect to see any name she knew and had moved over there rather from a wish to be unobserved by the Bridges if Rowland arrived and greeted her than anything else. But what she saw written made her heart stop beating for what felt like a

215

full minute and then thump loudly. For there, with an address in Green Park Buildings, was a flamboyant signature she recognized: E. O'Riley.

CHAPTER NINE

Joseph spent several days mentally turning over the possibilities of an abduction. He became reluctantly aware that whereas such things might be commonplace—even *de rigueur*—in a Gothic novel, in the ordinary environs of a respectable English town they were less easy to arrange. Night-watchmen in Bath had an inconvenient habit of patrolling the streets and not hesitating to blow a whistle to summon help if need be. The city fathers were well aware that Bath's continued prosperity was dependent on its visitors feeling safe and the town was unobtrusively but effectively policed. It was not, Joseph suspected, easy to bribe a couple of chair-men to abduct a lady and be sure of avoiding detection. Any number of things might go wrong.

He did not at first realize that fate had thrown him a lifeline when he met Lottie one evening sauntering in the Pump Yard outside the abbey. Lottie was finding life rather dull after her return to Bath. Her corporal had left with his regiment, her fellow-servants had grown weary of her tales of the highwaymen and Lady Wincanton's state of health meant that the household was unusually quiet. Furthermore, the housekeeper, a stern Methodist, believed in Satan finding work for idle hands to do, and kept Lottie cleaning grates and polishing furniture so that she never had a spare moment. Lottie, she thought, had slipped up once in allowing the attentions of a soldier—and everybody knew what their reputations were—and she had no intention of letting the girl repeat the offence.

However, this particular evening Lottie had managed to elude her vigilance and slip out. She had taken herself to the Pump Yard and wandered about, keeping her eyes open for any young man who might be inclined to buy her a drink and give her a good time. Lottie was a pretty girl with dimples and blue eyes and she knew she looked good in her pink print dress. Why should she not have some fun while she was young?

Joseph, too, was feeling the need for the attentions of the opposite sex. He looked Lottie over with an experienced eye. She was not a prostitute, he decided. Bath had its red light district down in the old quarter by the canal; a dangerous as well as a rough area. (The city fathers never thought to police there.) No, this girl was probably a servant, perhaps a shop assistant out for an evening's entertainment.

He stopped beside her and raised his hat. Lottie, recognizing her cue, artlessly dropped a glove. Soon enough conversation had passed between them to allow Joseph to suggest and Lottie to accept his escort to Sydney Gardens, one of Bath's pleasure gardens, with all the delights of fairy lights, music, a labyrinth and various secluded walks.

Lottie was thrilled. A real gentleman was taking her and that meant she wouldn't have to pay the sixpence entrance fee. Perhaps he'd buy her a drink or two and if he asked for a kiss, well, he was a nice gentleman, and what was a kiss, after all?

Joseph allowed Lottie her fun. She had a go on the Merlin swings, got lost in the labyrinth and exclaimed at the coloured lights.

'Oh, it's ever so pretty!' she exclaimed. 'My mistress is near her time and doesn't go out now, so it's ever so dull, you can't think!'

And who was this hard-hearted mistress? Joseph put his arm round Lottie and experimentally started to nuzzle her neck.

'Lady Wincanton.' Joseph's questing fingers paused. Lottie wriggled to encourage him to continue. 'I was in the country with Miss Hartfield, her friend you know, for a week or so, and it was ever so exciting, but it's been dull since I got back.'

'Oh?' Joseph's hand wandered to the strings of her bodice. 'Tell me about it.'

When Joseph eventually escorted home a

flushed and giggling Lottie an hour or so later he knew he had the information he needed. He kissed her good-night, slipped half-a-crown into her hand and walked back to Queen's Square locked in thought.

So, the question of the Hartfield inheritance was not quite as Merab had represented it, he thought with a flash of anger. Lottie's account was somewhat incoherent, but the bones of it were clear enough. If Sandiford married Merab before the stipulated date then the estate would be theirs, if not, it went to charity. Joseph wondered what on earth Rowland was about not to secure the fortune at once. Was there some other stipulation? His lawyer's mind wove to and fro. What would happen, for example, if Merab died before the six months were up? Would Sandiford inherit outright? There was something here that required his serious investigation.

The following morning he caught the mail coach to Cirencester on his way to Hartfield.

*   *   *

Merab was not able to go and see Eliza O'Riley immediately, as she had hoped, for Mrs Bridges went down with a feverish cold and for a few days Merab was fully occupied looking after her. Mrs Bridges usually enjoyed excellent health and this sudden collapse threw the household into unaccustomed chaos and caused Mr Bridges considerable anxiety. Merab, thanking her lucky stars that at least she could organize a household, did what she could. She oversaw the servants, reassured Mr Bridges and dealt with the doctor. She made some lemon and barley water for the sufferer, cooled her forehead with eau-de-cologne and saw that she got the quiet she needed.

Rowland came every afternoon to see his mother and offered to escort Merab to the Assembly Rooms. Merab shook her head. 'I could not go gallivanting whilst Mrs Bridges is ill.'

'Then may I come here, at least? I promise I shan't get in your way.'

Merab surveyed him hopelessly. His tone was polite and concerned, but he seemed more anxious to be seen to do the right thing than to have an opportunity for a tête-à-tête with her. 'Of course you may, Cousin. This is more your home than mine.' In fact, Merab had some scruples about staying there herself and it was only Mrs Bridges saying, 'It's such a comfort to know that you are here, Merab, and can look after things,' that relieved her conscience.

That precious moment in the doorway seemed to have vanished. Rowland made no movement towards her, nothing was said even when they were alone in the drawing-room which could indicate any special feeling for her. Sometimes she fancied that she heard a note of tenderness in his voice, sometimes she thought he looked at her when he thought he was unobserved, but afterwards she always doubted it again. That evening she had believed that she was beloved. But how could it be so? She knew how attached he had been to Kitty, an attachment which had been severed with such cruelty. Was she really allowing herself to believe that he had now a similarly special feeling towards herself?

The arguments went back and forth inside her head. If he did love her, then why did he not say anything? What ought she to do? Kitty might have understood the mechanisms of flirting and the importance of a covert encouragement, but Merab was completely unversed in these things. All she knew was that for the sake of her self-respect she must hide her feelings. She must be wrong and she did not think she could bear the humiliation of having her heart open to him if he regarded her as no more than an indigent relation who would soon get a teacher's post and vanish from his life.

And yet, there were times when Rowland dropped his guard and they enjoyed something of their former intimacy. He was amused to discover that Merab had been reading *Moll Flanders*.

'You found the book at Lady Wincanton's!' he exclaimed. 'I confess I am surprised. I would have thought she would consider it most improper.'

'It was in Sir Thomas's library,' corrected Merab. 'I'm not sure Sir Thomas knew it was there. It was wedged between Cicero and Herodotus and when I opened it clouds of dust flew out.'

'I read it one summer holidays when I was home from Eton,' said Rowland. 'I remember thinking that Moll was alarmingly mannish.'

'No, why? She was a survivor, that's all. She could only live by outwitting society.'

'But surely she breaks every moral code known to man?'

'But perhaps not every one known to woman,' countered Merab.

'And they are different?'

'Sometimes society makes them so,' said Merab seriously. 'If I were a man I could take my small inheritance and engage in some trade, do something to improve my situation. The fact that I am a woman both curtails my options and condemns me for being female and poor. If I were Moll I could see how theft and living off immoral earnings might prove attractive.'

'I'm beginning to think,' said Rowland with a smile, 'that you are far more Radical than I am! At Oxford I nearly got sent down several times for writing Radical pamphlets, but in your own quiet way your ideas are far more revolutionary than mine ever were!'

'Are they?' Merab smiled in her turn. She thought of those long years with her
222

grandfather. 'I have had plenty of time to think,' she said. And then something made her add, 'I often used to wonder about you, you know. I … I mean, you were the only member of the family Grandfather ever talked about. He never mentioned my father or Uncle Edmund. It was always you and your iniquities.' She laughed. 'It made me long to meet you.' She stopped, fearing that perhaps she'd said too much.

'Did you?' Rowland's voice was tender. 'I wish I'd known. It might have avoided a lot of misunderstanding.'

'I doubt whether Grandfather had any objection to our misunderstanding each other,' said Merab dryly.

'Probably not,' agreed Rowland. 'But if only I'd known you earlier, Merab, I might not have made such a fool of myself over Kitty.'

Merab's heart began to thud. Was this an opening? 'Oh?' she managed, hopefully. But Rowland, after a moment's almost tangible silence, said no more.

In spite of these oases of warmer feeling between Roland and herself, it was an uncomfortable few days for Merab. She could only be relieved when Mrs Bridges' rapid recovery meant that her hostess was able to return to the drawing-room.

Life slowly returned to normal. Mrs Bridges was now convalescent and able to take up the household reins again. She arranged for Merab to go out for a walk with Lavinia Heslop. Lavinia was a good girl, she told Merab, and she didn't like to see her always at Mrs Banstead's beck and call. It would be a kindness to ask her for her company for a walk. 'You've been cooped up here with me for too long,' she finished. 'A walk will do you good. What about Lansdown? I don't believe you've been up there yet, and the views are spectacular.'

Lavinia accepted eagerly; she was a country girl and used to long rambles at home and she couldn't help finding Mrs Banstead's dawdling style very irksome. 'Oh, Miss Hartfield!' she exclaimed breathlessly on their first walk as they passed Lansdown Crescent and came out into open country. 'How wonderful it is up here. You don't know how cramped I've been feeling in Laura Place—though Mrs Banstead is everything that is kind,' she added conscientiously.

Merab had tried to stifle her reluctance to see Lavinia. But she, too, was delighted to be out in the fresh air and found that she could not help responding to Lavinia's youthful admiration. She tried to banish the feeling that a match between Miss Heslop and Rowland must surely be perceived as a most suitable connection by both families.

And yet, whilst Rowland figured largely in Lavinia's chatter—he had helped her learn to trot on her first pony, he had rescued her from a muddy brook when she had lost her footing and fallen in—her feelings seemed to be largely (Merab hoped) that of a grateful younger sister.

She could not help probing a little about Kitty Parminster. 'I understand that Mr Sandiford once cherished warm feelings towards your friend, Miss Parminster,' she ventured. Lavinia looked alarmed and Merab added hastily, 'Mrs Bridges mentioned it. It is not known generally, I know.'

Lavinia sighed. 'As you're family I'm sure I may speak of it. Oh, Miss Hartfield, I felt so sorry for Mr Sandiford. Even while we were here in Bath, you know, Kitty allowed his attentions—in secret, of course. She has been my friend, but I cannot think it very kind in her. Once...' She stopped.

'Once?' said Merab encouragingly, knowing she should not.

'Once I saw them kissing behind a pot of palms.'

Merab's heart gave a sudden downward lurch followed by the wildest, most unreasoning jealousy.

'It was only a day or so before Viscount Claydon proposed,' went on Lavinia. 'And when I taxed her with it she only laughed and said that Mr Sandiford must look out for himself.'

It serves me right, thought Merab. I should not have asked. Rowland's kissing her shoulder that evening suddenly assumed a different, more casual significance, and one she found it very hard to bear. She had been wrong. It had meant nothing, a mere friendly salute.

When she got back to St James's Square she found Mrs Bridges looking flushed and agitated.

'Merab!' she exclaimed. 'Thank goodness you are back.'

'Whatever is it, dear Mrs Bridges? Oh God, no bad news from the Wincantons' I hope?'

'No, nothing like that. Mrs Tiverton has been here. I fear the rumours are starting again.'

'But what about? M ... my mother?'

'No. The will.'

'The will!'

Mrs Bridges put her hand to her forehead. 'Oh my dear, it's so dreadful...' and to Merab's horror she burst into tears.

'Oh, dear madam,' Merab rushed over and put her arms about her. 'Please don't cry. Tell me what Mrs Tiverton said.'

Mrs Bridges groped for her handkerchief and it was some time before she could speak. It was briefly told: Mrs Tiverton's story was that the will, which gave the estate jointly to Merab and Rowland if they married, reverted entirely to Rowland if Merab should die before the stipulated time. And, though Mrs Tiverton pronounced the suggestion to be impossible, rumour pointed out the sinister fact that Miss Hartfield had nearly been killed by a 'highwayman'.

Merab turned pale. 'You mean that people think that Ro ... Mr Sandiford tried to kill me?'

Mrs Bridges shuddered. 'This will ruin Rowland,' she cried. 'His parliamentary hopes will be gone. Who would support the candidature of a man suspected of murder? Of course I denied it all. But how could Mrs Tiverton have heard anything at all? And such lies too.'

'Is it?' said Merab slowly. 'I, certainly, have never heard of this extra clause.'

'Merab!' Mrs Bridges sat up in horror. 'You surely do not think that Rowland would...'

'No, of course not,' said Merab impatiently. 'But all the same, I wonder if it's true, about him inheriting, I mean. And if so, how they found out. Because that means that somebody, other than ourselves, must have had access to the will!'

Merab couldn't help thinking that the best solution would be for them to marry at once. But how could she possibly suggest it? She had already refused Rowland in no uncertain terms and he had shown no inclination to repeat the offer. Once the rumour reached his ears what would he do? Merab guessed that he would have too much pride to ask for her hand in marriage simply in order to save his

227

reputation.

It must be Joseph, she thought. It bore all the hallmarks of his devious mind. If he couldn't get at the Hartfield money through marriage with herself, then he was going to set up a situation where neither Merab nor Rowland could do so either. Rowland would not propose again and he would suffer all the slurs on his character. Mrs Bridges was probably right: his future was indeed blighted, unless somebody could find a way of scotching these rumours once and for all.

But how could Joseph's complicity be proved? And how could he be exposed?

* * *

Green Park Buildings, where Mrs Eliza O'Riley had rented her rooms, was situated in the Lower Town and overlooked Kingsmead meadows and the River Avon. It was a pleasant situation, within walking distance of the Pump Room and the baths, and not too close to the centre to suffer from the inconvenience and noise inseparable from the hub of a busy and popular city. Mrs O'Riley took four rooms for herself, her maid and a young man she called her nephew.

Eliza was a well-preserved woman on the very shady side of fifty, though she admitted to being thirty-eight, and had done so for some years. Like most of the facts about her life, her age was negotiable, as indeed was the 'Mrs' of her title and her 'nephew', who also figured, when occasion demanded it, as her man of business, a colleague from the Royal Opera and, even occasionally, her footman.

Eliza had learnt very early on in her career that she must look after herself and that what the world called 'respectability' was little more than a means of keeping females like herself in subservience. She always took care to preserve, so far as was possible, the veneer of respectability: not for her the wild supper parties pursued by some of the opera chorus girls, and she picked and chose her lovers with a view, not only to the furthering of her career, but also to their discretion.

Spoilt and wealthy aristocrats she avoided, feeling that they were too concerned to flaunt their own reputations for gallantry and intrigue to care about her privacy. Instead she went for dissatisfied married men of the sober merchant class, who were eager to mount a mistress, but preferred to avoid the threat of any matrimonial fracas. They were appreciative and supportive lovers, happy to sponsor an opera if she were guaranteed a good part, and generous to her when they parted.

Such were the benefits of this system that Eliza was able to retire from the stage with the respectable income of £400 a year and enjoy the fruits of her labour. One of these was her relationship with the ebullient Tim Heard.

Tim, the illegitimate son of one of the Theatre Royal's stage carpenters, had grown up in the theatre and Eliza had first met him as a lad, spreading sawdust on the floor of the Theatre Royal to catch any drips of paraffin or candle grease. She had immediately taken to him, liking the boy's liveliness and wit and later, when he grew up, was several times obliged to him for fending off some unwanted sprig of the nobility who tried to infiltrate her dressing-room, for Tim added being a first-rate amateur boxer to his other talents.

He was one of those men who look ageless and he could have been anything between thirty and fifty. In fact, he was thirty-eight and for the last twenty years had enjoyed Eliza's favours when circumstances suited. At this particular time Tim had an excellent reason for wishing to be out of London (some slightly shady business deal) and was happy to spend a month or so with her in Bath. He metamorphosed into her nephew, escorted Eliza to the Pump Room every morning to take the waters and generally looked after her. What they got up to in the privacy of their rooms in Green Park Buildings was nobody else's business.

It was Tim, in fact, who had found a terrified Abigail Cooper hiding backstage in the carpenters' storeroom after fleeing from a lecherous admirer, and he had promptly taken her to Eliza with the words, 'Here, Liza, another fledgling for you. Half-hatched this one is.'

Eliza had taken Abby under her wing, protected her, showed her the ropes and tried to see that she wasn't molested. It was uphill work. Abby was both enchantingly pretty and had an air of fragility that brought her admirers in droves. Few of the self-satisfied sprigs of the nobility could believe that the girl was serious in her dedication to her work. Bets were laid on who would be first to storm the virgin citadel.

Whatever her talent—and Eliza admitted her voice was exceptionally pure—she was plainly unsuited to the rough and tumble of theatre life. Eliza could only be glad when Jonathan Hartfield came on to the scene.

'I love Jonathan, truly I do,' Abby had wept on more than one occasion. 'But singing is my life! I was born to sing, Eliza.'

'Maybe,' Eliza had replied. 'But this constant harassment is killing you, Abby. Look how bad your cough has become since you got caught in the rain running away from, who was it? Lord Penrith?'

'Jonathan would never let me go on singing,' said Abby.

'No,' agreed Eliza. 'Not "respectable" enough.' She made a face.

Eventually Jonathan had prevailed and Eliza escorted her friend to the altar. After that their friendship inevitably faded. Eliza was aware that Jonathan, though he was always polite when they did meet and expressed his gratitude to her for her care of his wife, preferred it that way. Abby was too loyal to go against his wishes and only allowed herself the occasional visit and a letter every few months. The last Eliza had heard from her was the Christmas after Jonathan's death. She and Merab had moved to Hartfield Hall, she wrote. Her health was very poor. Both lungs were now affected and it could only be a matter of time. Her dearest love as always.

Somehow, since she had been in Bath, Eliza found herself thinking about Abby. Perhaps it was being with so many invalids or, perhaps, she thought later, it was some intuition from her Irish ancestry, but she was not altogether surprised when her maid came in with a card bearing the name *Miss Merab Hartfield*. Eliza was sitting in her drawing-room with Tim and she passed it to him. He whistled.

'Abby's daughter?'

'I imagine so. There can hardly be two Merab Hartfields!' She nodded at the maid. 'Ask Miss Hartfield to come up.'

Tim rose to his feet. 'You'll do better on your own, my dear. I'll come back later.'

Eliza didn't reply. She was studying the card with a feeling of sudden apprehension. What did this Merab Hartfield know? God forbid that she should have to explain the details of Abby's career to some starched-up miss!

Somewhat to the surprise of both of them, they found much to like and admire. Eliza's heart was touched by her guest's resemblance to her mother with the same lustrous dark eyes, but, she decided, Merab's determination was very much her own. She admired the way the girl tackled her most unenviable problems head on.

Merab, for her part, found Eliza both sympathetic and non-censorious. For almost the first time since her mother died she felt that she was truly accepted for who she was. Eliza allowed herself to be open about her part in her mother's life and it was impossible not to read between the lines and understand that Eliza's own life must have been far from the conventional notions of the respectable. Merab found that she didn't care. Suddenly conventional notions made her impatient. What was propriety compared with goodness of heart? And that Mrs O'Riley had in abundance, she felt sure.

Such was Eliza's sympathy that Merab found herself confiding about her childhood, her father's death and the last dreadful years with her grandfather.

'You poor thing!' cried Eliza. 'I wish I had known. But I fear I could not have helped you much. Until I retired I led a very ramshackle life. It would not have done for you at all.'

'I cannot help feeling,' said Merab with some bitterness, 'that being brought up as "a

233

lady" has grave disadvantages. By the end of the summer I shall have to find myself a post as a governess at thirty pounds a year—if I'm lucky. There is no other respectable option open to me. I once suggested to my friend Lady Wincanton that I was far more suited to being a housekeeper, which certainly pays better, but she was so horrified that I never dared to pursue it!'

Eliza laughed and surveyed Merab with interest. Now why does she need a job, she wondered. She's well dressed and plainly isn't short of a penny. 'Tell me why you have to become a governess,' she said, and added, noting Merab's hesitation, 'I can assure you that I am discreet. I have had to keep many secrets in my time.'

Merab, after a moment's silence did so. She told her everything: the will, Joseph Harrison, her situation. Though she forced herself to be open about the humiliating terms of the will, she could not bring herself to mention Rowland's name.

Eliza had been receiving confidences all her life and was experienced enough to recognize at once that there was a whole area around this mysterious other cousin which her guest was omitting. But that could wait, she thought. And Tim would certainly glean any information she wanted about this cousin. As an intelligence agent Tim was second to none.

'I have met Mrs Harrison, Dinah Cooper as

234

she was then,' said Eliza when Merab fell silent. 'She came up to London to remonstrate with your mother. Between you and me she was jealous. She thought that Abby was living an easy, luxurious life—at least, that's how she saw it—and didn't see why she shouldn't share it.' Certainly she had had her eye on some of Abby's admirers.

'I confess I am amazed,' said Merab. 'She is a very rigid, puritanical woman now.'

There was more, Eliza recalled. Dinah Cooper had become briefly involved with Sir Walter Tulloch, a vicious-minded fop who was pursuing Abby. Quite what had happened Eliza wasn't sure, but the affair, if affair it was, had been brief and not long afterwards Dinah left London in a storm of recrimination which had left poor Abby prostrated. Now, it seemed, Dinah had reappeared with the same envious disposition and a son who sounded all too like her.

'All this about Joseph Harrison sounds most unpleasant,' said Eliza. 'I think I shall put out a few enquiries of my own. Oh, don't be alarmed, nobody shall hear of them. But I have access to people and information . . .' She would say no more.

'Thank you for seeing me, ma'am,' said Merab, when she rose to go. 'It has been a great comfort talking to you. I have missed not being able to talk about Mama with anybody who knew her.'

'You must come and see me again,' said Eliza. 'But it would not do to acknowledge me in public, my dear. So we shall keep our acquaintance private, if you please.'

'I would like to acknowledge you in public,' said Merab wistfully. She was no fool; she realized that Eliza's past probably held a number of incidents about which it was better not to enquire too closely and that, for the sake of her own equivocal reputation, a theatrical acquaintance of her mother's was probably best 'forgotten'. But she liked Eliza and found her openness refreshing and her lack of hypocrisy admirable.

'Better not,' said Eliza briskly. 'Later perhaps.'

And with that Merab had to be content.

*   *   *

Babette was brushing out Amelia's hair one evening prior to her going to bed. There was a pile of curl papers to hand and Amelia's nightcap sat waiting on its stand. They were discussing the rumours about Rowland and Merab.

'So dreadfully worrying for them all,' finished Amelia. 'I confess I hardly slept last night since Lady Mandersby told me. Of course, nobody professes to believe them, and I certainly told Lady M. that there was not a word of truth in them, but it does make poor

236

Merab look as though scandal pursues her. Where on earth can these stories have come from?'

Babette picked up a curl paper, twisted it round a small lock of hair and neatly tied it, before answering. 'I wonder, *miladi*, have you thought to question Lottie?'

'Lottie?'

'She was the only other person who was there. And she's right off her food, *miladi*. Just nibbles at it.'

'But why would she spread such a rumour? She was delighted with the clothes Miss Hartfield gave her. Why should she wish to make things difficult for her?'

Babette shrugged. The ways of the English were frequently incomprehensible to her.

'You'd better call her, Babette,' said Amelia, when her maid had finished. 'I'll see her in my boudoir.'

When Lottie arrived, her hands twisting nervously in her apron, it was plain that she knew something. It took a long time for Amelia to coax the story out of her, but eventually, out it all came: the stolen meeting with her admirer, Sydney Gardens, everything.

'I didn't mean it, mum,' cried Lottie abandoning herself to tears. 'I wouldn't hurt Miss Merab for the world.'

Amelia was drumming her fingers on the table, trying to ignore a persistent ache in her back, and to think coherently. 'Who was this man?' she asked at last.

Lottie didn't know. He hadn't given his name. The description could have been of anybody. There were any number of tall, dark men in Bath—most of whom would, doubtless, be happy to trifle with a pretty servant.

'But I did notice he had a handsome pocket watch, mum, with his initials. I.H. or J.H. I think they was.'

Amelia sat up suddenly. J.H. Oh, my God! she thought. It must be Joseph Harrison.

She got up swiftly. 'My writing things, quickly!' she cried. 'No! I'll get them.' She got up, took a step and a sudden agonizing pang made her double up. She fell heavily.

Lottie's shrieks rang through the house.

* * *

Lavinia decided that she had learnt a lot since coming to Bath. Before, she had known nothing of the world and had only glimpsed society reflected through Kitty's eyes. Kitty's account of her first London season, with all the delights of beaux and billets-doux had seemed to Lavinia like a fairy-tale. How wonderful, she had thought then, to be beautiful and sought-after like Kitty, to have romantic meetings by moonlight, to dispense dances to adoring swains and have eager drapers' assistants spread out rainbow silks and muslins for you to choose from.

She had believed every word and naïvely taken Kitty's triumphs at Kitty's own valuation.

Reality, she saw, was rather different. She had no doubt that in Kitty's eyes her stay in Bath was another such triumph—had she not hooked a viscount? But Lavinia now suspected that there were many sensible men who were not taken in by Kitty and who had not taken her very seriously: Major Bendick for one.

And here was another puzzle. Since becoming acquainted with Merab Lavinia had got to know the major rather better. When she had first seen him she had given him all the virtues. Then she had discovered that he had feet of clay and begun to find his conversation somewhat tedious. Now, to her surprise, she discovered that she was changing her mind yet again. Or was it that something was happening to the major? On more than one occasion while she was walking on Lansdown with Miss Hartfield they had met him and he had turned round and accompanied them. His arrogance appeared to have softened. He no longer lectured them on what to think, nor indeed, told them how ladies thought, instead he seemed to want to know what they *did* think—in particular what Miss Hartfield's opinion was.

Could he be in love with her new friend? The more she watched him the more she became convinced that he was—and was pleased with

herself for this small step in understanding—
and still more pleased that her old unthinking
hero-worship had vanished.

It was the major who enlightened Lavinia as
to the rumours when he met her one morning
in the Pump Room.

'You mean that Mr Sandiford tried to have
Miss Hartfield murdered?' she cried.

'I fear so.'

'But that's preposterous!'

'It is right that a young lady like you should
be ignorant of the ways of this wicked world,'
said the major portentously.

'Nonsense, Major,' said Lavinia roundly. 'I
have known Mr Sandiford all my life. His
estate is part of my father's parish!'

The major was somewhat taken aback. He
had not thought very much about Rowland's
background, only that the damned fellow
seemed to be far too well acquainted with Miss
Hartfield for a cousin who professed barely to
know her. 'Of course,' he found himself saying,
'it is only a rumour.'

'Then you have no business to be spreading
it,' Lavinia told him crisply. 'Excuse me, I see
Mrs Banstead beckoning.' She gave him the
briefest of curtseys and left. It wasn't until
afterwards that she realized that she had
snubbed him—and didn't care.

The major looked after her with a dawning
respect.

While Mrs Banstead gently snored during
her afternoon nap, Lavinia spent a most

uncomfortable afternoon thinking about the major's information. She sat, embroidery idle in her lap, gazing out of the window and trying to think what she should do.

She did not want to be guilty of spreading rumours herself, and she realized that she had little opinion of Mrs Banstead's judgement and would not confide in her. But if Rowland did not know of it, she felt that he must be told. Mrs Bridges was not recovered enough to talk to and Lavinia did not think she knew Merab well enough to mention the subject—in any case, Miss Hartfield could hardly be expected to confront her own cousin with his supposed murderous intentions. But Rowland must be told of them, and soon, that much was clear.

Mrs Banstead was still asleep. Lavinia tip-toed over to the bureau and sat down to write. After ruining a perfectly good quill by chewing it, and several pieces of paper lay screwed up in the waste-paper basket, she managed eventually to produce a note. It was unsatisfactorily bald, she felt, and would certainly not pass the correct rules for ladies' letter-writing inculcated by her governess. But it would have to do.

The highwayman's attack is seen as being at your instigacion, she ended. *I am telling you this so thatt you may be on your Guard. Some Villain means you harm.*
Your sincere freind,
L. Heslop

241

She folded the letter, sealed and addressed it. She looked once more at Mrs Banstead. She would have to risk it, she decided. She dared not ask the footman to deliver it—young ladies did not normally write to young men—and he might easily inform Mrs Banstead. No, she would have to take it herself.

'Are you going out, miss?' asked the butler in surprise when a bonneted and coated Lavinia left the house some minutes later.

'I need some embroidery silks,' said Lavinia, glibly. 'I hope to be back before Mrs Banstead wakes.'

Rowland read the letter in growing anger. Lavinia's spelling was erratic but the message was clear and Rowland had no difficulty at all in pinpointing the villain. It must be Joseph.

As he paced up and down his room he began to consider fully, for the first time, the Hartfield will as it affected Merab. Initially, he had seen the will only as being damaging to himself and his hopes. Now, he saw very clearly that it could ruin Merab too. She would be the butt of every coarse wit. It was a will that used her as a bargaining point, and worse, he saw that his own behaviour in not initially acknowledging her could make her the subject of cruel jibes that she had been found unworthy of his proposal. And what could she say? If she said, truthfully, that she had refused him, she would not be believed.

That proposal had been shameful, he realised. How could he have even considered offering her so unequal a proposition, as if she had nothing of any value to offer a man? Rowland was bitterly ashamed. How blind he had been, how arrogant! And the worst of it was that he had destroyed any chances of making amends.

Rowland was not unmindful of his own position, either. This rumour would ruin any chance he might have had of one day being chosen as a parliamentary candidate. Joseph had effectively destroyed any hopes he might have harboured of a political career and put him in an impossible position with regard to Merab. Even if she liked him well enough, if she listened to his proposals, how could she consent to marry a man in order to save his political career? How could she possibly believe in his disinterested affection?

And worst of all, how far was Joseph prepared to go? Would he contrive another 'accident'? Rowland stopped his pacing and stared in horror at the thought which now struck him and made a cold trickle of fear run down his spine.

Was Merab's life in danger?

CHAPTER TEN

Major Bendick surveyed his reflection in the cheval glass in his dressing-room with less than his usual complacency. He no longer saw the tall, trim figure or the fine military moustache, instead he worried about his receding hair-line and the increase of crow's feet round his eyes. Would Miss Hartfield have him? He knew from a worldly point of view it was a match far beyond her claims, but he had been forced to learn that, desirable though his financial position was, it did not necessarily mean that a woman worthy of being loved would find him automatically acceptable.

He consulted his brother-in-law who had said, with what the major thought was a callous lack of feeling, 'Well, why don't you ask her?' The major did not like to voice his chief fear that proposing would mean that if she refused him all hope would be at an end. 'I shouldn't think she'd refuse,' went on Mr Harcourt, accurately interpreting the major's expression. 'After all, she's in an awkward position isn't she? If these rumours are true then she has no money and is at the mercy of a ruthless cousin. Not that I believe that last bit myself. Too far-fetched, if you ask me.'

'But the highwaymen!'

'Pooh!' returned Mr Harcourt. 'I was

assaulted by a footpad while I was courting your sister—you must remember my telling you about it. Am I to think that you set it up?'

'So you think I should risk it?' said the major, worriedly.

So here he was, standing in front of the glass, getting ready for the momentous occasion. He had prepared the ground with his usual military efficiency. The major liked to observe the proprieties and on this occasion he had consulted Mr Bridges as Miss Hartfield's most suitable male relative. (He was certainly not going to seek Sandiford's permission!) Mr Bridges had promised that Merab would be alone the following morning if he cared to call.

'Miss Hartfield is of age,' he finished. 'Neither Mrs Bridges nor I have any rights over her. The decision will be hers alone.' Mr Bridges had little faith in his wife's hopes of a match between Merab and Rowland and considered that the major, for all his pedantry, would be an excellent match for Miss Hartfield. It would also remove all possible speculation about the poor girl's future and give her an unimpeachable respectability.

When Mr Bridges mentioned the next morning that he was following the doctor's advice and had hired a pony trap to take his wife out for a little ride, Merab at once tactfully decided that she would stay at home—as Mr Bridges had known she would. Traps were not built for three, she said, and Mrs Bridges would be more comfortable without her.

She did not realize that anything was in the offing and when the butler announced Major Bendick she was taken by surprise.

'Good heavens! Major Bendick!' she exclaimed. 'Mr Bridges has just taken Mrs Bridges out for a drive. They will be so sorry to have missed you.'

The major, who had forgotten to hand his hat to the footman, now hastily took it off and began earnestly to examine the brim. 'Mr Bridges didn't mention my visit?'

'Why no.' All at once Merab realized why he had come. In considerable agitation she rose and went to the window. If only she could save him the humiliation of a refusal. If there were some way she could indicate her feelings without hurting him. 'Oh dear, how very awkward,' she murmured.

The major now came forward. He knew by the very pose she took, turned away from him, what the answer would be, and like the soldier he was he set his shoulders and met his fate.

'It's no good, is it?' he said. 'You won't have me.'

Merab turned. 'I am so very sorry,' she said. There was something about his straightforwardness, the lack of his usual bluster, that made her like him almost for the first time. 'I am deeply honoured, but it is not possible.'

The major bowed and expressed his regret.

He then left his compliments ... Mr and Mrs Bridges and went. The whole episode had taken perhaps three minutes. Merab sank down on the sofa hurriedly, hardly knowing whether to laugh or weep. Was she mad to turn him down? He was not Rowland, but he was a kind man, if a little rigid. He could offer her all the comforts of an elegant home. She would not have to be a governess. She would probably become fond of him.

But to go into a loveless marriage! One, moreover, where she knew they did not have a thought in common. No, she must be right to refuse. Teaching might be akin to drudgery, but at least it was independence. She could think what she liked without running the risk of offending the major's notions of feminine decorum.

In the end, though, Merab did cry. Major Bendick had had the courage to ignore her dubious reputation and offer her a proper marriage. It was a bitter contrast with Rowland who had offered her only its travesty. Merab realized that she was hoping against hope that Rowland would yet offer her what her heart wanted. But they were already halfway through May. There were only three weeks left before the six months since her grandfather's death was up.

She forced herself to face it: in spite of the fact that Kitty was officially engaged to Lord Claydon, that Rowland now acknowledged herself as his cousin, discussed his future with her, appeared to enjoy her company, he still did not want her as his wife. Even the thought of £20,000 did not tempt him.

Major Bendick's proposal only showed up her true position. Even with their new understanding, with the certainty of enough money to enable him to go into Parliament, Rowland did not think that what Merab had to offer was worthy of consideration. Merab's large dark eyes filled with tears and the world blurred over.

* * *

Contrary to Merab's expectations the major did not shun her company, instead he seemed to have constituted himself her guardian. Whenever she and Lavinia went for a walk, as they now did several evenings a week, they could be sure to meet the major, walking or riding up on Lansdown, and there would be a show of surprise and he would then join them.

The week wore on and it was late May. The trees had finally come out and the copper beech in the square had turned from the fresh green leaves to the beautiful burgundy of its summer foliage. This evening Lavinia had arrived while Merab was still upstairs changing into her walking boots and she was happy to chat to Mrs Bridges in the drawing-room.

'I expect we shall meet the major,' Lavinia

said resignedly, 'we usually do.'

'Do you?' Mrs Bridges knew from her husband that the major must have proposed and been refused, though Merab had preserved a strict silence on the subject.

'Oh yes. But nowadays he seems rather downcast. He doesn't say much, which is a relief, but he had this sad look,' went on Lavinia, who to her surprise had begun to feel sorry for the major.

'Perhaps he has had a disappointment,' said Mrs Bridges tactfully.

'I think he must have done.' Suddenly, things fell into place. So this was what it was to be grown-up, thought Lavinia. Mrs Bridges is telling me that the major has proposed to Miss Hartfield and been refused—but nothing is actually said. The idea that one could convey information obliquely was a revelation. She gave Mrs Bridges a brilliant smile and said, 'I do like my walks with Merab—she says I may call her that—she's such a nice person, isn't she?'

'Yes, she is a dear girl.' Mrs Bridges sighed, for time was ticking on and Rowland, it seemed, had set his face against his cousin. And yet, Mrs Bridges could not rid herself of the notion that he felt far more deeply involved with her than he would have anyone believe. The softening in his eyes when he saw her, the visits he paid every day. Mrs Bridges had a good relationship with her son, but she could

249

not believe that the visits would be quite so assiduous if it were only his mother to be visited!

'You know,' said Merab, when the girls set off some ten minutes later. 'We are really creatures of custom, you and I. Every time we go up past the chapel, go behind Lansdown Place and come back by Mount Beacon. Wouldn't you like to try a different route some time? We've never been over to Beechen Cliff, for example.'

'I know,' admitted Lavinia. 'But I like it up here. Besides, I can look at the shops in Milsom Street on the way. When I am with Mrs Banstead she never seems to want to look at the same things and, of course, I must do as she wishes as I am her guest.'

'We might go as far as Charlcombe, what do you think, Lavinia?'

'Oh yes. I hear it's such a dear little village.'

They had by now reached Beacon Hill and turned back to look at Bath. It was about six o'clock and the sun was just beginning to dip towards the western horizon and cast a golden light on the Bath stone of the city. It would be several hours yet before it was dark, but the heat of the day was going.

It was easy walking, the sheep-bitten turf was close-cropped and there were a number of trees to give shade. They were just approaching the Gloucester road when suddenly there was a shout, 'That's her', and two masked men leapt out from behind some bushes. Lavinia screamed and Merab hit out with her parasol, but they were swiftly overpowered. They were grabbed and handkerchiefs stuffed into their mouths.

The man who'd seized Merab hissed, 'Quiet now, and you'll come to no harm.' But Merab continued to struggle. She kicked hard with the heel on her boot. The man cursed, put his hand round her throat and squeezed. So this is it, was Merab's last coherent thought as the world turned red and she began to slide into darkness.

Lavinia had managed to get the handkerchief away from her mouth and screamed again.

'Dang ye,' cried her captor. 'Squeal, would you?' He hit her.

There was a sound of horse's hooves, a whinny and both girls were abruptly released. The major had been riding, keeping a weather eye out for Merab and had heard Lavinia's cries. The odds were two to one, but neither of his opponents were in a mood to fight. A couple of heavy punches from the major's punishing right, a kick or two and it was all over. The men picked themselves up and fled.

Merab fell back against a tree, one hand to her throat and gasped for breath. Lavinia, ignoring a rising bump on her head, was jumping up and down with rage. 'How dare they?' she shouted, waving her parasol dangerously near the major's eye. 'Cowards!'

'Miss Hartfield!' cried the major. 'Are you all right?'

Merab couldn't speak, but she nodded.

'I'll go and get help.'

'No!' It came out as a whisper. 'You must not!'

'But...' the major spluttered. 'To be attacked in broad daylight!'

Lavinia looked at Merab. They had not discussed the rumours, but Lavinia, like Merab, did not believe in Rowland's guilt. If this got out all hopes of scotching the rumour would be over. 'I believe that Miss Hartfield would prefer that this episode did not become known,' she said. Merab managed to nod.

'Nonsense, Miss Heslop.' The major felt it time to assert his male authority.

'No, Major,' whispered Merab, her hand on his sleeve. 'This has nothing to do with Mr Sandiford.'

'I suppose he has told you so,' said the major sarcastically.

'You know nothing about it,' whispered Merab. She leant back against the tree and closed her eyes. She dropped her other hand and they were both horrified to see a livid bruise round her throat.

'Major Bendick,' said Lavinia, eyeing Merab with concern. 'Please consider for a moment. Would Mr Sandiford really seek to harm his own cousin, one, moreover, who is his mother's guest? Miss Hartfield has already been the subject of several unpleasant rumours—which turned out to be completely unfounded—why should the new rumours be any more truthful?'

The major was silent. He could hardly say that his own murderous thoughts towards Rowland made him believe any ill of that young man.

'I think we should get Miss Hartfield home,' said Lavinia, sensibly. 'Are you able to walk, Merab?'

*　　*　　*

For a few days after her collapse there were the gravest fears for Amelia's recovery. She had gone into labour almost immediately, but it was nearly forty-eight hours before the baby, a minute scrap who hardly had the energy to whimper, let alone cry, was born. It scarcely seemed possible that the little creature, a girl, could survive. A wet nurse was found and a christening hastily arranged. The baby was named after her mother.

Merab called every day but there was always the same answer, 'Thank you for your kind enquiry, but Lady Wincanton is too ill for visitors.' Merab left her flowers and went away heavy-hearted and hurt. She couldn't believe that it would not comfort Amelia to see her and felt that she was no longer welcome there.

253

Sir Thomas, from his wife's bedroom window, watched her go.

'I should so much like to see Merab,' whispered Amelia.

'No, my dear. You are not well enough,' said her husband firmly. It was time, he thought, that this ill-judged friendship with Miss Hartfield ceased. There had been nothing but trouble ever since she had come. Sir Thomas acknowledged that it was not Merab's fault, but all the same, he told himself, Amelia's dangerous situation must, in part at least, be laid at Miss Hartfield's door. His wife's two other pregnancies had not been like this; this near catastrophe could be put down to his wife's concern over her friend. And now he had a sickly daughter who was not likely to live.

Amelia fretted dreadfully and bemoaned her uselessness. 'If he would but let me see her!' she said to Babette. 'I know Sir Thomas only wants my good, but oh! the relief if only I could see Merab for a few minutes.'

'I could ask Miss Hartfield to call when Sir Thomas is not here,' said Babette doubtfully.

Amelia shook her head. 'One of the servants would be sure to mention it, and I wouldn't put Merab in an awkward position for the world.'

'Would you like me to give a message, *miladi*? I shall tell her it is this Mr Harrison who is the problem, no?'

Amelia's eyes filled with tears. 'Oh, Babette, would you? It would relieve my mind so much

254

if I knew that she knew.'

Merab was sitting by herself in the drawing-room in St James's Square when Babette called. She was stretched elegantly along the day-bed, with a cushion behind her head and a silk scarf wound around her neck to hide the bruises.

She listened eagerly to Babette's account, but seemed much more concerned about Amelia's state of health than Mr Harrison's perfidy. 'Thank God she is getting better,' she cried. 'She *is* getting better, isn't she, Babette?'

'Indeed, mademoiselle. This morning she sat up and had some chocolate.' Babette was pleased that Merab's first concern was with her mistress. 'She has been very distressed at not being allowed to see you.'

'I cannot blame Sir Thomas,' said Merab with a sigh. 'It must seem as if I bring disasters with me.'

Babette sniffed. She had no opinion of Sir Thomas's fads.

'So it was Mr Harrison,' said Merab next. 'I own I am not surprised.' She must tell Eliza, was her first thought. She didn't know why, but she felt sure that Eliza was important in all this. 'And the baby, Babette. How is she doing?'

'She lives,' said Babette shortly. 'But such a wizened little thing, mademoiselle, she hardly looks human.'

'Poor little mite.'

'She is a fighter, her nurse says. Perhaps she

255

will survive.'

'I hope so. Amelia always wanted a daughter.'

When Babette left she took a hastily written letter to Amelia with her and promised to drop in a brief note to a Mrs O'Riley in Green Park Buildings on the way.

'I do miss Amelia,' sighed Merab. 'She is the one person I can talk to who I feel understands. I am very fond of Mrs Bridges, but the situation is so awkward there.' She made a hopeless gesture.

Babette tucked the letters into her pocket. '*Miladi* is getting better all the time,' she assured Merab. 'Soon, I think, she will take the waters and then you may meet her again.'

'My best love, Babette.'

It was about an hour later that the butler came in with a card on a salver.

'A certain male person is wishful to see you, Miss Hartfield,' he said. It was obvious from his tone that he did not approve of the visitor.

Merab took the card. *Mrs E O'Riley* read the legend. And on the back: *To introduce Mr Tim Heard who will escort you here*. Merab got up, throat forgotten. 'Tell Mr Heard I shall be down in a few minutes.'

She had dropped the note to Eliza begging for a moment of her time on a matter of urgency and Eliza had not failed her. Merab flung on her old pelisse, changed her shoes and went down to the hall.

She saw at once why the butler disapproved. Mr Heard, in his loud neckcloth, was plainly no gentleman, but on the other hand he looked as though he could protect her if necessary from any number of footpads. He was a stocky man with considerable breadth of shoulder, short rather grizzled hair and a nose that had once been broken. But as he bent over her hand Merab noticed that his eyes crinkled when he smiled and that, in spite of a couple of chipped teeth, he had the look of a man who could be trusted.

'How very kind of you to escort me, Mr Heard,' she said.

'And I'll bring you back safe and sound, never you fear,' he replied. He twitched one bushy eyebrow at the butler who did not deign to notice and they left the house.

Merab had taken the precaution of wearing her old shabby pelisse and a bonnet with a veil, for this was not an excursion where she wished to be recognized. She was pleased to see that Mr Heard had similar views, for he led her down the western side of Crescent Fields and cut across the Bristol Road.

Mr Heard was perfectly capable of switching on the charm with any number of females and by the time he had told Merab that he had known her mother and related a number of little incidents in which she had figured, Merab had relaxed.

Eliza greeted her with unaffected pleasure.

'Sit down, my dear. You don't mind Mr Heard being here, do you? He has been the greatest help.' The question was plainly rhetorical.

Merab murmured something polite. She had come here for help, she reminded herself. And Mr Heard looked as though he could keep his own counsel. She took off her pelisse and bonnet and in doing so her scarf came unwound. Eliza's look of horror was such that Merab felt obliged to explain. 'It looks dreadful, I know,' she finished, 'but I assure you that it's less painful than it was. Mrs Bridges has smothered it with arnica!'

'Mr Heard has been doing some investigation into Mr Harrison,' said Eliza. 'He has come up with something which I believe we can use. You remember my telling you about Dinah's visit to London?'

'Yes, ma'am.'

'She had an affair with Sir Walter Tulloch—one of the men after your mother. Of course, he was up to no good, but Dinah seems to have believed he meant to marry her.'

Merab stared. It was difficult to picture stout, prudish Aunt Dinah indulging in an affair of illicit passion.

'She went home when Sir Walter terminated the affair and almost immediately married Eli Harrison: on July 3, 1793 to be precise. In February 1794 your cousin Joseph was born.'

'Good God!' The Misses Goodison's arithmetic teaching might have been

258

elementary, but Merab was well able to work out the significance of this.

'Quite. But the original entry in the church register has been tampered with and Joseph's birth has been re-entered for May of that year.'

For a moment Merab could hardly make sense of it all. But then a thought occurred to her. Aunt Dinah knew very well that there was shame and illegitimacy in the family, but by a sort of displacement had tried to make it Merab's. She said as much to Eliza.

'You are very astute, my dear,' said Eliza, pleased that her guest was not succumbing to a ladylike fit of the vapours.

'What a risk, though,' continued Merab thoughtfully. 'Surely Aunt Dinah would have done better to have kept silence. Any exposure of the truth could only damage herself and Joseph. I wonder if he knows?'

'I don't believe that holding her tongue was ever Dinah's strong point,' said Eliza. 'Though I doubt whether she has told Joseph the truth.'

'But it doesn't explain Joseph's own animosity,' objected Merab.

'Harrison is jealous of what he sees as your undeserved social success, Miss Hartfield,' put in Tim Heard. 'He is an astute lawyer and doing well, but he has been refused by several young ladies of the rank to which he aspires and it—well—it rankled.' He grinned. 'I gather he was also refused by your fair self.'

Merab flushed. 'You are very well informed,

Mr Heard,' she managed to say.

Tim bowed.

'You will have to put up with that, my dear,' said Eliza. 'There is nothing Tim cannot find out.'

Merab gave a shaky smile. There was plainly no point in being affronted. 'Well, yes, he did propose,' she admitted. 'He was after my connections.'

'He does not seem to have taken his refusal well,' commented Eliza. 'But the one thing Tim has not been able to find out—yet—is how Joseph came by knowledge of the will.'

'I can tell you that,' said Merab, and she explained what she had learnt from Babette about Lottie.

Eliza looked at Tim and nodded. He rose to his feet. 'I have a little business, Miss Hartfield,' he said. 'I'll be back in about an hour to take you home.' He left the room.

'Merab,' said Eliza when he had gone. 'You will allow me to call you Merab, I hope? You will have to trust me if we are going to unravel this successfully.'

'But I do!' said Merab in surprise.

'Not quite, my dear. For there is also, I believe, another gentleman in the case.'

Merab studied the carpet.

Eliza eyed her tolerantly. 'Merab, when a young lady will do anything rather than mention a certain name you may be sure that it is the one name that is close to her heart.'

To her horror Merab felt her eyes fill with tears.

'You must tell me about this Rowland Sandiford, for you love him very much, do you not?'

'Yes,' Merab gulped. Gradually, amid a few sniffles and a dabbing of her eyes, Merab told Eliza all. And it was a sweet relief to do so. 'I never meant to love him,' she finished. 'But somehow I feel we are akin. I enjoy talking to him, I find him interesting. I would like to be part of his life and I share his aspirations.'

'I hope there are other, more improper desires!' said Eliza quizzically.

Merab turned pink. Somehow she thought Eliza would not be shocked at feelings about which she herself had hardly dared to think. 'I only have to look at him...' She could say no more. 'But I cannot see that there is any hope,' she finished. 'Sometimes I think he cares about me, but if so, why does he not propose again? If we married that would finish all the rumours and restore his good name. No, I fear that he doesn't care for me enough or else, in spite of his kindness, he still thinks underneath that I am an adventuress.'

'Interesting,' commented Eliza. 'A Radical in politics. I suspect your young man is being quixotic.'

'Quixotic?' Merab sat up and looked more hopeful.

'Well, idealistic, if you like. He accepts that

261

he insulted you deeply before and does not want you to think that he only wants you for the inheritance. I wouldn't be surprised if he proposed the day after the six months were up.'

Merab rapidly surveyed what she knew of her cousin. 'It's possible,' she admitted. 'But how idiotic! How stupid!'

'Men can be very obstinate sometimes where their honour is concerned,' said Eliza with a smile.

'But what can I do?' cried Merab in despair. 'I cannot force him to propose after all.'

'I can think of one thing you might do...' said Eliza slowly.

*   *   *

Rowland's rooms in Gay Street were the usual two-room accommodation Bath offered a single gentleman. There was a bedroom with a modern tent bed and a sitting-room with a couple of armchairs, a writing desk and a pembroke table by the window. Above the marble mantelpiece was a gilt-framed mirror into which Rowland had stuck various invitations, and a couple of not-very-interesting sporting prints hung either side.

Rowland was sitting on one of the armchairs with his head in his hands. Over the last couple of weeks he had felt pilloried. Whenever he escorted Merab to the Pump Room or sat by her during a concert in the Assembly Rooms, it seemed there were hostile eyes boring into the back of his skull. Most of his mother's friends remained polite, if cool, but he couldn't help noticing the whispered conversations that always seemed to stop if he went past.

Worst of all, he found he missed the growing intimacy with Merab. Perhaps it was his fault: for he found it quite impossible to mention the rumours to her and this seemed to place an embargo on every subject. At Hartfield they had begun to know each other and increasingly Rowland had come to understand how very much he had misjudged her. If only he had allowed himself to get to know her earlier; if only he hadn't been so wantonly ill-judging and hasty. More and more those large brown eyes, the creamy perfection of her skin and her slender figure were beginning to haunt his dreams—and it was all too late.

Joseph had won and there was nothing he could do to mend matters.

At last he raised his head, ran his hands through his unruly hair and got up. The room looked cold and unwelcoming in spite of a fire in the grate. The last thing he wanted, he realized, was another day spent alone and worrying. He would hire a horse and at least have a morning's ride away from it all. Just then a maid arrived with a letter. He stared down at it, frowning. The writing looked vaguely familiar but he couldn't place it.

He was thunderstruck to read the half sheet

enclosed:

Dear Mr Sandiford,
If you would do me the honour of calling any
time this morning, I believe I may be able to
help you in your present difficulties.
Yours sincerely,
E. O'Riley

His first feeling was of hurt that Merab had not mentioned meeting Eliza: for surely she must have done? When had they met? What had Merab said? Why had she not told him? There was only one way to find out. Rowland grabbed his hat and set out.

Eliza was curious to see Rowland. From Merab's description she had imagined a somewhat pompous, stiff man and was pleasantly surprised to see a tall, handsome figure, with unruly curly hair and a pair of quizzical grey eyes. She liked the way he bowed over her hand and expressed his pleasure at meeting her. He might easily have been one of the top-lofty kind, she thought, unwilling to offer the common courtesies to a woman of her profession.

'It would save a lot of time, Mr Sandiford,' she said, when they were seated, 'if we could omit the preliminaries. I shall simply say that Miss Hartfield has visited me a couple of times, has confided in me, and together we have been able to confirm the source of these rumours

264

that beset you, and I have the means whereby you may rid yourself of both Harrisons.'

Rowland lifted an eyebrow. 'You seem to know a lot about me, ma'am,' he said.

'You may choose to be offended if you wish,' said Eliza comfortably. 'But I think it would be more sensible to listen to what I have to say.'

Rowland gave a short laugh. 'Very well, I'll listen, but before you start you must tell me how you come to know Miss Hartfield. I was under the impression that she did not even know your name until a few weeks ago.' If Merab had been deceiving him, he thought, he did not think he could bear it.

Eliza noted the fact that Merab seemed to be his first concern and drew her own conclusions.

'Miss Hartfield saw my name in the Pump Room book and recognized it.'

'She said nothing to me,' said Rowland before he could stop himself. He could not keep the hurt out of his voice. 'I thought she trusted me. I see I was mistaken.'

'She is in a difficult position and it is not made easier by the fact that she was attacked a day or so ago.'

'What!'

'I gather she was walking with a friend on Lansdown and they were assaulted by two masked men.'

Rowland looked down at his hands. 'She believes that I instigated this?' Why else should she not mention it?

'No,' said Eliza impatiently. Really, young men in love could be so half-witted sometimes! 'In fact, she has some proof that Mr Harrison is involved. I thought it was time that you took a hand in the affair. I assume you are not unwilling?'

'I would like to strangle him,' said Rowland curtly.

Eliza laughed. 'That you may not do!' she said. 'However, I am giving you a far more effective weapon.' She rose, went to her writing bureau and extracted two pieces of paper. One was the copy of Mrs Harrison's marriage entry in the church records; the other a copy of Joseph's birth register with its clumsy attempt to alter the date.

Rowland stared at them for some time in disbelief. 'Mrs Harrison indulged in a bit of firkytoodling!' he exclaimed. He recalled the starched figure with pursed lips and well-corsetted bosom behind the black bombazine. 'I must say I find that incredible!'

'She came to London to see her sister,' said Eliza. 'I can assure you that there was a time when the lure of an easy life was most attractive to her. Joseph,' she indicated the paper, 'is the result. I think, if you mention my name, you will find her most anxious to leave Bath.'

'You said that Merab ... Miss Hartfield had proof that Harrison had set up these rumours?'

Eliza mentioned Lottie.

'Ah, Lottie,' said Rowland thoughtfully.

266

'Yes, I see.' He folded up the pieces of paper carefully and put them in his pocket. 'Thank you, ma'am.' He rose to go. 'I am most grateful to you. I hope I may call again when this business is over?'

'I should be delighted to further our acquaintance,' said Eliza formally.

* * *

Joseph was deriving a great deal of pleasure from watching Rowland's struggles under the cloud of rumour and suspicion. When Major Bendick all but cut him in the Octagon Room Joseph could hardly contain his glee. The cousins, he saw, whilst not estranged, were certainly ill-at-ease in each other's company. His mother, who occasionally played piquet with Lady Mandersby and her cronies, reported that Rowland was being cold-shouldered. Mrs Harrison would have been better pleased if it were Merab who was ostracised, but one couldn't have everything, and she contrived to drop her barbs into the conversation whenever the opportunity arose.

Joseph had learnt from his mistakes and, this time, instead of spreading the rumour himself had given his valet leave to do so. There was a tap room at the back of the Christopher Hotel which was much frequented by valets and footmen, for it was central, and it became a hot-bed of gossip. As Joseph knew, any

267

rumour told here would spread rapidly to every family of note in Bath. Footmen would whisper it to ladies' maids, valets to their masters. In no time at all, everybody who mattered would know.

It was even whispered to Joseph himself by an acquaintance in the Orange Tree coffee house. Joseph affected shock.

'This is beyond anything!' he exclaimed. 'I am sorry for Miss Hartfield, of course. My mother and I tried to help her when we first came to Bath, but no, Miss preferred her grand relations.'

'She'll be regretting it now,' suggested his companion.

'Of course it is only a rumour,' added Joseph conscientiously. Any moment, he thought, the news of the attack would come out and then the cat would be among the pigeons! He was half-surprised that it hadn't come out already. His two accomplices assured him that the girls had been rescued by a man Joseph had no hesitation in identifying as Major Bendick, and the major was not one to keep silence.

Joseph was hoping that Rowland would challenge him about it—preferably in public. He would do his best to provoke him and then sting him for libel. All in all the outlook seemed rosy. He mentioned his hopes to his mother.

'What!' exclaimed Mrs Harrison. 'Why, he might challenge you to a duel!'

'Not he,' said Joseph easily. 'If he did I

should have no hesitation in calling a magistrate. No, what I want is a nice, profitable libel action, don't you see? It would ruin him—even if he were acquitted. Mud sticks, you know, and he could say goodbye to his parliamentary career.'

Mrs Harrison had but a tepid interest in Rowland; her rancour was reserved for Merab. 'I'd like to see her taken down a peg or two. Setting herself up as gentry, indeed! Why, we all know what her mother was.'

'Cousin Merab,' said Joseph silkily, 'will not be gentry long, believe me. In two weeks' time all hope of the Hartfield inheritance will be gone and who will want her then? She is virtually portionless and nearly twenty-seven. No, it's a young ladies' seminary for her. And I wish her well of it!'

After leaving Eliza, Rowland made his way to the Pump Room where he saw, as he hoped he might, Joseph and his mother. He bought *The Bath Chronicle* and settled down to watch them under its cover. He had read about the impending visit of Queen Charlotte and the civic reception to be laid on for her about three times before the Harrisons left. It was about midday and after a fashionable lounge in the Pump Room most people went home for a light luncheon and to prepare themselves for the pleasures of the evening or to do some shopping. Rowland folded the paper and quietly followed his quarry.

They were going home. Good. He would give them an hour and then pay his visit. At long last the inaction was over. He could do something.

While Rowland was pondering his strategy Joseph and his mother reached their lodgings and prepared to relax for an hour or so. Joseph kicked off his shoes, removed his jacket and put on a splendidly frogged dressing-gown. Mrs Harrison summoned her maid, bid her untie her corsets and gratefully allowed herself to breathe more freely. She put on a large, loose wrapper and tied her hair under a morning cap. They would be going to the Assembly Rooms later on, but there was time enough to resume the discomforts of corset and whalebone.

The maid brought in the luncheon: ham, a veal pie and the remains of a shoulder of mutton and they both helped themselves liberally. Then Mrs Harrison sat down with the latest novel from the circulating library and a copy of Doddridge's *Rise and Progress of Religion in the Soul* in case anybody should call. Joseph picked moodily at his nails with a penknife. He had passed the time of day with Mrs Tiverton in the Pump Room and she had not said a word about any attack on Merab—and he was sure he had seen Mrs Tiverton talking to the major not ten minutes before. What the devil was going on? He must prime his valet to pump the major's valet for any tit-bits in the Christopher this evening.

There was a scratch at the door and a maid came in with a card.

'Aha!' Joseph's eyes lit up. He passed it to his mother.

'Mr Sandiford!' cried his mother. 'Is he armed?'

'Hardly, Mother, with the maid letting him in and having sent up his card?'

'I am not leaving,' announced Mrs Harrison, tying the strings of her wrapper more firmly around her ample waist.

'Why should you?' countered Joseph. 'Stay by all means. You'll enjoy it.'

Rowland came into the room, executed a curt bow in Mrs Harrison's direction and said without more preamble, 'I am here on a most unpleasant errand.'

'Indeed?' Joseph allowed himself a triumphant look at his mother. 'May I ask what about?'

'My good name.'

'And how may I be concerned with that?' Joseph was enjoying himself.

'You have been spreading malicious rumours about first Miss Hartfield and now myself. I am here to put a stop to them.' He turned to Mrs Harrison, 'You, madam, should at least have been concerned for the reputation of your niece. But I cannot find anywhere that you have stood by her.'

'Stood by her!' Mrs Harrison swelled

underneath her wrapper. 'The hussy! Why should I stand by her? Her mother was no better than she should be! And the bold piece tried to get her claws into my son!'

Rowland raised an incredulous eyebrow.

Joseph saw the opportunity for a bit of goading. 'If Miss Hartfield's reputation is so spotless,' he said smoothly, 'why have you not offered for her? You surely have much to gain?'

'Enough!' said Rowland harshly. 'I will not have Miss Hartfield's name bandied about and my relationship with my cousin is no business of yours.'

'You have just made it my business,' said Joseph. 'And I can see no reason why I should not report our conversation to whoever may be interested. And I am sure many will be!'

Rowland gave him a contemptuous look and handed him the two pieces of paper. 'I think you may find these interesting,' he said. 'I should warn you that there are other copies in existence.'

Joseph, frowning, looked at them. Then he sank down on to the nearest chair in silence. After a few moments he handed the papers to his mother.

Mrs Harrison took one look, threw herself back in her chair in hysterics and shrieked, 'It's a lie!'

'Is it?' said Rowland steadily. 'Perhaps I should mention the name of Mrs Eliza O'Riley. She is in Bath and has been most informative. I am sure she would be only too happy to confirm it, if it should become necessary.'

'Who is Mrs O'Riley?' asked Joseph heavily.

Mrs Harrison's sobs became louder.

'It seems your mother would prefer not to say,' said Rowland.

'What do you want?' said Joseph. He looked across at his mother and then averted his gaze.

'I want a written confession from you that you have been the instrument for spreading untrue and malicious rumours about Miss Hartfield and myself. At my dictation and signed and dated here in my presence. And you must both leave Bath—as soon as possible.'

'And if I write it?'

'Then I shall remain silent about these,' Rowland gestured to the papers.

'I have no choice.'

'None,' agreed Rowland.

CHAPTER ELEVEN

Rowland was fast discovering that there was a side to his nature which he had never previously suspected existed. He had grown up as the sort of boy who had been kind to those weaker than himself, detesting bullying of any sort. It was the brutalities of Eton which had first fuelled his Radical political opinions. Now he found himself positively looking forward to

Joseph's coming humiliation. The bastard had tried to ruin Merab and it would give him, Rowland, a very real pleasure to thwart him. If he could have horsewhipped him out of town it would have given him a still greater satisfaction. But one couldn't have everything and he must concentrate on, not revenge, but the most effective means of ensuring Merab's social acceptance and his own untarnished reputation.

Rowland surveyed his options and decided to approach Lady Mandersby. Her influence was all-pervasive and she would undoubtedly be affronted if she were not among the first to know.

Lady Mandersby was wary of seeing him but a brief note on the back of his card indicating that he would value her confidential advice did the trick, as he had thought it might. She greeted him with reserve. 'Mr Sandiford. And how may I be of assistance?'

Rowland took out Joseph's confession and passed it to her.

After a brief look at the signature, she said curtly, 'Pray, be seated,' and snapped open her lorgnette. 'Well, young man,' she said after reading it carefully. 'This seems to be comprehensive—and a relief not only to you, I am sure, but also to your estimable mother, who must have been greatly concerned.'

'I thought you would be the best person to advise me, Lady Mandersby, so I came straight here. Of course, I plan to visit my mother as soon as possible, but she believed in me anyway.'

'And I did not?' said Lady Mandersby humorously.

'Dear Lady Mandersby,' said Rowland, demonstrating a diplomacy which augured well for his political career. 'Naturally, a woman of your intelligence had her reservations. But damaging rumours do not just come from nowhere, and you had to be careful.'

'Leave it to me, dear boy.' Lady Mandersby became almost skittish. 'I shall see to it. I never took to those Harrisons, never. And I am almost sure that Mrs Harrison is not above cheating at cards. Who are they, after all? Pooh! A Bristol lawyer! But Bath has grown so lacking in discrimination that nowadays one is expected to accept just anybody. Now, let me see ... I hope you mean to attend the Assembly Rooms this evening?'

'Why yes, I shall go with my mother and Mr Bridges, and Miss Hartfield, if she cares to come.'

'That will do very well. Make sure that Miss Hartfield comes too. And be sure to bring that piece of paper with you.'

It was almost the end of the season and the Rooms would normally be somewhat thin of company, but thanks to Lady Mandersby having the foresight to send out a number of confidential notes, it was very well attended. The Tivertons were there and Major Bendick. Lavinia and Mrs Banstead came and even Sir Thomas Wincanton put in an appearance.

Joseph's confession was the object of everyone's conversation. Suddenly, nobody had a good word to say for him. Joseph, who had been the object of a certain amount of interest from mothers with daughters to dispose of, now became 'a shabby fellow' and 'a confidence trickster', and many a mama discovered that there had been a certain something about his countenance which she couldn't quite like.

Whilst Mrs Bridges' mind was now relieved of care, and she was being assured by her friends that they had never believed a word of it, Merab was not feeling so sanguine, for she had almost quarrelled with Rowland again.

Earlier, Mrs Bridges had left Rowland and Merab to discuss the affair when her mantua-maker had arrived. 'You can tell Merab all the details. Forgive me, but Mrs Preston is so busy that I must see her when she comes!'

When she had gone Rowland's first words were, 'I am sorry that you couldn't trust me enough to tell me about your visit to Mrs O'Riley, Miss Hartfield.' What he wanted was reassurance, but the words came out cold and distant.

'You've seen her?' Oh, my God, what had Eliza said? Surely she had not betrayed her

276

confidence?

'How else do you think I came by the knowledge to screw a confession out of Harrison?'

Merab felt weak with relief. 'I ... I thought you must have threatened him—physically, I mean.'

Rowland shook his head. 'I'd have been up on a charge of assault. No, I blackmailed him with exposure about his illegitimacy.'

'Oh!' Merab did not know what to say. Apart from that momentous evening in the moonlight she felt that the old intimacy had largely gone and she had not dared to presume on his feelings towards her. 'I ... I would have told you,' she managed to say at last, 'but I have been too aware that my existence has been the cause of all your problems. Especially recently.'

'Nonsense,' said Rowland, more curtly than he meant.

'If I did not exist then you would have inherited Hartfield and might have married Miss Parminster.'

It's not Kitty I want, his heart cried. 'I cannot see, Miss Hartfield, that my relationship with Miss Parminster is anything to do with you.'

'No, you are right,' whispered Merab. 'I am sorry.' What else could she say? I wanted to know because I love you? And I dared not mention Eliza because I feared what you might say? It all seemed hopeless.

It was with reluctance that Merab went to the Assembly Rooms that evening. Rowland recovered his composure enough to call her 'Cousin Merab', but his conduct, though irreproachable, was scarcely warm. He appeared to have retreated behind a sheet of glass.

But it was better than Merab had feared. Lavinia flew up to embrace her enthusiastically. 'Oh, Merab! I am so pleased it has all turned out right. Now you may relax.'

Merab tried to look relaxed. 'At least we may now go for walks without fearing to be attacked!' she managed.

'Major Bendick will no longer have any excuse to bump into us,' said Lavinia, slyly.

The major very handsomely went up to congratulate Rowland and expressed his satisfaction at the outcome.

'I gather you were on hand to rescue my cousin and Miss Heslop,' said Rowland, shaking his hand. 'I must thank you for keeping silence.'

'Miss Hartfield asked me to do so,' said the major briefly. But there was a limit to the major's civility and shortly afterwards he moved away.

'I think the major is somewhat enamoured of your cousin, Mr Sandiford,' observed Mrs Tiverton with a smile.

'Major Bendick!' Rowland was most

unpleasantly surprised by the news. Would Merab really marry the fellow? Why he was a blockhead!

'Certainly. It would be a good match for her if he should pop the question. I believe his estate to be worth some four thousand a year.'

Rowland glared across at the major.

Sir Thomas came up to Merab armed with compliments and an invitation from his wife. 'She would be glad if you would call,' he said with a somewhat ponderous bonhomie. 'She's feeling much more the thing now, you know.'

'I'd be delighted to!' exclaimed Merab. 'Dear Amelia! I've missed her so much.'

'Most ungentlemanly thing for Harrison to do,' observed Sir Thomas next. 'To try to destroy a man's good name—and yours too, my dear. Disgraceful!'

Sir Thomas, Merab saw, was wishful to make amends. 'I am pleased that my mother's name has been cleared,' she said quietly. 'And if Amelia is well enough I should like to visit her and the baby tomorrow.'

'I shall tell her,' promised Sir Thomas.

*   *   *

Amelia was lying on her day-bed in her boudoir when Merab came the following morning. The two women embraced, Amelia shedding a few glad tears.

'Dearest Merab,' she wept. 'I'm sorry to

greet you like a watering can. You know how easily I cry!'

Merab sat down next to her and looked carefully at her friend. When she had last seen her, heavily pregnant, Amelia had had dark rings under her eyes and her face had been pinched with strain. Now she looked rested, though her hair still lay pale and wispy against the cushion. 'How are you, Amelia?'

'Better, truly. This was not an easy baby from the beginning.'

'No, I remember you never felt well. How is she?'

Amelia sat up and smiled. 'We think she will be all right. She was so tiny when she was born it scarcely seemed possible that she could survive. But now she does nothing but feed and sleep and her nurse tells me that she is beginning to put on weight.' Sir Thomas had found a wet nurse, the buxom wife of a toll-house keeper, who had just lost a baby and was willing to nurture little Miss Wincanton.

'May I see her?'

Amelia smiled and rang the bell. The baby was brought in and duly admired. 'I've never seen a baby so small,' said Merab in awe. 'But she's perfectly made. Look at her tiny fingernails!'

When the nurse had taken the baby back to the nursery Amelia said, 'But Merab. About you. Those dreadful tales! I have felt so much for you.'

'It was awful,' agreed Merab. 'I began to feel like some outcast. Wherever I went I trailed scandal after me. It was almost worse this time as I am staying with Mrs Bridges and such dreadful things were being said about her son.'

They discussed the events of the last few weeks and then Amelia said, coyly, 'Rumour has it that the major is growing very particular in his attentions. Now, don't think me inquisitive, Merab!' Merab threw her a quizzical glance. Amelia laughed but added, 'You know I only want to see you happily settled.'

'I refused him.'

'Oh ... dear,' Amelia said in dismay.

'I couldn't love him.'

'But you might have been happy nonetheless,' said Amelia practically. If only she hadn't been so uselessly ill, she thought, she might have been able to hint to the major on how best to win her friend. Amelia had been truly fond of Sir Thomas when she married him, but 'love'? That was for impractical romantics. Merab was surely sensible enough to have considered the major's offer seriously? She looked at her friend.

Merab was staring down at the carpet and there was a look Amelia had never seen on her face before. A look of quiet agony, of someone who thought she had lost what she most cared for.

'Merab! You're in love with somebody else!'

281

Merab was startled into saying, 'He doesn't think of me.'

'But ... who is it?' Amelia's mind ran swiftly through the possibilities. 'My God, it's Rowland Sandiford, isn't it?'

Merab burst into tears.

'Oh dearest Merab! But surely he cares about you too? Why, you told me you had made things up when you were both at Hartfield.'

'I thought so too. But he doesn't care about me enough to want me for his wife,' said Merab hopelessly. 'There is now only a week till the six months are up, Amelia. It's far too late for banns.'

'He would need to see a bishop for a special licence,' said Amelia thoughtfully. 'Oh dear, Merab. I am so very sorry. I always thought he was right for you. Are you sure he doesn't care? I don't see how he could help it!'

Merab left Amelia feeling somewhat comforted. True, Amelia had not been able to alter anything, but it was a relief just to be able to talk it through, and to be assured of her friend's affection and understanding. Apart from having everything dragged out of her by Eliza, she had had no other confidante: to talk to Mrs Bridges would not have been appropriate, and she didn't know Lavinia well enough. All the same, she felt agitated by the conversation and decided that instead of walking straight back to the Pump Room she

282

would stop at the abbey and have a few quiet moments.

Merab entered the abbey and settled herself in the corner of a pew near the choir stalls. She was, she hoped, unobserved, and could sit in peace without having to make polite conversation. The abbey was not very busy. A couple of women were polishing the lectern and a harassed-looking canon was talking to a man Merab recognized as the dean. Fragments of their conversation floated past her.

'So the bishop will be here for the chapter meeting next Wednesday?' the canon was saying.

'Yes. Three o'clock sharp he wants it.'

'Oh dear, it will clash with the archdeacon's meeting about the Queen's visit.'

'That can't be helped. In any case, the bishop also wants to discuss Her Majesty's visit. Perhaps, I'd better have a word with the archdeacon myself.'

'I'd be grateful if you would.'

'The bishop will be here about noon. I'll give him luncheon and bring him to the meeting. It'll have to be over by half past four because of the building committee meeting.'

'What are you going to do with the bishop then? Is he staying for evensong?'

'I imagine so. I don't know whether he has anything in mind. We shall have to see.' The dean bustled away and after a few moments the canon too left.

Merab found she had almost stopped breathing. The bishop would be in Bath on Wednesday. He would be free at half past four. What she was thinking was so alarming that she found her heart palpitating and she had to take a few deep breaths and try to calm herself down.

She had not wanted even to think about Eliza's revolutionary suggestion—she certainly had not dared mention it to Amelia—but now, it seemed that fate was taking a hand. She stayed in the abbey for another ten minutes and then made her way to the Pump Room where she had arranged to meet Mr and Mrs Bridges.

*   *   *

Mrs Bridges looked at her son in exasperation. Here he was on the brink of wilfully losing £20,000 because he wouldn't apparently consider marrying a delightful young woman, whom he liked, knew to be intelligent and who was in every way suited to be his wife.

Naturally, she was pleased that the stigma on his name had been removed and that the Harrisons' rout had been complete, but it looked as though everybody else was getting settled advantageously and he alone wasn't. Kitty, for example, would be a viscountess—little though she deserved it: even Lavinia with only a couple of thousand pounds seemed to be attracting the attention of Major Bendick—the major had lately taken to squiring Lavinia around, perhaps feeling that he must conquer his affection for Merab.

'I know,' said Merab, when Mrs Bridges mentioned it that weekend. (She had eventually told Mrs Bridges of the major's proposal.) 'And I am glad of it. I really would not be a suitable wife for him. But Lavinia! I do not know whether she is fully aware of his attentions and she often scolds him amazingly.'

'Yes, I confess I rather enjoy watching it,' smiled Mrs Bridges. 'The major used to be so conceited but you and Lavinia have cut him down to size.'

'Lavinia treats him as an elder brother, though,' said Merab doubtfully.

'Young women of eighteen rarely regard handsome older men as elder brothers!' observed Mrs Bridges dryly.

Merab laughed. 'You may be right. I am not in Lavinia's confidence but I cannot say that I have observed any signs of a partiality for him.'

'Well, she is enjoying herself at all events,' said Mrs Bridges. 'And I am delighted. She was always under Kitty Parminster's shadow before. Thank goodness she is out of the way. I did not relish the idea of having her as a daughter-in-law!'

'I think Cousin Rowland may still cherish warm feelings for her, though,' said Merab hesitantly. Talking about Rowland was a painful pleasure and one she rarely indulged in—certainly not with his mother.

'I'm sure he doesn't!' Mrs Bridges responded emphatically. 'He said only the other day that he thought he was well out of it.'

'Oh!' said Merab.

Mrs Bridges gave her a searching glance. She had begun to suspect that Merab was not indifferent to her son and, in spite of her husband's scepticism, she was fairly convinced that her interest was returned.

'Rowland can be very quixotic, you know,' she said in as disinterested a voice as she could manage. 'He is quite impractical where his honour is concerned. He nearly got expelled from Eton for refusing to sneak on another boy and taking the blame on himself. Fortunately the other boy decided to tell the truth just in time.'

'Oh!' said Merab again.

Mrs Bridges picked up her sewing and appeared to be absorbed in it. She could do no more. She had done her best to hint that Merab should take the initiative, but they must work out their own destinies. All she could do was see that they had time to be private together if they wished it.

It appeared, however, that this was something Rowland was determined to avoid. They saw him briefly in church on Sunday, but that was all. He declined an invitation to dine

286

with them that evening on the grounds that he had just received a letter from his estate manager and must answer it forthwith. If either his mother or his cousin noted that the post did not arrive on a Sunday both forebore to point it out. He seemed further disinclined to make a positive engagement for Monday either. 'I thought I'd go riding,' he said vaguely. 'I'm not sure when I shall be back.'

By Tuesday evening Merab was feeling frantic. She thought endlessly about the conversation with Mrs Bridges and decided that, in so far as her hostess could, she was being encouraged to take things into her own hands. But if she failed? If Rowland repudiated her? Could she bear it?

She slept badly and woke on Wednesday morning feeling haggard, desperate but resigned. She had but two options: to remain passive, and wait until Rowland proposed—if he ever did, or to take matters into her own hands and know the worst. If he thought her unfeminine and abandoned, so be it. He could hardly think worse of her than he had done in the past.

At least this time she would have the comfort of Amelia, Mrs O'Riley and Mrs Bridges. She would have to turn her mind seriously towards finding a teaching position, but that, in a sense, would be a relief. Solid drudgery would surely help to blot out heartache. Rowland would go back to Merryn and she need never see him again. She would never have to face utter destitution. Thanks to her father's £1,000 and Mr Camberwell's efforts on her behalf she could count on an income of about eighty pounds a year. Many families would feel themselves rich on that.

Pale, exhausted, but determined, Merab got out of bed, went to the davenport in the corner of her bedroom and sat down. Mrs Bridges had provided her guest with pen, ink and paper. Merab pulled a piece of paper towards her and wrote:

Dear Cousin Rowland,
I would be most grateful if I might have a few private words with you this afternoon. Would it be possible for you to meet me by the stairs to the Gravel Walk at half past two?
Yours etc
M Hartfield

It was not ideal but it would have to do. She folded it, sealed it and inscribed it. When she was dressed and before she could change her mind she went downstairs and gave it to one of the footmen.

'I want you to take that to Mr Sandiford, please,' she said crisply, to hide her terror. She gave him a shilling.

'Certainly, miss. Shall I wait for an answer?'

'No—wait, yes.' Merab didn't think she

could spend the rest of the morning wondering whether her letter had been delivered, and if so, whether he would come.

It was done. There was nothing she could do to stop it now.

*　　　*　　　*

Merab looked at herself carefully in the glass and pushed a curl into place. A pale face with huge dark eyes stared back at her. She sighed. It would have to do. A glance in the cheval glass showed a tall slender figure in a violet walking dress with a light black lace shawl draped over her shoulders. She put on her bonnet, a fetching light straw creation with violet ribbons, and picked up her gloves.

Rowland was already waiting as Merab came down the steps. Her letter had exercised his mind considerably and he was worried. Had she taken a governess's post without telling him? Were there, God forbid, further revelations about her past to come? He was looking pale and a little stern. The sight did not reassure Merab.

The cousins shook hands. Rowland noted that she was trembling and his own apprehension increased. 'You said that you wished to speak to me in private,' he said, formally.

'Yes,' whispered Merab. However was she going to say what she had to say? Already the palms of her hands felt clammy with nerves. She swallowed. 'Perhaps we might sit on one of the benches,' she suggested.

Just above them was a bench under some trees. It was reasonably secluded for there was a laurel bush which screened it from the Gravel Walk.

'Very well.' Rowland turned towards it in silence. His senses were now fully alert. Whatever she had to say it was plainly something she found difficult. They sat down. There was a long-drawn-out agonized silence while Merab stared down at her hands and wondered how to begin.

'Is it something about your mother, perhaps?' suggested Rowland gently.

Merab shook her head. She took a deep breath and turned towards him.

'Rowland,' she began.

All Rowland's senses suddenly quickened. Merab had never before called him by his name and a suspicion entered his head. 'Yes?'

'It is only two more days until the six months since Grandfather's death.'

'I know.'

'Oh!' said Merab, disconcerted. 'Well, I wondered ... I mean ...' She suddenly realized a new danger. She did not want Rowland to think she was only after the money. 'No, well, that's not important,' she said hastily. 'What is important, I mean, it's important to me, of course it may not be important to you ...' she

290

floundered on.

'Yes,' said Rowland again. He took hold of her hand.

Merab clutched it convulsively and said in a rush, 'I love you. I know you probably don't feel the same way...'

'But I do.'

Stunned, Merab looked up and met his eyes. What she saw there made her heart turn over.

'Merab, darling,' he said, laughter in his voice, 'are you by any chance trying to propose to me?'

'Yes!' cried Merab desperately. 'Oh! I know it's dreadful of me and not what any respectable female is supposed to do, but I didn't see how else it was going to happen.'

'I take it that you think we should marry in time to claim the Hartfield inheritance?'

Merab nodded. 'Only if you want to,' she said conscientiously.

'Of course I want to,' said Rowland impatiently. 'I haven't said anything because I made such a mess of it before and why should you believe me now? I was going to wait until Saturday. I wanted you to know that I wanted you more than Cousin Julian's damned estate.'

'You could have both,' ventured Merab.

'Sweetheart, it's too late.' Rowland took hold of her other hand.

'No it isn't,' said Merab. 'The ... the bishop is in Bath today. He has a meeting with the dean and chapter about now. He will be free at half past four.' All Rowland could see was one pink cheek.

Rowland gave her a look of mingled amusement and admiration. 'You mean that we should beard him in his den, get a special licence and marry at once?'

'I know it's a bit hasty...' began Merab.

'Hasty! Darling, it's outrageous!' He looked at Merab and laughed. 'We'll do it!' He gave a quick glance round, tugged at her bonnet strings, pushed the bonnet away impatiently and pulled her into his arms. 'I know I don't deserve this,' he whispered. 'But I swear to God I love you. Kiss me, Merab.'

* * *

It was six o'clock. Mrs Bridges and her husband had had some tea and were sitting in the drawing-room wondering where Merab was. They were all due to go to a concert that evening in the Assembly Rooms.

'She left the house shortly after two,' said Mrs Bridges. 'I daresay she only went shopping, but it's unlike her to be late.'

At that moment there were sounds in the hall.

'That's her voice,' cried Mrs Bridges in relief. 'And I think Rowland is with her.'

A moment later Merab and Rowland came in. Merab held her bonnet by its strings. They were holding hands and both were smiling.

'I hope this won't come as too much of a shock, Mama,' said Rowland. 'But we are getting married in about an hour and a half.'

'By the bishop,' added Merab.

'We're exhausted,' finished Rowland. 'Is there any chance of tea?'

Gradually things quietened down. Mrs Bridges recovered from her shock and sank back in her chair with relief. Of course such a hasty marriage would cause talk, but it would die down. Such things always did. If she and Samuel were there that would help and they seemed to have got the bishop on their side.

'He was delightful,' said Merab. 'Of course it all took a bit of time to explain things, but in the end he said that the best thing he could do to help us was to marry us himself. He was acquainted with Grandfather, so he knew all about his reputation, which helped.'

'I'm sorry we are so late back,' said Rowland. 'Merab wanted to write to Lady Wincanton and there is an old friend of her mother's in Bath who we hope will come as well. And then we had to get a ring.'

'You will give me away, won't you, sir?' said Merab anxiously to Mr Bridges.

'I'd be honoured. May I ask what you are going to do afterwards?'

'We shall have to set out at once for Hartfield,' said Rowland. 'I daresay we may make ten miles before dark.'

'No! Certainly not,' said Mrs Bridges

293

decidedly. 'You cannot start your married life in some poky tavern on the Gloucester road. In any case I don't suppose either of you has eaten much today. Merab only pecked at her lunch. Besides, you both look exhausted. Merab will stay here tonight and have a good night's sleep, which is what she needs—especially if you have a full day's driving ahead of you. And you, my son, will sleep at Gay Street.'

Rowland looked at Merab. She had told him she had hardly slept the previous night for worrying about their interview. He, too, was tired and needed to pack and settle his account with his landlady.

'Very well,' he said. 'I suppose we must be sensible.' And he and Merab looked most indignant when Mr and Mrs Bridges burst out laughing.

'What time is this wedding?' asked Mrs Bridges.

'Half past seven, after evensong. In the Lady Chapel.'

At first Sir Thomas had been adamant that Amelia should not go and only changed his mind when Amelia showed him the note and he learned that the bishop would be performing the ceremony.

'There will be a good deal of talk,' he said gloomily.

'There will be less if we are there,' his wife pointed out.

'But I do not like you to be mixed up in

gossip.'

'My best friend is being married in a quiet, private ceremony because of mourning in the family,' said Amelia. 'Who is to say that it has not been arranged some time ago? If the bishop marries them I really cannot see that there is any cause for scandal.'

'Very well,' said Sir Thomas heavily. 'I shall come too.'

'I am sure that will help,' said Amelia demurely.

At twenty past seven a small knot of people gathered inside the abbey. Mr and Mrs Bridges, together with Merab and Rowland, Eliza O'Riley in a startling hat with pink ostrich feathers, Tim Heard and Sir Thomas and Lady Wincanton.

One of the vergers came up to them. 'If you would come this way, please,' he said. 'The bishop is ready now.'

*   *   *

Mr Camberwell sat in his office and surveyed the calendar gloomily. Friday. On Monday he would have to write to the two charities and tell them of Julian Hartfield's legacy. He sighed. Old Hartfield had succeeded in death in being as obstructive and difficult as he had been in life. Two nice young people were being deprived of the inheritance which in natural justice they had every right to expect would be theirs.

At that moment there was a knock at his door and his clerk entered.

'Mr Camberwell!' he said excitedly. 'Mr and Mrs Sandiford are downstairs and wish to see you.'

'Mr and Mrs ... show them up at once.'

Merab and Rowland might have been emotionally and physically exhausted on Wednesday evening after the alarms and excursions of the previous weeks. On Friday morning, however, after a night spent at the King's Head, Cirencester, things were different. Merab's cheeks were delicately flushed, and Rowland was looking extraordinarily pleased with himself.

They shook hands and Mr Camberwell expressed his delight.

'We were married on Wednesday,' said Rowland as Merab reached into her reticule and took out a folded piece of paper which she handed to Mr Camberwell. 'So we have come to claim the Hartfield inheritance. I daresay you will want to see the certificate.'

We hope you have enjoyed this Large Print book. Other Chivers Press or Thorndike Press Large Print books are available at your library or directly from the publishers. For more information about current and forthcoming titles, please call or write, without obligation, to:

Chivers Press Limited
Windsor Bridge Road
Bath BA2 3AX
England
Tel. (01225) 335336

OR

Thorndike Press
P.O. Box 159
Thorndike, Maine 04986
USA
Tel. (800) 223–2336

All our Large Print titles are designed for easy reading, and all our books are made to last.

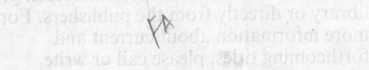

We hope you have enjoyed this Large Print book. Other Thorndike Press or Chivers Press Large Print books are available at your library or directly from the publishers. For more information about current and forthcoming titles, please call or write, without obligation, to:

Chivers Press Limited
Windsor Bridge Road
Bath BA2 3AX
England
Tel. (01225) 335336

OR

Thorndike Press
P.O. Box 159
Thorndike, Maine 04986
USA
Tel. (800) 223-2336

All our Large Print titles are designed for easy reading, and all our books are made to last.